Our Dream Home

ALSO BY JESSICA HUNTLEY

Horrible Husbands
Room 21
Our Dream Home

OUR DREAM HOME

JESSICA HUNTLEY

JOFFE BOOKS

Joffe Books, London
www.joffebooks.com

First published in Great Britain in 2026

Cover art by Nebojša Zorić

ISBN: 978-1-80573-527-4

PROLOGUE

My whole life has been a complete and utter lie. For every second I've been alive, my parents have lied to me. I hate them! How could they do this to me? What makes them think it's okay to treat their own daughter like this, like someone who doesn't matter enough to know who they truly are and where they came from? Don't I deserve the truth? I don't understand what I've done wrong.

Despite my recent problems, I've always done what's been asked of me, stuck to my curfew. Okay, there were a couple of times they don't know about when I sneaked back in a little later than planned after one too many drinks at a party, but overall, I've been a good daughter. I don't steal or swear or sleep around. I'm starting the next phase of my life in a matter of months and now they drop this bombshell on me, destroying my love and trust in them.

This is how they repay me.

Earlier, when they told me, I screamed at them. I stamped my foot like a toddler throwing a tantrum, said I hated them, grabbed my bag and stormed out of the house, slamming the door hard. I thought my blood was boiling, steam escaping from my eyes. I've never been that angry before.

They ran out after me, begging for me to come back so they could explain and talk some more, but what's the point? I don't want to know the details. I don't want to *talk*. They don't deserve my attention. I'm done with them. I'm old enough to look after myself now. I don't need them, not anymore. My new life awaits and I'm never talking to them ever again.

When I left the house, I didn't have a plan. I thought about knocking on my friend's door a few streets over. Lucy's parents would let me in, allow me to stay as long as I needed, but that's the first place my parents will look. I need to hide somewhere that would never occur to them, so I make a wide circle around the neighbourhood, making sure to stay out of sight, then hop over the wall to the back garden and climb up to my old treehouse.

It's hilarious. Here I am, safely tucked away in my childhood hiding place, and they're still in the house, shouting at each other, wondering what the hell to do. Granted, it's a little cold. Scratch that. It's *very* cold. And wet. The storm that everyone's talking about is now here, and it's buffeting the tree like a plastic bag caught in a tornado. The treehouse has seen better days. I haven't played in it since I was around ten, but it's enough to keep me relatively dry for the next few hours until the storm's passed. Enough to let my parents sweat a little at the thought of me out in this terrible weather.

Ha! That'll serve them right.

Maybe now they'll realise what horrible parents they are for keeping such a huge, life-altering secret from me.

Damn it, I wish I'd thought enough to grab a coat on my way out, but I'd been too furious, too intent on getting as far away from them as possible to think about needing an extra layer of protection. I wedge tight into the far corner, the furthest from the open window and door, and attempt to make myself comfortable, but that's impossible since I don't have a coat or anything to sit on. My short skirt barely covers my bum, so my cheeks are squished against the cold, damp wood of the treehouse floor. Goosebumps bristle over my bare legs.

The storm is only supposed to last a few hours, so I'll just grizz it out here for a while, then I'll climb down and go back home to get warm and dry. Oh, how I'll laugh when I tell them I've been hiding out in the back garden the whole time.

I'll only stay with them for a few more weeks until I can move out into my new accommodation. Then I'm free. I'll get a job and be one of those kids who have no contact with their parents. I'll change my number too.

A car door slams.

I scuttle to the window and peer over the sill, keeping low in case an errant beam of light from somewhere picks up my pale face. Looks like they're getting in the car. Possibly going over to my friend's house to see if I'm there. I presume some phone lines are down in the storm.

A few minutes later, the car headlights disappear into the gloomy darkness and rain. God, it's really coming down out there. I've never seen it rain this hard before. Huge rivers of rainwater are flooding the roads beyond our garden. A streak of lightning illuminates the treehouse in a flash, followed closely by a rumble of thunder.

I shriek, ducking back into the far corner and pulling my jumper cuffs over my hands, which are shaking from the chill.

Maybe this wasn't such a good idea after all. I kind of wish I was tucked up in bed right now with my nightly hot chocolate and listening to Britney Spears' new album, but no, my parents had to go and ruin that, didn't they? I didn't think I could hate them any more, but the more I think about it, the more the hatred grows inside me, like a flame feeding on timber.

I don't want anything to do with them. Can I emancipate myself? Is that possible? It's certainly an idea that I'll explore. Or maybe I don't need to now I'm eighteen.

I spend the next couple of hours hunkered down in the corner, eventually drifting off to sleep, curled up on my side when the storm quietens. When I wake up, it's raining and still pitch black, but at least the wind has settled. The worst is over.

The family car isn't in the driveway. They must still be out searching. Ha!

Time to make them feel extra guilty and stupid.

I climb down the ladder to the ground, which is saturated with rain. As soon as my feet touch down on the grass, my trainers are soaked through. I'm so cold my teeth chatter as I sprint across the lawn towards the back door of the house. I lift up the flower pot and retrieve the spare key, slide it into the lock and enter the house.

The instant warmth is the best feeling ever, but not as good as how I'm going to feel when they finally turn up, tired and wet from their long search to find me safely tucked up in bed. I quickly take a hot shower, put on my pyjamas and crawl under the covers.

Sleep comes within minutes.

* * *

The next morning when I wake up, the bright sun is beaming in through the slit in my curtains straight onto my face. I groan and rub my eyes as I sit up.

I didn't hear my parents come back home during the night. I slept like the dead. They must have looked into my room, seen me snoring and closed the door, happy to have their precious child back home. I snort as I fling back the bed covers. Time to cause a little more hell for them.

As I pad into the hallway, I can't help but notice how quiet the house is. They're not still asleep, are they? I push open the door to their room to find their bed empty, still made from the day before. They haven't been home yet.

Yeesh, they've been out all night.

Sucks for them.

I flick on the television downstairs, half expecting to see a news alert about my disappearance. That would be so typical of them, to contact the police and set up a missing person alert. I was only gone like four hours!

I begrudgingly make myself some breakfast, stick on my favourite show and eat on the sofa, my legs tucked underneath me, still in my pyjamas.

But three hours later, they still haven't come back home. There've been no phone calls either.

I'm not worried. Not really. I mean, this is the first time I've had the house to myself in forever, so I'm actually enjoying it. I guess I could invite my friends round to hang out, but I decide against it. In fact, I'm bored of staying in on a weekend. I'm going out to visit Lucy. We'll have a proper laugh about it all.

I grab my things and throw open the front door.

Two police officers are walking up the driveway, stern looks on their faces.

Oh shit, they've called the cops on me! That's just typical of them!

I fold my arms across my chest and lean on one hip. 'Whatever they've told you, don't believe them. I'm not missing. I'm fine, okay? I just wanted to make them sweat a little. That's all. I was hiding out in my treehouse this whole time!'

The officers reach the bottom step and stop, looking up at me as they both take off their hats.

'I'm sorry,' one of them says, 'but we have some bad news about your parents.'

PART 1

CHAPTER 1

Reaching my fingers up to my dark brown hair, limp and dank from five days without washing, I grasp a small strand by my forehead, twirl it around my fingers for a few seconds, then tug at it until I hear a satisfying snap. The hair that frames my face is already short and split, but I keep doing this until my breathing rate slows and I feel the tension dissipate, like a balloon deflating.

It's a condition known as trichotillomania, a hair-pulling disorder that's usually triggered by stress and anxiety. It started many years ago during a time I don't like to talk or think about. It's best I keep those monsters at bay. We all have them, don't we? The demons we'd rather keep hidden than allow to see the light of day for fear of being ridiculed or crucified. Even my husband doesn't know the origin of my hair pulling, and that's the way I intend to keep it, thank you very much. So yes, I'm stressed and anxious, but what mother of two teenagers isn't?

At the age of thirty-six, apparently older if not wiser, I still pull and break my hair when I'm nervous or bored or have had a particularly bad day. Sometimes, I don't know I'm doing it. It's an unconscious reflex, as normal as swallowing or blinking. I'd go so far as to say it soothes me even at the most troubling of times.

My husband of thirteen years, George, often comments on my habit or tells me to stop because it's distracting him, but who is it hurting in the grand scheme of things? Other than perhaps my hairdresser, who always complains about the short, broken strands on either side of my face and the split ends it causes. He still gets paid, so again, *who is it hurting*? I may have those awkward strands of hair that I never know what to do with, but if that's the price I have to pay to keep my anxiety and stress levels under control, then so be it.

'Heather! We're going to be late!' I call up the stairs, but get nothing in response. I glance at my watch. Why is every school day a constant race where I'm constantly playing catch-up?

Liam stomps down the stairs, dragging his backpack behind him. 'Please pick up your bag. No wonder the bottom of it is wearing away if you drag it around all day.'

Liam barely makes eye contact with me. Somewhere along the way, I've lost their love and support and now I'm merely the person who feeds them and washes their clothes. Oh, and taxis them around, picks them up, reminds them to brush their teeth, buys them new clothes, makes their packed lunches . . .

A few seconds later, Heather emerges at the top of the stairs, her face caked in make-up, her skirt hiked up as short as it could possibly go.

'Heather, you are not going to school looking like that. Pull your skirt down and take off some of that make-up, please.' I've had more than enough emails and calls from the school, warning me about Heather's attire.

Heather rolls her eyes as she passes me and walks straight into the living room, where George is finishing up his cup of coffee. Apparently, I have turned invisible.

'Bye, Dad,' she says.

'Bye, Heather,' he replies. 'Have a good day.'

I enter the room. 'Heather, please take off your make-up and lengthen your skirt,' I say again.

'I think she looks fine,' says George.

Heather beams and plants a kiss on his cheek. 'Thanks, Dad.' She glares at me. 'At least someone in this family likes the way I look.'

'I'm not saying I don't like the way you look, but it's not appropriate for school!' I say, my voice a high-pitched squeal. 'George! Back me up here!'

George takes another look at Heather. 'Maybe take off the false eyelashes, love.'

Heather sighs. 'Okay, Dad.'

My jaw drops open as a flurry of rage simmers beneath the surface. I don't have time for a full-on argument with George right now.

My watch pings with an email. I've got no idea where my phone is, so I quickly check the screen. The subject line is all in bold.

Be quick! Enter now to win a brand-new car and a luxury holiday! Don't miss out!

Seriously? This is the fifth email in two days. Why are these not going straight into the spam folder? I've flagged them repeatedly, but they continue to plague my inbox like a horde of flies over an animal carcass. I don't bother opening the email this time. I send it straight to the bin. I'm no stranger to spam, having to complete a mandatory online course on recognising fraudulent emails as part of my yearly employee training, but whoever is sending this stuff isn't even trying to be subtle about it. All from suspiciously similar email addresses and all excitedly announcing I could win various different amazing prizes. Who the hell falls for these scams?

The kids eventually climb into the car, Liam in the backseat and Heather in the front. I back out of the driveway and turn in the direction of the school.

Heather leans forward in her seat and, using the visor, starts pulling off her lash extensions.

'Why didn't you remove them when I asked you to?' I'm not ready to let this go yet.

'Because you didn't ask nicely,' she says, a hint of sarcasm in her voice.

I grind my teeth. 'You should know better,' I say. 'I've had far too many warnings about the way you dress. You're lucky you haven't been suspended or sent home yet.'

Heather shrugs. 'Who cares?'

'I care!'

'Well, I don't.'

'Well, maybe you should.'

'Or maybe you should just stop caring, Mum. No one cares what you think anyway.'

I stop behind a car and turn to her, but find I have no words. She's knocked the breath straight out of me. How is she my own flesh and blood?

I look back at the road.

'That's what I thought,' mutters Heather.

I feel like I've been slapped across the face. How have I let it get to this point? I've lost their respect.

The kids have George wrapped around their little fingers. Always have done. Unfortunately, my dream of having a daughter as a best friend hasn't worked out how I planned. I thought when Liam came along, he might be a mummy's boy, but alas, I was wrong about that too.

I'm stuck between a rock and a hard place with Heather though. I do try and suggest things to do together — shopping trips, salon visits. She refuses everything, but as soon as George offers to take her out and do something fun, even if it's something as unsophisticated as grabbing lunch, she jumps at the chance like he's offered her an all-expenses-paid holiday. Is it my fault? Did I do something wrong?

I don't know, is the answer to that.

Liam, on the other hand, is my little boy and always will be, despite him now being almost the same height as me. He's fourteen and an absolute whizz with computers, gadgets and electronics, taking after his dad. He even takes coding courses at school, and wants to be a famous YouTuber when he grows up. He's begged and begged George and me to let him start his own YouTube channel because, apparently, there are kids as young as five making content, but we've firmly said no, not until he's sixteen. And even then, we'll be closely monitoring his videos and interactions online, which he's agreed to. I've seen that series on Netflix. It scared me half to death and I didn't sleep properly for a week, waking up in the middle of the night to check that Liam was still asleep in his bed, and not online with some women-hating extremist group.

The past year my relationships with my kids seem to have got worse. Maybe it's because they're growing more independent with every passing second, but nothing I do seems good enough. They avoid me at all costs, preferring to ask their dad whenever they need something. The constant monologue in my head doesn't help, telling me I'm a bad mother. I know that already. I don't need reminding.

I drop the kids at school and watch them run away from me as if I'm a contagious leper.

I can already tell that today is not going to be a good day.

* * *

'Hey, Fiona, is payroll done yet?' asks a gruff voice from the office behind me, several long hours later. My boss, Alan — a straight-talking, forty-year-old mechanic who can strip a car apart and put it back together with his eyes closed, but can't make a decent cup of coffee if his life depended on it. He's saved me a fortune on my MOT and services over the four years I've been working at Alan's Automobiles though.

Ah, crap.

'Almost done,' I reply, quickly navigating to the payroll folder on the screen and double-clicking.

I haven't started it yet, too distracted by reading an online click-bait article that caught my attention due to its disgusting headline.

Mother Sleeps with Son

I don't know why I read it. Morbid curiosity, I suppose. I'm not saying I have a sick mind, but it does seem to jump to conclusions rather fast and I get an addictive jolt of adrenaline reading outlandish articles.

Turns out, the article is exactly that. Clickbait. The son in question is six months old and it's about a single mother who raves about co-sleeping with her infant. Whoever wrote the headline should be sent to prison. Maybe I should be sent to prison for reading it . . .

A lump forms in my throat as I close the tab and turn my focus to the damn payroll that was technically due over an hour ago. It's not a hard job to do, just boring. But reading the article has brought back a lot of memories from when I did co-sleep with my daughter back in the very early days of being a young mother. George was away so much at the start. Not his fault, but it made me feel very isolated because I didn't have anyone I could rely on for help, not even a close friend. Back then, it was just me and my baby, together forever. Me and her against the world. Stupidly, I thought it would always be that way, but now, at nearly sixteen years old, she's practically a stranger to me.

I push my unwanted, guilt-ridden thoughts away before they consume me. The ones every mother gets at one time or another. Probably several times a day. The ones that overwhelm her with the dreaded 'mum guilt' and tell her she's a bad mum because she has a freezer full of chicken nuggets and doesn't cook meals from scratch. The ones that play on repeat in her head until she begins to believe them. I need to finish my work, then I can go back to internally beating myself up over the state of my relationship with my teenage daughter.

Alan's Automobiles only hires ten people, including the man himself, so I breeze through payroll, finishing in record time, and send the final numbers to Alan for him to sign off.

I stretch my arms above my head, feeling my right shoulder pop and crack, an old sports injury from that time I thought I'd take up tennis in my early twenties. To be fair, I did start to get good, but then I sprained my shoulder, took a few months off to recover and then got pregnant for a second time. I said goodbye to my dreams of winning Wimbledon, and threw myself into being the best mother I could be.

Look how well that turned out.

Another email notification pops up on my watch.

Congratulations! You have won a dream home in the country! Click here!

Oh yay! Lucky me. Now, I can move to the country and forget all my problems. Maybe while I'm at it, I'll win a million quid too.

I find my phone.

Delete. Block.

I push myself away from the desk, rolling across the floor in my swivel chair. I need a strong caffeine fix.

One of the downsides of working in a garage is that there are no other women employed here, so I've no female friends who I can chat with during the day. It's extremely sexist and I've raised the issue more than once with Alan, but his response is always the same: if a woman applied for a job as a mechanic, then he'd be more than happy to hire her. That's me told, then. Maybe I should have been a mechanic. Believe it or not, I do like cars and I have learned a lot about them since working here.

Before this job, I worked in sales at a clothing store, as a barista in a small coffee shop and in a local Waitrose. It's safe to say I'm a jack of all trades, but a master of none. I dropped out of university early on, and I was never able to get my dream career in fashion design back on track. I had a lot of dreams as a fresh-faced teenager, but they all went to hell in a single day that will haunt me for the rest of my life.

I found out I was pregnant with Heather only four weeks after starting a three-year course at Kingston University, London, studying Textiles and Fashion Design. That wasn't the day my life went to hell. That was before. I don't regret having her, but I do regret dropping out of studying, but back then I couldn't see any way of making it work. Thank God for George. He saved me. He saved *us*.

He stood by Heather and me, and a couple of years later we had Liam. I was a stay-at-home mum until they were both in school and then cautiously entered the world of part-time work, grabbing any job I could get. Luckily, I didn't have to worry too much about money because George made enough to support us all, working for a tech startup in London which specialises in creating gadgets and machines to help make the home a more 'homely' place to live. Their tagline. Not mine. He's worked for them ever since, and hasn't shown any desire to change jobs.

He earns a decent wage, but we still live in a modest townhouse in the centre of Leicester. I have floated the idea of moving once or twice. Not far. Just . . . somewhere else. Anywhere else. But George is set in his ways, and trying to get him to step outside his comfort zone is like trying to convince a toddler to eat a green vegetable. It's not worth the stress and effort.

I walk into the sorry state of a kitchen and flick on the kettle. Only two more hours till school pick-up. George used to do the school runs since he works from home four days a week and his hours are much more flexible than mine, but after one too many late collections, not to mention the forgotten lunches and homework, I took over. Nothing against my dear husband, but he'd forget his head if it weren't attached to his body. And yet, despite that, he's still the best dad in the world in their eyes.

I don't know many of the mums and dads at school, and I often feel out of the loop with what's going on with their education, especially when all I get in response to questions is, 'Fine,' or 'It was okay.'

Maybe that's half the reason I've been feeling so stuck lately with regards to my life. The truth is, I'm invisible to everyone around me, including my family. They know I'm there, of course, but sometimes I fantasise about what would happen if I suddenly disappeared and everyone was left to fend for themselves.

Would George get out of bed? More often than not, I have to kick him in the shins to get him to wake up, despite the three alarms he sets every morning.

Would Liam remember to take his inhaler to school? The number of times I have to tell him is beyond a joke, and a part of me wants to let him go without it, but then I beat myself up for thinking such a horrible thing about my own son. If he had an asthma attack at school and didn't have his inhaler because I decided to teach him a lesson, I'd never forgive myself.

Would Heather eat proper food, other than whatever crap she buys from the corner shop after school with her friends? Would any of them remember to feed the cat?

I love my family. Truly.

But I've been lying to every single one of them for the past seventeen years.

Maybe that's why I allow them to treat me the way they do — ignoring me, barely acknowledging I exist. I can't risk it. I'd rather that than risk them finding out the truth. Especially George. He's unpredictable. Dangerous.

I've seen it a few times before, in his younger days.

If he ever found out that Heather isn't his biological daughter, I don't think he'd ever forgive me. There's no telling how he'd react, which is why I'll take the secret to my grave.

No matter what — I cannot let him find out.

It would destroy the family, and that's all I've ever wanted — a family.

I'll do whatever it takes to keep us together.

Whatever. It. Takes.

CHAPTER 2

Time ticks by at its usual glacier pace while I'm at work. I finish at three during the week, except for Tuesdays and Thursdays, when the kids have after school clubs and I stay till four. Nine times out of ten, I can get to the school gates on time, but it's cutting it close, and I'm often the last parent to arrive. Not late. Just the last one to arrive.

Today, I find Liam standing outside the gates with his teacher, who gives me a weak smile before allowing Liam to bimble towards me, scuffing his shoes on the concrete, like it's an effort to pick up his feet.

'Did you have a good day?' I ask him.

'It was okay,' Liam replies without taking his eyes off his phone screen.

I look up at the teacher, whose name I don't remember. 'Thanks for waiting with him.'

'No problem. Um . . . might I have a quick word?'

Oh God. Here we go.

I leave Liam staring mindlessly at his phone. I'm surprised the kid doesn't have a permanent neck injury. Smiling through the anxiety swirling around in my gut, I resist the urge to reach up, grasp a strand of hair and feel the soothing snap.

'Has something happened?' I ask, keeping my voice low.

'Liam . . . has been spending time with some of the older boys at the school, and I just wanted you to be aware of that.'

'Older?'

'Year elevens.'

'Oh. Um . . . okay.'

'Some of them have been caught in the past smoking at the back of the school.'

'I see. Thank you for letting me know. I'll have a word with him.'

The teacher nods and walks away, leaving me feeling like the worst mother in the world. Nothing new there.

'Hi, Fiona!' says a particularly cheery voice from behind me.

Fucking hell. What now?

I turn and see one of the other mums rushing towards me. She's the one who always has a spray tan and looks like she's stepped out of the pages of a fashion magazine. How the hell does she have the time to look so good? She's dressed in smart yet casual clothing that accentuates her tiny figure and has her long, dark hair tied back in a tight ponytail with a cute butterfly clip on one side. She's wearing oversized sunglasses and shiny pink lip gloss.

'Hi, er . . . Linda.'

'Laura.'

Damn it.

'Sorry, Laura. How are you?'

'Fine, thanks. Did Liam tell you about after school tomorrow?'

I glance at my son, who doesn't seem to have heard. It would be so much easier if I had the power to read minds. 'No, sorry, not yet. What's happening after school tomorrow?'

'I was going to take the boys for pizza and ice cream, if that's okay, after the sports day.'

'Oh, yes, that's fine. Sounds lovely.' I stop, my brain catching up with what she's said. 'What sports day?'

'Tomorrow is the school's annual sports day,' Laura replies, with a condescending tone I've heard many times before. The thing is, it's not unusual for me to forget things or be kept out of the loop. I'm not part of the school mums' WhatsApp group, which apparently is the place to be for all the gossip. I did get sent an invite, but honest to God, I can't deal with all the drama. Besides, the school keeps me updated with their weekly newsletters and emails, but I don't recall anything about a sports day. Shouldn't I have least received a reminder from the school about it? Or have I somehow missed it? And I used to give George a hard time when he forgot things.

'Oh gosh, yes. Of course it is. Uh . . . what time does that start again?' I ask, knowing for a fact I'm not fooling anyone.

'Two. Over on the sports fields.'

'Right.'

'I assume you don't have a partner for the mum's three-legged race, so would you like to team up? I'm happy to run a second time.'

I get flashbacks from my own school sports days where I'd watch my mother attempt to run the mum's race and end up falling flat on her face, flashing her knickers to the whole crowd. It was hilarious, obviously . . .

'Ah, I would, but . . . I twisted my ankle yesterday and it's really sore, so I think I'd better give this year a miss.' At this point, Liam looks up from the screen and gives me one of his infamous eyebrow raises.

'What a shame,' says Laura. She's probably remembering the scene I caused last year when I tripped over my own feet and took out three other mums in the process, accidentally dislocating one of their shoulders. I didn't flash my knickers though. Silver lining and all that.

I've learned my lesson the hard way.

We say our goodbyes — hers chirpy and pleasant, mine high-pitched and awkward — and then Liam and I walk to the car, which I had to park halfway down the street because of course I arrived too late to get the decent spots close to the gate. Parking around here is a free-for-all fight to the death. All bets are off, and God forbid you block the road with your car at the wrong time and meet the ice cream van coming in the opposite direction. It's one of those extra stresses in life I could do without.

Heather usually meets us at the car (she finds it herself), but when we arrive at the older-than-my-teenage-son Volvo, she's not there. I glance left and right, scanning the crowds for a glimpse of my daughter's naturally auburn hair. I tell people I've no idea where she got it from, because I'm not auburn. Nor was anyone else in my family.

My hair is dark brown, flecked with grey (thanks, mid-thirties — couldn't have waited till my forties to make your first appearance, no?). Her father . . . well, let's just say, I don't remember much about what he looked like, other than he was somewhat decent-looking. Even in my severely intoxicated state, I like to think I still had standards.

I don't even know his name. Dear God, I'm a walking cliché. I was somewhat liberal with my choices of sexual partners back then. I was careful, but I wasn't on the pill because it gave me a bad reaction, and I hadn't got around to booking in for a coil fit. It was one of those adult things that, at the time, I didn't think I'd need. Ha-ha!

Anyway, after the one-night stand with whoever his name was, I carried on with my studies, but then ran out of a lecture one day and hurled my guts up in the hallway in front of a gaggle of other students. It didn't take long for me to realise I was pregnant, but I had no way of contacting my mysterious and fleeting shag, so I resigned myself to never knowing who the father of my baby was.

A few weeks later, I met George and everything clicked into place. I made my choice. I fell in love with him and he with me. We slept together, and the timings weren't too far apart to announce my pregnancy. He was shocked, yes. Perhaps a little more than shocked, but he stood by me and promised he always would. I got my happily ever after and Heather got a doting father. George is a wonderful dad. I don't regret what I did, but as the years have passed, it's been harder and harder to keep it from him. From all of them.

I blink out of my internal thoughts as Liam says, 'Oh, I forgot. Heather said she's meeting her friends after school and won't be home until later.' He climbs into the passenger seat and slams the door.

'How much later?' I ask, opening the driver's door and peering in at him.

'I dunno. Later.'

'Is she going to be back for dinner?'

Liam looks up from his phone, his face deadpan. '*I don't know*,' he repeats, slower this time with a hint of sarcasm as if explaining to a child what one plus one is.

I narrow my eyes at him, and he returns his focus to the screen. I want to reach over, grab the damn thing from his hand and throw it into a nearby bush, but I don't. Because I don't want to initiate the end of the world as we know it.

Sometimes, it's just not worth the effort.

CHAPTER 3

As soon as we get home, Liam disappears upstairs like a bolt of lightning, but not before he's thrown his shoes haphazardly into the corner and dumped his school bag in the entrance hall. I'm not quite sure what's happened to him in the past year. He always used to hang up his coat, put away his shoes and empty his bag of all the papers and whatever else he'd collected during the day as soon as he stepped through the door, but lately, none of that's been happening.

Perhaps his change in behaviour has something to do with those older boys he's been hanging around with. I wonder how long he'd been interacting with them before his teacher felt the need to inform me. Should I question him about it or will it just piss him off? God knows I don't need any further abuse and moodiness in this house, but I can't just ignore it. This is one of those times where I need George as my backup, so I decide to speak to him first and then we can plan our course of action together. As a team.

Sometimes I do wonder if my family think I'm their personal assistant, only put on this earth to serve them and their fifteen million requests. Nothing ever changes. Every day is like a monotonous car ride on an empty motorway. What I wouldn't give for a car or two to pop up, just so I have something to focus on instead of the never-ending stretch of road ahead of me.

Of course, it wasn't so long ago that my stretch of road threatened to come to a very abrupt end, and I thank my lucky stars every day that it didn't. Ten years ago, I was diagnosed with breast cancer and my whole world came crashing down like an avalanche. The kids were still small, and it was a struggle to hold myself together in front of them as I attempted to explain what I was going through, knowing they might have to grow up without a mother.

George did that thing where he made jokes to lighten the mood and laughed off the serious talks my doctor had with me, but I knew, deep down inside, that he was as terrified as I was. I couldn't imagine never seeing my babies grow up, couldn't imagine them changing into adults and navigating their lives without a mother, so I fought for my life, while keeping on top of the mum stuff and hiding my struggles from the world. I was given the option of having a double mastectomy with a small amount of chemotherapy afterwards, so I took it. It was either that or a massive dose of chemotherapy, which would have rendered me incapable of looking after my children and run the risk of the cancer returning to my breast tissue one day. Yes, George was there, but he also wasn't. I still felt like I had to be the one to do everything. That's my mentality: it has to be me.

So, I may not have my C cups anymore, but at least I'm alive and kicking. It was caught early enough and I get yearly check-ups and tests, but I'm in the clear.

Fuck you, cancer.

Fiona: one. Cancer: nil.

Soon, the kids will be grown and then they'll flee the nest and I'll be here wondering where the hell the time has gone and why I've suddenly turned grey. I may complain about the grey hairs, but I'm actually hugely thankful for them because it means I'm still here, growing old.

I catch my reflection in the hallway mirror and check out my flat chest. Oh yes, I get a lot of strange looks from people (mostly women) when they see I have nothing up top, but hardly anyone knows I had them removed. To them, I'm just a woman who hasn't been blessed with large breasts. To me, I've someone who's been blessed with a longer life. Who needs breasts to be a woman anyway?

I tidy Liam's shoes and hike his school bag into the lounge, where I dump it on the floor. He can bloody well sort it out himself when he eventually emerges from the cesspool he calls a room. Since he's entered his teenage years, I'm reluctant to peer into his school bag or his room too often, for fear of being called overbearing or nosey, or discovering something that will either gross me out or shock me to my core. I'm terrified my baby boy is slowly becoming a man.

But what if he's got something *bad* in there? Like . . . cigarettes? Alcohol? Drugs? Dear God, please not condoms. He's fourteen! Does every mother think like this or is it just me? It can't only be me, surely. Plus, if he did have something in his bag that he didn't want me seeing, he wouldn't take the risk of leaving it in the hallway. He'd hide it, make sure there was no chance of me rooting around inside and finding out his secret.

Momentarily convinced that my son isn't hiding anything dodgy or dangerous, I get to work preparing dinner.

Thirty minutes later, I enter that strange time between pick-up and dinner where I'm at a loss of how to occupy myself. I decide to send my daughter a message, asking her what time I can expect her home and to remind her that dinner is at six. Just like it is every single night.

She reads it. She doesn't reply.

So, I push my luck and call her. She doesn't answer.

I put my phone on the kitchen worktop and stare out the window at the overgrown back garden. My hands clench around the edge of the cracked worktop, as I attempt to get my blood pressure under control. It's then that all the jobs I've been meaning to get around to start popping up in front of my eyes like phone notifications.

The wonky picture frames in the lounge need straightening.

The lawn needs cutting.

Boots's cat litter box needs emptying and changing.

Most of all, the corner of the lounge needs sorting. It's currently known as the vortex of doom because once an item lands in it, it often disappears forever. I think there's a chair buried underneath all the stuff somewhere, but I can't be sure. This rental house has been our home for ten years. We moved in and the very next week I got diagnosed with cancer, so the renovations and projects all got put on hold and then forgotten about — hence, the paint is peeling in almost every room and the carpets are fraying at the edges. Before this, we lived in a tiny flat, but as Liam started walking and becoming more and more mobile, we quickly realised that we'd outgrown it, so we scraped together a small deposit and rented this house. Of course, we have dreams of owning our own home one day, but a mortgage has never been possible.

George has a steady job with decent pay, but we've never taken that next step, mainly because there's always been something else to pay for, to save for. He spends a lot of time ensuring we have a comfortable life. We're not poor. We can afford new uniforms for the kids whenever they need them, and can take them on a yearly holiday. We do okay, but we're far from buying a new house — or a new car, for that matter.

Lately, it feels as if the walls are squeezing closer and closer. The house is too small, or maybe we just have too many things crammed into it. I even applied to be on *Sort Your Life Out* with Stacey Solomon, but I haven't heard back. I guess that means we haven't reached crisis point yet. I do try and keep on top of the cleaning and the sorting, but with no help from the kids or George, I often let things slide. I only have two hands, not ten.

I'm not saying George is lazy. He's just very work-orientated. He's closed-minded with regards to who should earn the money and who should look after the kids and the home. Doesn't take a genius to work out who he thinks should do what. He's always said he'll take care of me, and I love him for that.

I just wish . . .

I let out a long sigh as tears brim in my eyes, making my vision blur. What's going on with me today? Why am I feeling so . . . disconnected from my life? I've been in a never-ending loop for the past seventeen years, since I found out I was pregnant with Heather. I haven't thought about my own well-being, my own happiness since then. I'm not depressed (trust me, I've had that particular conversation with my doctor and once with my therapist, who I no longer see), but I am a bit . . . I guess the word would be *tired*.

Yes, I'm tired right now. In more ways than one.

Tired of being ignored. Tired of being treated like a servant, like I'm just that random person in the background who does everything without asking, without question. Tired of not hearing a please or a thank you. Tired of never being asked how *my* day was, if *I'm* okay.

Something needs to change.

I don't know what, but I know it needs to be *something*.

And I know for a fact it won't be my family who change, so that means I have to be the one to take the first step. I reach up and grab a strand of hair.

Then stop before I fiddle and tug at it.

No.

No more.

I'm making a conscious effort to stop.

Removing my fingers from my hair takes monumental effort, but I do it. Maybe a haircut is in order. More and more grey hairs are springing up, framing my face. Yes, I know I said I don't mind them, but who am I kidding? They can be the first to go. They make me look ten years older than I actually am. I grab my phone, call my local hairdresser and book an appointment for tomorrow afternoon. Luckily, they can squeeze me in as they've had a cancellation. They promise it will only take thirty minutes. We'll see.

Feeling momentarily elated, I next decide to empty Boots's litter tray. He's part house cat, part outside cat. Some days he won't leave the sunny spot on the windowsill, preferring to watch the world go by from his pedestal, whereas other days he spends his time prowling the neighbourhood, eventually coming home with a small, furry dead animal in his mouth.

Today, he's on the windowsill and hasn't yet acknowledged my presence. Even the cat doesn't care about me, only demanding attention if I happen to be late with his food.

Boots is a rescue and joined our family a year ago. He's now two years old, still full of mischief, and looks down on everyone (mostly me). It's sad really, that I crave attention from the cat as much as my own family. Just a meow of appreciation would be nice once in a while, or perhaps a cuddle on the sofa, but no, I have to work for everyone's affection around here.

Dinner is ready at six, yet not one member of the family is at the table. George messaged earlier to say he was running late, so that's fine, but Heather is yet to arrive home and Liam hasn't appeared from his room. I sit at the head of the table and glance at the three empty seats.

This is my life.

I suddenly get a glimpse into an alternate reality of what it would be like without them. Yet another reason to keep my secret to myself. What if George walked out and took the kids? They would, in a heartbeat, choose him over me. I know they would. There wouldn't be any sort of competition. George is the fun one, especially lately. The past year he's been letting them get away with murder, whereas I've had to try and rein them in and set some ground rules. George and I aren't on the same page anymore, and it's slowly working a wedge between me and my children.

Despite all I do for this family, it's never good enough.

Is it too late to change?

CHAPTER 4

That night, George eats his dinner cold. Liam appears from his pit half an hour late and eats without a word, taking his pudding of ice cream up to his room, where no doubt the empty bowl will be forgotten about until it starts to smell and grows fluff. Heather returns two hours after dinner and says she's already eaten at her friend's house.

I'm standing at the sink, finishing the last of the washing-up. Sometimes, I do it straight after dinner, other times I leave it an hour, whereas when I really want to push the boat out, I leave it until the next morning. Depends what sort of mood I'm in. Sometimes, I'd rather poke hot needles into my eyes than tackle the mountain of dishes. We have a tiny draining board, so I end up playing the precarious game of washing-up Jenga, which usually ends with the whole tower crashing to the floor, making the cat bolt up the stairs, hissing and spitting.

Heather takes the entire plate of sausage and mash I left on the side for her and dumps it in the bin.

'Hey!' I shout.

'I told you, I already ate,' Heather snaps back.

'There's no need to throw it away! You could have put it in a Tupperware and put it in the fridge.' I sigh, taking my hands out of the suds. 'How was I supposed to know if you'd eaten or not?

Despite what everyone thinks, I'm not a mind reader.' I snatch her now empty plate away with wet hands and drop it in the sink. Soapy water splashes over the counter and down my top.

Heather rolls her eyes and stomps upstairs.

'Thanks for the backup,' I say to George, who has been lingering in the doorway to the kitchen for the past few minutes.

He looks up. 'Like my opinion even matters to you,' he replies bluntly. His coldness makes me do a double-take.

'Of course it matters!'

George scoffs and crosses his arms.

'What's going on?' I ask.

'Nothing,' he says, a scowl on his face.

'Clearly it's not nothing. Come on, out with it.'

George grinds his teeth. 'It's just . . . fuck it, why even bother? You never listen, do you? You don't care what I have to say. You act like your opinion is the only one that matters around here.'

I swallow the hard lump in my throat. 'I . . . I've never said that . . .'

'No, but you think it. You just expect me to agree with you all the time.'

'No, I expect you to back me up.'

'What, the way you back me up all the time?'

My mouth opens, but no sound comes out. I'm floored. Is he right? 'I'm . . . I'm sorry if you think that . . .'

George laughs. 'There you go again. Fucking hell, Fiona.'

'What!' My voice rises several octaves. I feel like I'm being attacked by my husband for something I have no idea about.

'Let's drop it, yeah?' he asks, his own tone of voice dropping to a much calmer one.

'Fine,' I say with a long, drawn-out sigh. I don't want to drop it because there's clearly something still bothering him, but I don't have the energy to deal with it now. Maybe that's half the problem between us. Neither one of us is willing to stand and fight it out, get it out in the open in case our marriage derails completely.

'Did you know about the sports day tomorrow?' I ask, changing the subject.

'Yeah. I can't make it. Sorry.'

'How did you know but I didn't? Did Liam tell you?'

'Yeah. Last week.'

'And you didn't think to mention it?'

'I thought you knew.'

I bite my lip, causing pain, deciding to quit while I'm ahead. Maybe it's my fault. Maybe Liam did mention it and I forgot. It's not unheard of. It's impossible to remember everything. I don't pretend to be the perfect mother. There is no such thing, but damn it, I try my hardest to keep on top of things.

Sometimes stuff slips through the net — a net whose threads are fraying, the holes widening with time. Sooner or later, something much bigger than a sports day is bound to fall through.

* * *

I'm late for the fucking sports day because my haircut overruns, so I miss Liam's first race but manage to catch his second. He's amazing! He wins the 400 metres a full ten seconds clear of anyone else, and makes it look effortless.

A gaggle of other parents clap and congratulate me when he crosses the line. I had no idea he was so fast. When did this happen? Whenever I ask him how he got on at PE, all I get in return is a shrug of the shoulder or a grunt or two.

How do I get through to him that I genuinely want to know all about his day? Neither of my children seem to understand that. By the look on his face when he wins, he loves running and competing, so why hasn't he spoken to me about it? The school hasn't mentioned anything either. Neither has George, and the kids seem to tell him everything. I mostly get information second-hand.

Liam spies me standing at the edge of the field. I wave and he quickly avoids eye contact, making a wide circle to avoid me.

I attempt a bit of small talk with two of the other mums, who both gush about my hair. I've gone for a choppy bob, slicing off at least four inches from the bottom. It's now dyed a gorgeous chestnut brown, covering those pesky greys. It's taken at least ten years off me, meaning I now actually look my real age. But no amount of haircuts or cosmetics procedures will ever make me look twenty-five again.

'Thank you,' I say, blushing. I can't wait to show George later. Maybe even Heather will notice. Miracles can happen.

* * *

Turns out, miracles don't happen. Not to me, anyway. Liam shuffles into the car carrying his medals and two trophies, ignoring me completely. Heather, when she eventually turns up and sits in the passenger seat, pops her earbuds in and looks down at her phone.

She's silent the whole way home.

'I'm so proud of you, Liam,' I say, glancing at him in the rear-view mirror.

'Thanks,' he mutters.

'No, really, I am. I never realised you were so good at running. Are you on the running team at school?'

'Yeah.'

I wait a few seconds, hoping he'll elaborate. He doesn't. 'I'm happy to take you to races and things. I'm not sure how it works, but if it's something you want to—'

'Don't bother,' he says with a sigh. 'Can you drop me off at Steve's house?'

'Uh . . . do his parents know you're going there?'

'Yes.'

'Okay, well, sure. I'll just double-check when we get there.' This receives an eye roll from the back seat. 'Um . . . your teacher says you've been hanging out with some older boys.'

'Yeah, so?'

'It's just . . . I don't . . .'

'Mum, relax, okay? Yes, I hung out with them a bit, and yes, they were smoking, but I didn't join in. Besides, I prefer hanging out with friends my own age. All the older boys are interested in are girls.' I see him roll his eyes again.

I smirk. Seems even at fourteen, he's not quite there yet with regards to girls. Thank goodness.

'I mean, I like girls, but . . .' He stops, as if realising he's saying too much. God forbid he open up and talk to his mother about how he's feeling or anything personal. He lapses into silence, so I take that to mean the conversation is over.

Satisfied that Liam isn't about to start having sex and smoking himself into an early grave, I turn to my daughter. 'Where can I drop you, Heather?' I ask, keeping my tone light.

Heather doesn't reply, probably because she's got the volume up too loud. I reach over and tap her on the knee. She flinches away as if I've burned her with a match, then rips out one of her earbuds.

'What?'

'Can I drop you anywhere?'

'Home. No, actually, on second thoughts, drop me at Willow's.'

I wait for a please or a thank you, but none come.

I snap like an elastic band stretched beyond its limit.

'You know,' I say with a frustrated chuckle. 'I'm getting really tired of your attitude lately.' At this, she bows her head, eyes on her screen. I slow to a stop at a set of traffic lights. Feeling bold from out of nowhere, I continue. 'It would be nice for you to use please and thank you, or, I don't know, answer my questions with more than a grunt or a sarcastic comment. That goes for the both of you.'

Nothing.

Not even a grunt or a sarcastic comment.

I've never felt more insignificant or useless as a mother than I do right now. I drive without a word to Steve's house. Liam mumbles something that sounds like a 'thank you', but I can't be sure. I quickly unbuckle myself and follow him to the front door.

He knocks. We wait in silence.

The door opens and Steve's mum looks out. 'Hi!' she says.

Liam rushes past her.

I shake my head. 'I'm sorry about him. He's a boy of very few words lately.'

'Aren't they all? Your hair is gorgeous!'

I automatically reach up and touch it, grabbing a small strand and tugging. 'Thank you.' It seems only people outside of my immediate family can see my new hair. At least it proves I'm not invisible.

'I'll drop Liam round about six. Is that okay?' she asks.

'Yes. Fine. Thank you.'

I back away and give her an awkward wave, questioning myself why we've never become closer friends. I hate to admit this, but I don't even know the woman's name. How do I have two teenage children, yet hardly know any of their best friends' parents?

This is my fault. I'm a useless human being in general. I've made it my mission in life to do what's best for my children, always put them first, always ensure I take them to playdates, yet never bothered to make friends myself.

I get into the car with a heavy sigh, start the engine and point it in the direction of my next destination. Heather remains silent beside me. Her earbuds are in, so I don't bother wasting my breath trying to speak to her. She won't hear me.

I pull up by the side of the house and she reaches for the door handle. 'Thanks,' she mumbles before slamming the door.

I sit and watch my teenage daughter go into her friend's house. I'm taking those two small thank yous as a win.

I hit rush-hour traffic on the way home. There's also roadworks up ahead and a four-way traffic light system in place, so I'm here for a while. Just what I need to settle my already high blood pressure.

I catch myself in the rear-view mirror, allowing myself a small smile at my new haircut and colour. It looks lovely, I'll admit. Bouncy. But, despite taking a few years off me, the dark bags and wrinkles around my eyes are doing their utmost to add years on. I'm hopeless with skin care, always have been.

A random radio station is on. I'm not even sure which one it is, but the presenter begins talking about a new competition that starts today.

'Win your dream home in the country!' she says in a chirpy voice. *'A multi-million-pound country house in the Cotswolds is the prize. All you have to do is answer the following question: What is the name of the female, teenage popstar who released the song "Lucky" in 2000? Text your answer to 15467 before midnight tonight to be in with the chance of winning. This house is being given away to one lucky winner, completely mortgage free, plus all bills paid in full for the next year and a bonus one hundred thousand pounds in spending money to do with as you like. Enter now and good luck!'*

The correct answer immediately pops into my head because I used to play that damn song on repeat when I was a teenager. In fact, the whole album would be played over and over until the CD became so scratched, it was unusable.

The traffic ahead hasn't moved in the past five minutes. Horns are blasting around me. People are impatient. Then, my brain catches up to what I've heard.

Win a dream house in the country . . .

What are the odds? Is this the universe trying to tell me to enter? First those emails flood my inbox for days and then I just happen to be listening to this radio station, which happens to have a similar prize . . .

Granted, the emails were clearly spam, but I swear it's like a huge light bulb has just been lit above my head.

I stare down at my phone.

'Text your answer to 15467 before midnight tonight. You never know, your new life in the country may just be one text away!'

My eyes remain on my phone. I don't really believe in the universe sending me messages, or karma or anything like that, but this seems different.

I'd be a fool not to at least try . . .

'Fuck it,' I say as I pick up my phone.

I type in a new text message and send it off, my fingers trembling.

A car horn sounds behind me.

Damn it, the traffic is moving.

CHAPTER 5

When I finally arrive home — fifteen minutes later than I planned — I'm flustered. After being stuck in traffic and being diverted down a different road, I had to go all the way round the houses to get back on track. My new bouncy hair is sticking to my sweaty face, even though I had the air con on full blast. It's not even hot outside, so God only knows why I'm getting hot flushes. There's no way I'm old enough to be entering . . . *Nope, don't say it.*

I may be a sweaty mess but I'm still on a high from entering that radio competition. It's given me tingles all over. I can't explain it, but I feel hopeful for the first time in forever, like there's a flicker of a flame coming to life. There's no guarantee I'll win because things like that just don't happen to me. Ever. As a kid, I entered a drawing competition at school and there were only two entries, including mine, and I still lost. But . . . it's nice to dream, isn't it?

I can't even remember where the house in the prize draw is located. Somewhere in the country. It's a pipe dream because there's no way George would want to move. Getting him to switch from full-fat to semi-skimmed milk was hard enough. I suppose I'm like that too, but not as extreme. I like to stay on my toes, and can adapt quickly, but during the past year or so, I've got a weird itch that I can't seem to scratch. I'm not sure what needs to change, but I know it's something. My hair was just the start.

It's a surprise to see George's car in the driveway. I'm not expecting him home so early. He hasn't parked far enough up the driveway as usual, so when I pull up behind him, the back of my Volvo sticks out onto the pavement. I sigh in annoyance because I've asked him to make sure he parks higher up so many times. So. Many. Times. Sometimes I wonder if I'm speaking English to my family.

What's he doing home early? I thought he was working late or he had some sort of meeting that was going to run long, or . . . To be perfectly honest, I don't always pay attention when George tells me about his work, but I'm almost certain he told me he was working late. There's been a lot of miscommunication with us lately. Perhaps one or both of us are losing our memories or maybe we're both too far stretched and information just doesn't stick like it used to.

Maybe George has started dinner and chucked the hoover around the house since he's been home. Ha! As I say, I can dream, but I think there's more of a chance of me winning that dream house than George picking up the hoover. I'm not even sure he knows where it's stored.

As soon as I slide the keys into the lock and push the front door open, I know my dreams have not come true. George is sitting on the sofa with his feet on the ottoman, his laptop resting across his thighs, a cup of tea balanced on the arm of the sofa.

'You're home early,' I say, setting my bag on the side table. 'That's nice.'

'I told you I was going to be home early today.' He doesn't lift his head when he speaks to me, just keeps his eyes glued to the screen.

I remain where I am, standing just off to the side, in full view, waiting for him to look up and notice my hair. I told him I was getting it done before he left for work this morning, but all he did was grunt at me.

'No, you didn't,' I say, frowning. 'You said you were working late.'

'Pretty sure I didn't.'

I open my mouth to keep arguing, but then decide not to waste my breath. 'The kids are at their friends' houses for a bit.'

'Cool,' he replies.

'I'll start dinner, then. Um, by the way, I had to use the credit card today.'

At this he looks up. 'Why? I told you it was maxed out.'

'I know, but I got a haircut and a colour . . .'

George rolls his eyes and goes back to the screen. He mutters something about me spending money again.

I know he told me not to use the credit card for a while, not until we've paid some of it off, but when I went to use the debit card, it was declined. I barely check our bank accounts. I know it's a bit old school, sexist even, that I let George sort all the finances, but I trust him. Besides, I do enough, and it's nice not to have to worry about when the car insurance is due, when the rent is changing, and all that malarky that I don't have time for. George is the expert in finances, after all. It's part of his job description. I think . . .

I love George to bits. He's my person, my soulmate, but our relationship has drastically changed since we became parents, which is probably the same for all couples over the world, but George and I seem to have lost ourselves along the way and we're struggling to find each other again.

He's there, right in front of me every day, but he doesn't *see* me anymore. Not like he used to. I wonder if it's because I've maybe lost my looks — I'm not as fit and toned in certain places as I was — but I don't think that's it. It's not even the fact I don't have breasts anymore. He said he doesn't care. Or . . . that's what he said ten years ago. Maybe he's changed his mind. Men are visual beings, after all.

Try as I might, I can't seem to work out what it is we've lost.

The spark.

Whatever that means.

We have sex maybe once or twice a month. That's still decent for a couple in their second decade of marriage, but it's more of a routine than anything else. There's no passion. It's another job, another chore, that needs ticking off the list to keep our marriage on track.

And it's fine.

It's *fine*.

I turn and start dinner. I don't know what to cook. I didn't get any meat out of the freezer to defrost overnight and, by the looks of it, we're out of pasta, so I can't fall back on good old spag bol, a meal that's guaranteed empty plates in this house.

I've done my best over the years to feed the family wholesome, nutritious meals, but when the babies started eating proper solid food, I quickly realised it was all a load of bollocks. Kids don't care about wholesome, family meals cooked from scratch with fresh ingredients and fancy names.

No. They want chips. Nuggets. And peas. And ketchup. Don't forget about the ketchup.

On repeat every day.

Forever and always.

The end.

Except when they turn around out of the blue, five years later, and say they hate chips and never liked peas or ketchup, and have no idea what I'm talking about when I say I now have shares in ketchup because I've bought so much of the stuff over the years, I could fill a swimming pool.

Now though, they're out of their kiddie phase and well into their teenage phase and I'm even more at a loss of what to feed them. Liam will basically devour anything and everything put in front of him except mushrooms, seafood and peppers. He's allergic to seafood, so it never comes in the house.

Heather, on the other hand, can get by on a few picky mouthfuls of whatever I happen to make. She never says she likes it or asks for more, so it's difficult to tell if she enjoys what I cook. She spends a lot of time with her friends at their houses, so I assume their parents feed her.

'What's for dinner?' asks George.

I turn and see him standing in the doorway of the kitchen, leaning against the doorframe. 'I have no idea,' I reply.

'That's not like you. You always have dinner planned out.'

'Yes, well . . . I'm having an off day. Is that okay? Am I allowed to have an off day?'

George raises his eyebrows at me. 'All right, all right, keep your hair on.'

I whip my head round and give him my trademark stare.

'Speaking of hair . . . You look different,' he says. 'Have you done something to your hair?'

I turn my back on him, bite my lip and count to ten, reminding myself it's wrong to murder your husband over something as menial as him not noticing a new haircut.

Murder is wrong. Murder is wrong.

* * *

Liam is dropped off home at six, and he retreats to his room until I call him down for dinner, which, in the end, is rice, green beans and fish fingers. Liam and George discuss Pokémon trading cards and George regales him with tales of the time when he had over a thousand. I know when I'm not wanted or needed.

I tried to get excited about the whole *Pokémon Go* thing back in lockdown, but Liam preferred to go out with George, not me. Apparently, having a mum who enjoyed playing *Pokémon Go* with you wasn't cool.

Washing-up done and kitchen surfaces wiped, I take up my position on the sofa, the same sofa we've had for fifteen years. It's so old that it has an imprint of my bum that, no matter how many times I shake out the padding or wash the covers, refuses to budge.

George is watching a DIY programme on the television and I'm half-heartedly reading my Kindle. I've recently got into dark romance books. The darker the better. The more spice the better. In fact, screw the romance. I like it downright dirty when it comes to reading. I do read thrillers on occasion, but I prefer to escape into a hot and spicy romance fantasy than read about blood and lies and secrets.

My husband has no idea the filth I read. If he did, he'd probably be a bit worried or feel insignificant compared to the hunks on the covers of most of the books. That's why I read on Kindle. He'll never know . . .

There's a lot of things about me that I keep from George.

It's for his own good.

Including the origin of the scars high up on my inner thighs. I told him they were from attempting to climb over a barbed wire fence at the age of fifteen.

That's not true.

I self-harmed when I was at school. A lot. That's why I try and keep such a close eye on both Heather and Liam. Self-harm may not be hereditary, but I know all too well how addictive it can be. I never told anyone, but my parents did find out eventually and they helped me through it, made me see a therapist. It was just a thing I did. It felt wrong, bad, dangerous. I don't condone what I did and I'm well aware that self-harm is a lot more talked about and prevalent these days, but it was never to end my life. It was a way of controlling my emotions, but a lot of people would never understand it if I told them that.

I do wear skirts, but never above the knee, just in case I happen to flash too much leg. I do go swimming, but I wear longer swim shorts over the top of my costume. George thinks I'm being silly, that no one will care about my scars, but I care. My kids have never seen them and they never will.

Every marriage and family have secrets.

Some secrets are bigger than others.

I'm sure George keeps secrets from me too. I doubt any of them are as shocking as mine, but I never pry.

My parents died when I was young and I've never really got over it. Their deaths forced me to grow up fast, especially when I found out I was pregnant only a few months later. I'm fast approaching the age my mother was when she died, and thanks to my close call ten years ago, I do think death itself scares me more than most.

The worst thing is the thought of leaving my children behind. I've got too much left to teach them, but all they do is push me away.

When Heather was a baby, I never let her out of my sight. When it came to nursery and pre-school, she was more than happy to leave me, never giving me a backwards glance, but I refused to leave the building, convinced she'd fall apart without me by her side. She never did. She's always been my independent girl, and I can't help but feel slightly resentful that her friends' mums seem to spend more time with her under their roofs than I do under mine.

Liam, on the other hand, loved me and would throw a hissy fit whenever I left the room. I loved being needed, but the fear of something bad happening kept creeping up on me when I least expected it. Sometimes, the fear would overwhelm me and I could hardly catch my breath. I didn't want the kids to leave the house without me, constantly shouting at them whenever they stepped too close to the kerb, even though I knew they had no intention of crossing the road without me.

George is the opposite. He's so laid back, he may as well be horizontal.

That's not his fault. He had a stable, normal upbringing. Whatever that means. That's another reason why I can never tell him the truth about my scars. He wouldn't understand. How could he? He once told me, while we were watching a reality programme that involved suicide and self-harm, that people who self-harm or end their own lives are only doing it to get attention. I must admit, I hated him a little bit that day.

No one can understand, so that's why I avoid talking about it altogether. The only person who sees the scarring is George and he's used to it now, so never makes a comment. He's never second-guessed my cover story. Clearly, the sight of my scars doesn't bother him, but it bothers me and, try as I might, I can't get over how ugly they look now. I thought they'd fade with age, but no. They're like a constant reminder of my youth. Mottled, lumpy lines all over my upper thighs. My lack of breasts are a reminder of how strong I am, yet the scars on my legs remind me of how weak I am.

I see so many mumfluencers on social media promoting the whole 'love the skin you're in' message, but how can I love the skin I'm in when it's a daily reminder of the worst time in my life?

I thought cutting would make me feel better about myself, but it's done the opposite. Therefore, I cover up.

Heather comes home at just after eight that evening. She pops her head round the lounge doorway. George doesn't bat an eyelid.

'Hi, love. Did you have a good time at Willow's?' I ask, putting my Kindle down.

'Yeah. Goodnight.'

'Wait. Hold on. Did you do your homework there?'

'Yes,' she replies with a moan.

'Have you eaten?'

'Yes.'

'Okay, then. Goodnight, love.'

She stomps up the stairs. I look over at George. He's asleep. No wonder he didn't say anything. I roll my eyes and get back to my Kindle. Now that both the kids are safely back under my roof, I can relax for the evening and enjoy reading.

For a moment, I close my eyes and imagine winning that dream home in the country. A smile creeps across my lips and I get back to my smutty book.

CHAPTER 6

The next morning, the school run goes off without a hitch and I'm on my way to work when my phone rings. It's hooked up to my car via Bluetooth, so I answer the call, thinking it may be the school already. Maybe I forgot to give the kids something to hand in. It wouldn't be the first time, but again, like I repeatedly tell my family, I'm not a mind reader, and if they need me to sign a form or do something, then they need to physically ask me, not attempt to telepathically transmit the words in the hopes I'll decode their silent messages.

'Hello,' I say, keeping my tone bright and cheery.

'Hello, is this Fiona Howden?'

'Yes, speaking.'

'Hi, Fiona. This is Julia from Radio West. How are you doing today?'

'Uh . . . I'm fine.' I turn left down a road. 'I'm sorry, but where are you calling from?'

'Radio West. It's about your entry to the prize draw yesterday.'

'Oh . . .'

'Congratulations! You've won the Cotswolds multi-million-pound house draw!'

The line crackles slightly.

Silence follows her loud, excited outburst.

'I'm sorry,' I say, turning the volume up. 'What did you say?'

'You've just won a multi-million-pound country house in the Cotswolds!' Julia shrieks again.

This is a joke.

'I . . . I . . . I'm sorry, but . . . Wait. Are you sure?'

'Quite sure!'

'Is this a joke?' I ask with a chuckle.

Julia laughs. 'No, I can assure you it's not. Don't worry, we get that a lot.'

I pause for a moment, words failing me. Why can't I think of anything to say? 'I . . . I can't believe it. Wait, am I live on the radio right now?' A wave of fear crashes over me. Public speaking has never been my forte. One time, in one of my previous jobs, I had to get up and make a quick sales pitch, and I messed up so bad that I forgot the name of the product I was selling.

'No, not yet. We like to get the initial shock over with first.'

'Oh, right. That makes sense.'

'But we are due to go live in less than five minutes. Can you stay on the line? Are you at work or in your car?'

'Um, yes, I'm in my car at the moment, but I can pull over now. I'm just arriving at work, actually.' I pull into a parking space but keep the engine running. 'Are you sure this is real? This sort of thing never happens to me. I've never entered a radio competition or any competition before . . . ever! So this is all a bit . . . Sorry, I'm blabbering. I don't know what to say.' I burst out laughing, covering my mouth with both hands.

Julia laughs too, her cackle instantly setting my jingling nerves at ease. 'It's perfectly okay. How about I give you a couple of minutes to compose yourself? Grab some water. Then, we'll have a chat live on the radio — please don't swear! Would you like us to call anyone and surprise them or would you like to tell them yourself?'

The question shocks me for a moment because I hadn't given it a hint of a thought. Everything is happening too fast and I can't catch my breath. I've never been on the radio before. Thank God it's radio though and not television!

'Um, no, thank you. I'll tell my family myself tonight.'

'No worries. I'll just put you on hold for a couple of minutes, then we'll make a start, okay?'

'Yeah, sure. Thanks.'

The line changes to some smooth country music, leaving me staring open-mouthed at the brick wall ahead of me. I'm going to be late for work, but screw it.

I fan my face with my hand to stop the heat rising in my face. It doesn't help. The blood is rushing around my body so hard and fast that I can feel it pounding in my head. It feels as if I'm submerged yet my mouth is dry, so I reach for my trusty water bottle in my bag and take a swig.

What the fuckity-fuck has just happened?

I barely remember sending that text yesterday. It was a spur-of-the-moment thing because I happened to know the answer, but I always know the answer to competition questions on the radio, so what the hell possessed me to enter that particular competition?

Like I told Julia, I've never entered one before. I don't gamble. I don't waste money on things like this because the likelihood of winning is too remote to even bother. But someone has to win, right?

And today, that person is me.

The emails. It was the emails that made me enter, wasn't it? They were like a sign from the universe. Could it be that the universe is answering back, telling me I deserve this after all the shit I've put up with? No, not shit, but . . .

Another laugh erupts from my mouth and I rub my eyes, which are brimming with tears. Happy tears. Confused tears. I want to laugh and cry at the same time and I have no idea how I'm supposed to get through a live radio interview now when all I want to do is scream with joy, maybe throw up a bit.

My hands go to my head and I start nervously tugging, snapping my new hair like it's an injection of heroin. Over and over and over, I twirl and tug and tug and pull.

Stop it!

It's fine. It's just a live chat on the radio. Damn it, what if my work colleagues are listening? Does anyone ever listen to Radio West? Why was it on in my car yesterday? I don't think I've listened to it before. I usually listen to Heart or Capital.

Should I jump out and go and tell my boss first? I'm already late, but maybe he'll understand when I tell him what I've won.

Holy crap, I've won a massive multi-million-pound country house. Is this real? Maybe there's a catch. There's always a catch, but what if there isn't one?

My mind starts whirling with images of what it could look like. I've seen those Omaze houses on TV adverts. Swimming pools. Games rooms. Huge bars and basements. Even tennis courts and acres of grounds and gardens.

And I've just won it all.

* * *

The next fifteen minutes are a complete and utter blur. A mix of emotions that I can barely keep under control. I blubber and stutter my way through the radio interview, even forgetting the names of my own children, then question myself whether I should have revealed their names live on air. I kick myself. What if one of their friends' parents are listening and they tell their kids and then their kids tell my kids and they find out before I tell them? They'll be so confused, thinking it's all a big joke.

When I finish the interview and get off the air, I walk on shaky legs into the garage and say hi to Harry, one of the mechanics, who's tinkering with an engine on a Vauxhall Corsa, and head straight to the back office where Alan is usually sat drinking his first coffee of the day.

'Ah, there she is. I was beginning to get worried,' he says as he takes his feet off the desk.

'I'm so sorry I'm late, but I promise you, I have a very good reason.'

'Let's hear it, then. I'm intrigued.'

* * *

I somehow make it through the day, but by the end, I'm so exhausted from repeating the story to my colleagues that I'm looking forward to picking up my children, who will most likely not utter a word to me. Unless they've somehow found out from a parent or teacher, but I'm hoping that's not the case. I'm assuming George hasn't found out through the grapevine either because he would have called me, even to ask if it was a joke.

I'm not sure why I told Julia not to call and tell him live on the radio. I suppose I thought it would be best if he heard it directly from me. I want to see the look on his face when I tell him. Plus, George has never liked being put on the spot and I know he'd hate to be blindsided like that.

I've already received a long email from the radio station, explaining what's going to happen next. The house itself is empty and ready to be moved into. All I need to do is sign the deeds and it's mine, bar a few other forms and various housing hoops that I'll need to jump through. I have the option of living in it for a year, all bills and expenses paid, or selling it, pocketing the money and using it how I wish. If I did that, I'd be a millionaire overnight. Apparently, it's worth close to three million pounds. Not only that, but I also get gifted a hundred thousand pounds as a cash prize, tax free.

I need to speak to George before making any decisions, obviously.

It's going to be a massive life change, no matter which option we choose.

As predicted, both children get into the car without a single word. I savour the silence while I drive home, but can't help but smile as I do.

'Can you drop me at Steve's again?' asks Liam.

'No,' I say decisively, turning right. 'Tonight we're having a family dinner, which means we all have to be seated at the table at the same time.'

'Why?' asks Liam.

'Because it's a nice thing to do and I have some news that I'd like to share with you all.' I half expect them to ask what news, but that would mean they were interested in anything I have to say.

Heather avoids eye contact and can't hear me anyway because of her earbuds.

* * *

The kids retreat up to their rooms the second they walk in the door, leaving me to prepare dinner and sort out their school things. George is still at work.

Boots meows at me from the back door, so I let him in. He rushes straight to the fridge and meows again. *Yeah, yeah, I'm getting to it.*

I make a mild curry using a jar of sauce and place a plastic tub of poppadoms in the middle of the table. George walks in the door bang on six, kicks his shoes into a corner, drops his bag on the arm of the sofa and plonks himself down in his chair, putting his feet straight up on the coffee table.

'Hi,' I say from the kitchen doorway.

He looks up in surprise. 'Hey,' he replies. 'Good day?'

'You could say that,' I reply with a coy smile. Again, I wonder if he cares enough to ask me what I mean, but he doesn't.

Sometimes I wonder why I bother.

It takes several attempts to get the kids downstairs from their rooms. It seems they've gone deaf again, so I'm forced to walk upstairs, bang on each of their doors and yell over their loud music that dinner is on the table.

By the time they make it downstairs, George and I are halfway through our meals and theirs are going cold. Liam starts shovelling the curry and rice into his mouth as if it's a race. I'm surprised he doesn't give himself indigestion more often.

I clear my throat. It's now or never.

'I have something very important and exciting to tell you all.'

Silence. The sound of crickets chirping in the distance.

'I said, I have something important and exciting to tell you,' I repeat.

George looks up from his food. 'Oh yeah?'

'Yesterday, there was a competition on the radio and I knew the answer to the question, so I entered. And this morning, I received a call from the station telling me I'd won.'

George's eyebrows raise half an inch. 'That's great, Fi. What'd you win?'

I glance at the children, neither of whom are paying me any attention, so I decide to carry on regardless. Maybe when George starts jumping up and down with excitement, it will shock them out of their comas and they'll understand that something big has happened in their lives and they actually have to pay attention to their mother, for once.

I smile. 'A multi-million-pound country house in the Cotswolds and a hundred thousand pounds in cash.'

George's hand pauses with a forkful of food just as he's about to put it in his mouth, which drops open and stays there. He blinks. Then, his fork crashes down onto his plate, splashing drops of curry sauce everywhere.

'You what?'

'It's true, I swear,' I reply with a giggle. A part of me still doesn't believe it. All of a sudden, I'm going to wake up from this crazy dream, but it hasn't happened yet.

'You're serious,' he says.

'Yes, I was even on the radio today. Radio West. I have the documents already. All I need to do is sign them, and the house and money is mine. Ours.'

George snaps out of his bemused look and bursts out laughing. He stands and rushes to my side. I barely have the time to stand up before he takes me in his arms and swings me around in a tight hug, like we're newlyweds. We laugh together and kiss.

'This calls for champagne!' he says, putting me down on the ground.

'It's already chilling in the fridge,' I say.

George races to the kitchen, leaving me alone with the children. Heather and Liam are staring at me like I have horns growing out of the top of my head.

'Wait . . . What's just happened?' asks Liam.

'Mum's won a big house in the country,' replies Heather coolly. 'It's a scam, right?'

'It's no scam. No joke. I can promise you that.'

'Cool!' replies Liam.

Heather locks eyes with me. I can see she wants to react in some way, but perhaps her teenage hormones and persona won't allow such a large show of emotion in front of her mother.

'Yeah, cool, I guess,' she says with a mere shrug of one shoulder.

George returns, carrying four flutes and the bottle.

'Oooh! Can I have some?' asks Liam.

'Just a sip, buddy,' replies George, already tearing into the gold foil around the top of the bottle. I picked the bottle up en route to school pick-up. I'm sure George won't mind me splurging a bit, considering we're about to come into an enormous sum of money.

Heather's eyes finally light up at the prospect of drinking alcohol. It's not her first time; we allow her some on special occasions as long as she's around us, but I expect she also drinks with her friends. I'm yet to be called up in the middle of the night to fetch her from a drunken party, but it's bound to happen sooner or later. I've tried my best to teach her right from wrong and warned her about the dangers of drinking, drugs and partying, but it falls on deaf ears. Plus, and I'd never admit this to her, but I feel like a hypocrite because I had her at nineteen due to a drug- and alcohol-fuelled one-night stand at a party.

George disrupts my thoughts by popping the cork. It makes me jump, but I also laugh again as the frothy liquid spills over the rim of the bottle and onto the carpet. I don't even care.

'So, tell me everything,' says George, pouring. He gives Heather half a glass and Liam a small splash, then fills our glasses up.

'Wait!' he says just as Liam is about to chug it down in one. 'Here's to your mum taking a chance and winning!'

'Cheers to that,' I mumble as we all clink glasses.

This is the closest I've felt to my family in a long time, even if Heather is still looking like she'd rather be anywhere else, but she seems to have mellowed slightly because her phone is face down on the table and she's waiting for me to start talking. For the first time in God only knows how long, all three of them are staring at me, and I have their undivided attention.

I must admit, I'm a little nervous.

CHAPTER 7

I start at the beginning and tell them everything. At least, all the parts I can remember because it's still all a blur. Liam eventually loses interest. It's easy to spot because his eyes glaze over and wander to his phone, but he soon perks back up when I announce the size of the house and what rooms and gadgets it has.

'It has a *swimming pool*?' he says with a gasp.

'It has two,' I reply proudly. 'One indoors and one outside, which is heated. It also has a games room and a home cinema.'

'Oh my God, that's so freaking cool!'

I then reach the part about the bills and the no-mortgage clause, explaining again about the tax-free cash prize.

'Are we actually, like, getting a suitcase full of money?' asks Liam, his eyes the size of saucers.

'Erm, I'm not sure that's how it works,' I say. 'It'll probably be a lump sum transferred directly into our bank account.'

'Hang on,' says George, holding up his hand to stop me. 'Are you saying that we get to live in this house completely mortgage free *and* have our bills paid for an entire year?'

'Yep,' I say, taking a smug sip of fizz.

'So . . . the cash prize isn't to use towards paying for this enormous house for the next year? Because I've heard of these types of prizes. The cost of running a house that size is ridiculous and most people end up putting it on the market, but then it takes years to sell because of its size and cost and they end up getting less than what it's worth.'

I've seen those stories on the news too. It's all well and good winning a three-million-pound mansion, but it must cost several thousand pounds a year to run if you include council tax, electricity, gas, insurance, utility bills, not to mention the cost of hiring people to take care of the property — gardeners, cleaners and so on.

'I know,' I say. 'But this prize includes everything for a whole year. We wouldn't need to pay for a single bill.'

George's mouth drops open. 'I mean . . . I don't even . . . Wait, where did you say it was again?'

'The Cotswolds.'

At this point, Heather pipes up. 'Hang on. We're not *actually* moving though, are we?' She makes it sound as if I'm asking her to move to the Sahara Desert and live under a canopy, not a hundred miles away to an idyllic country house.

'We'll have to talk about it, I suppose,' I say, glancing at George for some backup. 'Your dad can easily work from home and I'm not tied down with my job, so . . .'

'Oh, yeah, of course, it's all about you, isn't it?' Heather snaps back. 'What about me? What about my life, my friends, my school? I'm not leaving! I've got my GCSEs!'

'Heather's got a point, Mum,' says Liam. 'I don't want to leave my school and friends either. It's really close to the end of the school year.'

'You'd rather live in this cramped old house that's overflowing with stuff and stay in your schools than move to a luxury mansion in the country?'

'Why can't we just sell it, then use the money to buy somewhere just as good around here?' asks Heather.

I stand up, glass in hand. The bubbles have gone to my head a little, so my vision swims. 'It's a chance to start over somewhere new and—'

'I don't want to start over somewhere new,' says Heather.

'I don't give a damn what you want!' I gasp at my tone of voice and harsh words. 'I'm sorry,' I say quickly. 'I didn't mean—'

'Yes, you did,' mutters Heather. 'You don't care about me. You never have.' She storms out of the room, leaving her glass of champagne untouched in front of her.

Liam eyes it. 'Can I have the rest of her glass?'

'No,' say George and I in unison.

Liam grumpily folds his arms, then picks up his phone again.

I glance at George. 'I didn't mean to snap at her like that.'

'I know, but she does have a point. We don't have to move there, do we? We could sell it and buy something slightly smaller around here. Plus, we'll have the extra hundred grand to make life easier.'

It's like a bucket of ice water has been dumped on my head, shocking me out of my dream-like state. The excitement of moving to a new home has been washed away, leaving bitter disappointment and a slight resentment towards my family, who are doing their best to hold me back.

I thought they'd be excited to move, but I was wrong. Rather than looking at it as a fresh start, a brand-new opportunity for a better life, they'd rather stay here. Change scares them.

I take the bottle of fizz and my almost empty glass and wander out into the garden, plonking myself down on the little foldout chair on the tiny patio. It's in dire need of a good scrub, having built up grime and dirt over the winter, but I haven't had the time to spruce it up. The garden is overgrown and small, the lawn mostly moss, and the shed at the bottom is crammed full of junk that needs sorting, most likely all covered with mould from the leaking roof.

If we moved to the new house, I could quit work for a year and focus on myself for a change. I'd have time to do all the things I've missed out on since having children. Plus, with our bills taken care of, any money from George's work could be used for fun things, like holidays and trips away to spectacular places. Hell, George could even quit his job for a year.

The downside of selling and buying a house near here is that, while we'd have a bigger home and no mortgage, the bills would still need paying, which means we'd be using a chunk of the prize money and it would take much longer for everything to happen. Houses don't sell overnight. Julia said on the radio that we could move into the Cotswold house in as little as two weeks. Selling and buying could take months, maybe even up to a year, and we may not get what the house is worth due to the state of the market. Yes, we'd have leftover money from the sale, but then what?

'Penny for your thoughts?' asks George as he sits down on the stone step beside me. We stare at the tiny garden ahead, at the long grass, the weeds, and the array of footballs and other items Liam has left lying around.

'Am I a bad mum for wanting to uproot the kids and move somewhere else because it would make me happy?'

George scoffs. 'Of course not! Heather's just being Heather. At the end of the day, it's you who's won the house, so you have the final decision.'

'Thank you, but I don't feel that's right. The decision should be made as a family.'

'Then you have to realise that someone in the family is going to come out of this disappointed, no matter what we choose.'

'And that's what I'm afraid of,' I reply, tipping back the last drop of fizz. I pick up the bottle beside me and fill my glass. 'What do you want to do?' I ask, turning to look at him.

George sighs. 'Honestly?' He stops and stares at the garden again. 'I want to ditch this place and move to the Cotswolds.'

The dwindling flame inside me flickers back to life. 'Really? This, coming from the man who hates change?'

He nods enthusiastically and throws up his hands. 'I don't hate change.'

I give him a look he knows well.

'Okay, so maybe I do hate change, but fuck it. Something like this doesn't happen every day, does it? You're right. Other than the kids' schools, we're not tied down here, are we? I can work anywhere. It would be an adventure for us. Plus, to not have to pay bills or a mortgage . . . it would ease the pressure for sure.'

I've never wanted to fling my arms around my husband and give him a massive squeeze more than I do right now.

'Thank you,' I say quietly. 'If it doesn't work out after a year, then we can sell up and buy something smaller, either back here or somewhere else. We'll have money left over to take the kids travelling and do all the things we've never had the chance to do.'

I'm already making an internal list of things we need: a new car, an all-expenses-paid holiday, trust funds for when the kids turn eighteen.

George nods. 'Sounds like a plan. The kids will come around. I guarantee you the second Liam sees the gaming room and the pool, he'll forget all about his friends. And Heather will love having a whole wing of the house to herself.'

'She can even move into the separate cottage if she wants.'

'There's a separate cottage?'

'Yeah. It has two bedrooms.'

George chuckles. 'Bloody hell. This is going to be one amazing year.' He reaches out without another word and takes my hand. We hold hands as the darkness closes in, the warmth of the day dwindling, but I couldn't be happier right now. I'm warm and cosy thanks to my alcohol buzz and I feel closer to George than I have done in a long time.

I've never seen him so animated, so excited. It's the longest conversation we've had in well over a year. It's at this moment I realise I haven't been happy for a while.

I don't want to make it sound like I'd only be happy with a big house and money because it's not true. It's the freedom. The release of pressure on my chest. That's what's making me happy, making my heart feel full.

I don't have to work for a year. I can spend more time with the kids, rekindle our close relationship, even if it's going to take a lot of work. Maybe I can home school them. Although, then again, maybe not. I'm not sure which one of us would snap first.

Yes. This move is going to be life-changing for us as a family.

I'm sure of it.

CHAPTER 8

The money lands in our joint account a day later and George and I waste no time in buying a brand-new family car. George's eyes bulge at the sight of all the shiny sports cars, but I manage to talk him down out of the rafters and we end up with a new top-of-the-range Audi A6 Avant. I say my goodbyes to the Volvo, which has been a very faithful addition to the family over the years, and hello to the Audi, beaming like a Cheshire cat as I pull out of the garage forecourt. George is clearly quite jealous that I get a new car to drive and he has to keep his old company car, but apparently he's due an upgrade soon.

The next day, I hand in my notice at work. Alan says I don't even have to work out the week's notice, which is very nice of him. George decides that he's not going to quit his job, which I think is a sensible option, considering he's worked so hard to get where he is today, but he is cutting back on his hours. He does have a few away trips that he can't get out of because they've been in his work diary for months, but he assures me he'll be around as much as possible over the next year.

Two weeks later, the deeds are signed and the paperwork is complete.

The kids' current school is very understanding and I'm able to get them enrolled to the nearest school to the Cotswolds house, but they won't be starting for another week. The timing isn't great because of Heather's GCSEs and it being so close to the summer holidays, but I think we can make it work.

We inform our landlord about moving out of our rental house. There's still four months left on the tenancy agreement, but since we have a large lump sum in our bank, we don't squabble over it. I even agree to pay for a cleaner to come in once we've moved out to spritz the place up because I can't be bothered to do it myself.

The radio station have been in touch to arrange everything. I've spoken with Julia a few times, but no one else. She's been a great help and answered all my silly questions. It feels a bit weird, to be honest. I keep asking myself the same question: why me? Why has the universe decided to grace me with this life-changing opportunity? Do I deserve it more than everyone else who entered the competition? Do I deserve it at all?

One thing I do find a little peculiar is that we're not filmed or photographed for the paper. Not that I'm complaining. I can't think of anything I'd like less, but don't big prize winners usually get interviewed or something? Apart from the radio interview I did on the first day, there's no other announcement, which means no one is aware of our win until either me or George tells them.

The parents at the school gates have clearly heard because all of a sudden I'm like a local celebrity at morning drop-off and afternoon collection. I get asked so many questions, but all of them are laced with an underlying tension.

'Must be nice to never have to worry about money again.'

'Wow, what have you done to deserve that, then?'

'Don't forget about the rest of us when we're still here slaving away to pay the bills.'

I don't know these people. I don't owe them anything, yet every single one makes a comment that slowly chips away at my good mood. On the last day of school, I stay in my car outside the gates because I can't deal with any more thinly veiled insults.

Laura knocks on the window. I begrudgingly lower it. 'Ooh, is this your new car?' she asks, sticking her head through the window and taking a look at the leather seats.

'No, I stole it,' I reply with a chuckle.

She laughs back. 'Just wanted to say good luck with the move and everything. It must be very hard on the kids, having to leave their school.'

'Yes, very hard,' I say with a sweet smile. 'But I'm sure they'll be okay.'

When George and I told Heather and Liam about the move, it did not go well. Heather has barely said a word to any of us in two weeks and has spent most of the time out of the house with her friends. Liam, on the other hand, is slowly warming to the idea, but he does make sly comments every now and then, making sure we know this is clearly upsetting his social life and schedule. I'm certain he'll get over it. I've managed to sweeten the deal by telling him we'll invite all his friends for a massive pool party in the summer holidays, which are fast approaching. He agreed and instantly started texting them all.

Laura gives me a thin smile. 'Hmm, well . . . I'm looking forward to my invite to your house-warming party!'

I laugh out loud. 'Yes, as soon as we're settled, I'll be in touch.'

'Perfect!'

We say our goodbyes and I push the button to raise the window.

Over my dead body.

* * *

The day of the big move arrives. I'm a jumble of nerves, anticipation and excitement. I haven't slept properly for three days. We haven't visited the house yet, but I've seen pictures. It looks like a show home, something out of a fancy magazine or a house belonging to a celebrity. It's mine. Ours. I still can't wrap my head around the idea, but whether I'm ready or not, we're about to move into our new home today.

The moving lorry drives away down the street, leaving me, George, Heather and Liam standing by the Audi (where Boots is currently residing in his travel box, meowing in protest) with our empty old house behind us. It's the end of an era. Despite its damp corners, small rooms and narrow hallways, this house has seen us through a lot. The kids may not have taken their first steps here, but many firsts have happened within its walls, including first teeth falling out, first wins at school, first kisses happening outside the front door (as far as I know it was Heather's first kiss, I could be wrong). I can't help but think back on the happy memories as I pull away, following George in his work car. The kids have opted to ride in the new car for one reason and one reason only: it has all the cool gadgets and mini TVs built into the headrests. Heather has her earbuds in, staring blankly out the window. Liam is playing a game on the TV screen, linked up through his iPad. Boots is in his cat carrier on the passenger seat.

A couple of hours later, we're almost there. Three minutes to the turning, according to the trusty built-in satnav. I glance at the kids in the rear-view mirror.

'Heather, Liam, we're nearly there. Please take your earphones out. Phones down.'

This receives an eye roll from Heather and an excited squeak from Liam. He may be fourteen going on eighteen, but really he's still an overly excited little kid who's about to get his own gaming room and home cinema system, not to mention all the open space he could ever need to play football to his heart's content.

George signals left ahead when we reach the road leading up to the house. Apparently, it's a quarter of a mile on the right with a short driveway leading up to it. Every house around here is massive. I feel like an outsider, an intruder. I shouldn't be here. People who live here have bought their homes with hard-earned money. Perhaps they have well-paying jobs or are business owners, worth millions. You'd have to be a millionaire to live in any of these houses. Now, there's me and my family moving in.

From Leicester.

Up until this morning, I'd lived in rentals my whole life. I was a minimum-wage worker who used discount coupons to get a few pence off her favourite food items, who shopped at Aldi, who wore the same clothes so often and for so long that they'd get holes in them.

And now I'm here with my family driving towards this enormous seventeenth-century house. We're situated a stone's throw from Cirencester, but far enough into the countryside to be classed as rural. There are other houses nearby, all within walking distance, but there's no chance of ever hearing the neighbours arguing or stomping around, like our previous house. More than once, we had people living next door who were so noisy and disruptive we had to put in a noise complaint, which didn't go down well. There's nothing worse than coming face to face with a neighbour who knows it was you who dobbed them in to the landlord or council, who in turn gave them a verbal warning to keep it down or they'd be kicked out.

George slows as we round the corner. I follow as the driveway opens up ahead and the house expands in front of us in all its glory.

Holy. Mother. Of. God.

CHAPTER 9

'Holy crap!' says Liam.

I don't tell him off for his language because I'm thinking the same thing. I roll the car to a stop in the gravel driveway just as my eyes flood with tears, and before I know it I'm sobbing and laughing at the same time, covering my mouth with both hands to stop from making a complete fool of myself. I very rarely show a great deal of emotion, other than anger and frustration, so this is a whole new experience for me.

George is speechless as he gets out of his car, his mouth opening and closing like a fish. As I climb out of my car, my eyes are glued to our brand-new home, which looms in both directions, stretching out as if to say, 'Ta da!'

It's easily the most stunning building I've ever seen. Yes, I've seen the pictures, but they by no means do it enough justice. It's a quintessential Cotswold property, combining traditional charm with modern amenities throughout. I did my research before arriving, so I know a little about its history and what lies inside, but nothing could have prepared me for the sheer magnitude of its honey-hued stone exterior. Cascades of wisteria adorn the outside of the property, framing several of the windows in beautiful, bright blooms of lilac. I can smell the sweet fragrance of the flowers from the car, which I'm clinging on to for dear life, afraid my legs are going to collapse beneath me if I take so much as a single step.

Inside, I know it has five bedrooms and five bathrooms, a cinema and games room, a modern yet classic cottage-style kitchen, several living areas, massive hallways and a laundry. Outside, a heated pool and pool house are situated off to the right, an indoor pool and spa area are somewhere round the back, and a large triple garage is attached on the left. There are two greenhouses and stables in the grounds, which consist of almost two acres of beautifully landscaped gardens with a large pond. Oh, and the separate two-bedroom cottage is across the yard, its own little home away from home. It has its own front gate and garden.

'This is . . .' begins George, but he stops speaking, coming instead to stand next to me. I've finally made it a few steps away from the car.

'What do you think, kids?' I ask, without taking my eyes off the property. I'm too worried that it's all going to go *poof* in a cloud of smoke and I'm going to wake up any minute.

'It's . . . big,' says Liam. 'Can I go and explore by myself?'

George and I glance at each other and say 'Yes' in unison.

Our son doesn't need telling twice (unusual for him because it often takes at least three attempts for him to do as he's told). He lunges forward, leaving his iPad behind (there's a first time for everything) and stampedes up the stone steps towards the front door, which is unlike any front door I've ever seen. Elegantly carved with swirling motifs, it's embellished with a large, ornate handle and a wooden porch, similarly draped in wisteria.

The moving lorry hasn't arrived yet, despite leaving before us, but there was hardly any need to pack all of our furniture from home because this property comes fully furnished with everything we could ever need. Our old, worn, cheap items will look out of place here, ruin the tranquil ambience and perfect decoration.

Heather is snapping pictures on her phone and hasn't said a word yet, but I catch her eye before she runs after Liam and she gives me the smallest of smiles.

I'll take it.

George grabs my hand and squeezes. 'Shall we?'

'We shall,' I say with a smug grin.

We burst out laughing and practically skip towards the front door like a couple of lovesick teenagers, following the kids into the house, straight into our dream home. Upon entering the hall, which is the size of an entire house, we gasp in unison and crane our necks up at the spiralling wooden staircase that looms ahead. All it needs is a red carpet down the middle and it would look like something out of a Hollywood blockbuster. The decoration in the hallway is tasteful, with calming tones of colour, but with a modern twist.

There's a lot of technology in this house, most of which I doubt I'll know how to use. Next to the front door is a large white box that looks to hold all sorts of wires and cameras and buttons. No doubt George or Liam will be all over that later, figuring out what everything does. I'm glad to see there are CCTV cameras set up everywhere I look. We never had that at our old house and several times there were attempted break-ins or damage done to our property and we weren't able to catch who did it. Seeing the level of security this house has instantly sets my mind at ease. A house this size needs it.

The smell of fresh jasmine tickles my nostrils as we explore downstairs. I may take a moment to myself and explore upstairs later. I don't know where the kids are, but I don't care. They're safe here. They're content. And that makes me beam with warmth and happiness.

George and I take everything in, holding hands as we enter the kitchen. I burst into laughter and tears again as my eyes soak in the splendour — the wooden beams, fresh flowers on the vast island counter and the bitter-chocolate-coloured units, set off by pristine black-quartz countertops that sparkle in the sunlight.

A smoked mirror splashback, an enormous oven that has four different doors and an induction hob with eight sections finish off the luxury that is my new kitchen. There are six rattan stools tucked under the central island. I don't think I'll ever complain about cooking ever again.

I open the double American-style fridge. There's a matching freezer next to it. The fridge is fully stocked with top-of-the-range food and fresh vegetables, so I don't have to worry about going shopping for at least the next week or so. All the cupboards are full too and there's even a walk-in pantry, the shelves laden with tins and jars and everything a family of four could ever want or need.

I step out of the pantry and close the door, gulping back the hard lump in my throat. My heart starts thumping and I can't catch my breath. George lays a hand on my back, noticing my sudden change of demeanour.

'You okay?' he asks soothingly.

'It's . . . It's just all a bit sudden,' I reply with a weak smile.

'I know what you mean. Hey, how about you take a seat and watch me attempt to make us a coffee using this . . . this . . . monstrosity of a coffee machine.' George gestures to it and I laugh. I must admit I'd missed it.

'It looks like it belongs in a café! The size of that thing.'

'I'm going to go and get Boots first,' I say, hastily backing out of the kitchen, allowing me a few seconds to catch my breath. I'd forgotten all about the cat, who's probably thinking about reporting me for animal cruelty as we speak. I only left him a few minutes ago. I'm sure he'll be fine.

He yowls at me as I lift his cage from the car and carry it into the house. I don't want to let him out straight away because you have to be patient with introducing a cat to a new house. We did the same thing when we first adopted him, keeping him in a single room while he adjusted to the new smells and sounds around him. I bring him into the kitchen and place his cage on the floor by the French doors. I quickly fill his bowl with water and slide it through.

Boots instantly begins scratching to be let out, but then he resigns himself to the fact that he's stuck in there for a bit longer and sits watching the birds outside.

I turn my attention to George as he scratches his head and studies the enormous coffee machine while I perch on one of the stools at the island/breakfast bar. He presses random buttons and finds the fancy cups and bags of expensive dark roast in a cupboard above the machine.

It takes him twenty minutes, but he finally hands me a hot cup of steaming, fresh coffee.

We clink cups and drink.

I know we have the rest of the house to explore, but here, in this moment, is where I want to stay forever. It's perfect, and with the late afternoon sun beaming in through the French doors leading to a perfectly manicured garden, it feels as if I'm in a movie, or living someone else's life.

'Helloooo?'

George and I swivel our heads towards the sound at the same time. George gets up to investigate, but just as he reaches the door leading out of the kitchen, a face peers round it.

'Ooh, I'm so sorry, I didn't mean to intrude. The front door was open and I saw you drive up. I'm Glory Hamilton, your closest neighbour.'

A woman of around my age steps into the kitchen, carrying a bottle of red wine and a box of biscuits wrapped in a red bow. She's elegantly dressed in a pair of white linen trousers and a long-sleeved, floaty floral blouse that's open at the collar, revealing her rather large and perfect breasts. My eyes go straight to them, and if *my* eyes head straight there, then I know where George's have gone. I don't blame him and, despite my acceptance of my own lack of breasts, I feel a surge of envy.

George's face lights up when he sees her. 'It's no problem at all,' he says, approaching her with a bounce in his step. 'I'm George, and this is Fiona.'

I stand up and give her a slight hand wave. 'Hi, nice to meet you.'

Glory steps closer to George and gives him a great big hug, still holding onto the wine and biscuits, her huge breasts pushing up against his chest. I stifle a smirk as I watch his awkward reaction. Next, she approaches me and does the same, but not with as much enthusiasm, quietly kissing the air on either side of my face.

'So lovely to finally meet you,' she says in an excited sing-song voice. 'Here, these are for you.' She sets the wine and biscuits on the counter, pushing them towards me. 'I heard the house had been won in a prize draw and was so excited to see who the lucky winners were.'

George chuckles. 'Yes, well, we still can't believe it, to be perfectly honest. This house is like a dream come true.' He's blushing, a tell-tale sign he's a little taken aback by this woman.

'Would you like a coffee?' I ask her.

George throws me a look, which tells me he'd rather not make another coffee after spending so long making ours. I give him a slight shrug.

'Ooh, yes please,' says Glory, clapping her hands together.

George puffs out his cheeks and approaches the coffee machine. 'It's rather larger than our instant espresso machine,' he says.

Glory skips up and stands next to him, her hips brushing against his. 'Here, let me show you. I have one exactly the same. There's a knack to it, but once you know how to work it, you'll never want to drink coffee from any of those nasty high-street shops again.'

Glory shows George how to use the machine, explaining all the knobs and dials, but I'm barely listening because I can't take my eyes off this new neighbour of ours. There's something about her that's drawing me in, and it's not her perfect appearance or peppy personality. It's something else. Something I can't put my finger on.

She's fascinating. The way she moves around the kitchen is like poetry in motion. She even opens the box she brought and removes some dainty macaroons (turns out there aren't biscuits inside), serving them on a plate. She strikes up an easy conversation with George as if they've known each other for years. Clearly, this woman doesn't have any problem with making new friends. I find myself a little envious of her again, now in more ways than one.

We sip our drinks and chat for a few minutes.

'Top-up?' she asks, finally taking her attention off George and putting it onto me. She's been eyeing my husband for the past twenty minutes like a succulent piece of meat.

'Oh. Um. Please.' I hand her my empty cup and she shoves the plates of macaroons at me. I take one with a tight smile, feeling like a fish out of water. This woman oozes wealth and poise and here's me dressed in old slacks, a baggy t-shirt and dirty trainers. I'm still sweaty from the humping and dumping of boxes this morning and can slightly smell my own armpits. Delightful.

'Shall we take these outside on the patio?' she asks George, who nods enthusiastically and follows her like an eager puppy. I head outside, and finally there's something magnificent enough to draw my focus away from Glory.

The garden.

Standing at the top of the stone steps, which lead down to the manicured expanse of lawns, I see a wildflower meadow and an orchard stretching out to the side, a paved path leading through it. It's a south-facing garden, and even I know that means it gets the most sun all year round (thank you, *Gardener's World*). A huge greenhouse is situated in the middle of the back garden. Glory explains that it has mains power, running water and fancy automatic roof vents, just like hers. Are our houses carbon copies of each other?

Glory points out various other features too. George is lapping it up like a dehydrated dog, whereas I just stare in wonder at the beauty around me. I'm looking forward to exploring the orchard and grounds by myself one warm, sunny evening.

I sit down on the lavish six-seater corner patio sofa. Eventually, Glory and George join me. George makes a show of sitting close beside me, our legs touching.

'So, tell me everything,' says Glory. 'Where are you from? Do you have kids?'

'We have two,' I say. 'Heather and Liam. Almost sixteen, and fourteen.'

'Oh, that's wonderful. I also have two. Ryan is nearly eighteen, and Jess is twelve, but she's away at boarding school at the moment. I'm sure Ryan would love to meet Heather.'

I smile, already knowing that Heather will perk up when she hears there's a seventeen-year-old boy living next door. She's had a couple of boyfriends lately, but no one serious. She gets fed up with them quickly. I'm reluctant to tell her that that's men for you, sweetheart. They don't change even as they get older.

I listen as Glory tells us in detail about Ryan and Jess's education and hobbies. Jess loves horses and has two of her own. Ryan is an expert archer and has won many a championship since the age of eleven, even pipped for the Olympics in 2028.

Her husband is called Victor and he's an important businessman who works in London mostly. She doesn't expand on what exactly he does, but it doesn't take a genius to know they're loaded. He commutes back home at weekends and is often away on long trips, so we aren't expected to see a lot of him. George keeps quiet during this part. Ryan attends a local private school and, as she's already said, Jess is at a boarding school down south, which I already know costs more than my and George's salary combined.

I listen and smile and nod in the right places. Glory intimidates me, I can't deny it. She's everything I wish I was and the more she talks, the more I realise that this is my chance to not only better my family's life, but my life too. My body. My brain. My soul.

I'm going to do better. Be better.

Nothing can derail our new perfect life.

CHAPTER 10

Glory leaves an hour later with a friendly wave and another hug for George (not for me). She's invited us for dinner at theirs tomorrow night, so Heather can meet Ryan and as a "welcome to the area" type of gathering. Plus, her husband's home from London, so we can meet him too. She says that Ryan is into his gadgets and technology, so I have no doubt Liam will get on well with him.

I must admit, it's nice to be invited to dinner. I didn't know any of the neighbours at our old place, not in a friendly way. They did have kids, but much younger, just toddlers, and the women never made an effort to chat when we ran into each other on the driveway. In fact, they often avoided eye contact with me, pretending like I didn't exist. They clearly had their own lives to worry about.

Fine by me, but this house means a fresh start for the family, including me and my tendency to shy away from socialising.

Glory is different. She's put herself out there to be friendly and welcoming towards us from the start and doesn't seem entitled, nor does she look down at us in any way just because we won the house and didn't buy it with our own wealth. There've been no sly comments about how lucky we are or how we haven't worked hard enough to deserve a place like this. She may be a little showy, and she still intimidates the hell out of me with her appearance, but there's a genuine kindness there. Perhaps we can be good friends one day.

The kids eventually join us as George and I finish unpacking the car after Glory leaves. I let Boots out into the living area, but make sure to tell the family to keep the doors closed so he doesn't escape into the rest of the house or outside just yet. Boots finds a sun spot on the windowsill and lies stretched out, paws in the air. He seems happy.

The moving men arrive with the lorry, but since we don't need anything they dump it all in the large garage, which still has space left over after all the boxes have been unloaded. I'm not sure what we'll end up doing with the extra furniture, but for now it can stay out of sight.

'Mum, there's a seventy-inch TV in the cinema room! Plus, the game room has a brand-new PS5, a Nintendo Switch 2, and a brand-new Xbox. Plus, a pool table, a ping-pong table and a racing game like in the arcade!'

I raise my eyebrows at Liam's outburst. He's been begging us for a PS5 for over a year and, this Christmas, we were going to surprise him with one because we've been secretly saving up, but now I guess that's out the window. He's got everything a boy his age could ever want.

'That's amazing!' I say, trying not to let disappointment flood my voice. I feel disgruntled that I didn't buy the game console myself. It's silly, I know.

'Oh, and get this . . . There's an actual full-size replica of Thor's hammer on the wall!' he continues.

'Okay . . .' I say, unsure whether or not I should be impressed. I turn to Heather. 'Have you found a room you want?'

'Yeah. It's the one furthest away from the master suite.'

Of course it is.

'Great. And hey, you can even move into the separate cottage if you want to, you know, have some more space.'

'No, thanks. I'm good.'

I take that as a small win. Perhaps she realises if she lived in the cottage, she'd have to do all her own cooking and cleaning and washing. Then again, I have been trying to encourage her independence more and more as she nears adulthood. It destroys a little piece of my soul every time she moves away from me, a little further out of reach every day, but it's an inevitable bridge I have to cross, so I may as well get used to it now.

* * *

I explore the upstairs of the house by myself a little later. George is playing with Liam in the games room, absorbed by the gigantic screen and surround sound system that is surprisingly quiet once the doors are closed. Liam explains that the games room is soundproofed. This place just keeps getting better and better.

Heather is sunbathing by the pool. It's almost five in the afternoon, so I plan to start preparing dinner soon, but first I want to see my new bedroom.

The master suite is exactly that: a suite. The ash wood bed, covered in ivory linen, is big enough to sleep six people side by side comfortably — four posters with dark red silk drapes over a wooden canopy. At the bottom of the bed is a characterful stone mullion, complete with a cushioned window seat below, which enables you to look out across the vast grounds.

There's a separate seating area with a pop-up television, cleverly hidden behind a secret panel, as well as an adjoining vanity room with a thick wool carpet and bespoke shelving set into muted mauve walls. I'm half expecting it to be filled with beautiful, designer clothes, but of course, that would be a step too far. It seems wrong to hang my tatty clothing in such an exquisite dressing room, but I'm determined to rectify that soon and buy myself some trendier outfit choices.

The heritage en-suite is more like a full-scale bathroom, with a rolltop bath and a revitalising rainfall shower in an immaculate corner of marble and glass. With dark wood, intricate painting and gold accents, it sets an opulent tone — a nod to French elegance. I swear I've seen this house in a magazine or on a movie before.

I twirl around in the middle of the room, still not quite believing that this is all mine.

* * *

An hour later, George and I open the bottle of wine Glory brought round and I drink it while preparing dinner. I haven't seen the kids in over an hour, but George has gone off in search of them again, wine glass in hand.

There's so much food in the fridge and cupboards that I'm at a loss what to make. I eventually decide on a home-grown salad and some extravagant-looking fresh pizzas, so all I need to do is figure out how to turn on the oven. I stand in front of it, studying the vast array of knobs and digital buttons.

Is there a manual for this thing?

I push what looks like the on button and the whole thing lights up, followed by an airy tune. *What the* . . . I push another button, but nothing happens. I fiddle and turn one of the knobs on the far right and the digital display in the middle changes. Okay . . . so I think that's a timer, which means if I accidentally forget to turn the oven off, like I have done in the past, it will do it on its own after the time has elapsed.

Okay . . . but how do I actually start the damn thing?

I open one of the four oven doors and stick my hand inside. Nothing. Not even getting warm. This is stressing me out.

I make a mental note to ask Glory tomorrow night how to use the oven. Maybe I'll invite her round at the weekend to show me how everything works. I've never felt so out of my depth in my entire life, even when I turned up to Liam's school day raffle event when he was six, not realising I was expected to run one of the stalls.

After several long minutes and countless curse words, I finally get one of the ovens heating up. I stick all four pizzas in at once (oh yes, it's big enough for four pizzas), then prepare a fresh salad, using the lettuce, tomatoes, cucumber and various other ingredients in the fridge. They're all from the garden, so the vegetable patch is one place I'll be exploring tomorrow.

Are we supposed to look after the grounds by ourselves? I wonder who's been tending to the gardens before now or if the house comes with a garden maintenance team and a cleaner. I don't remember there being anything about that in the paperwork. Oh God, am I supposed to clean this whole house myself? It'll take me hours! Since I no longer have a job, I can keep on top of things here, but the thought of cleaning this place is enough to send my nerves tingling. I reach up and tug at my hair, something I haven't done since arriving here.

I know it seems like a good problem to have, but the sudden reality of owning such a large house is dawning on me. How much does it cost to run this place? Our bills may be paid for the next year, but after that, George and I will need better-paying jobs to be able to afford to run it. Or I will at least.

But that's a future problem. Not a now problem.

The pizzas go down a treat. The kids are happy for the first time in I don't know how long. They have smiles on their faces, and, when I tell Heather over dinner that next door has a son called Ryan who's slightly older than she is, her eyes virtually bulge out of her head. I explain we're going over for dinner tomorrow evening and neither of them make any complaints or talk in their usual moany voice. Success.

* * *

A few hours later, I find the sumptuous snug — a cosy room with cast-iron radiators and painted panelling, adding a period charm. It also has a mahogany bar in the corner, complete with a proper beer pump and a wine fridge. But it's the sheet of glass in the floor that stops me in my tracks.

Under the glass is a spiral staircase leading down to a . . .

'Oh my God . . .'

It's an underfloor wine cellar, like I've seen in adverts and movies. The sheet of glass covering the hole is thick enough to stand on. The lights below flicker on, beaming icy light onto the hundreds of wine bottles snugly fitted into every nook and cranny.

I step behind the bar and find a control panel. I press a button that says *open* and the sheet of glass in the floor slowly slides away, enabling me to climb down into the wine cellar. The steps are steep and it's not large, but it's big enough to fit three people comfortably side by side. The wine bottles are all grouped by type — rosé, red, white, then there's the champagne, prosecco, cava and other various sparkling wines.

There must be close to a thousand bottles, all ranging from the most recent year to almost a hundred years old. Yeesh. They must be worth a fortune.

George is going to go nuts when he sees this. He often brags that he's a budding wine connoisseur, always complaining when I buy a cheap bottle from Aldi rather than a more expensive brand.

Back in the snug, I plonk myself on the generous cushions of the corner sofa and snuggle up with my Kindle as the cool evening air breezes in through the open window. There's a set of double doors leading to a small patio covered in plant pots, but I opt for the sofa, tucking my legs under me and staring out at the garden and the slowly dimming light of the early summer evening.

But I can't focus on my book. I read the same sentence at least five times, never once taking a single word in. My mind is on overdrive about everything that's happened today and is due to happen tomorrow. It's the start of a brand-new life for me and my family. It's going to take some getting used to.

After giving up on reading, I set my Kindle aside, stand up and stretch my legs. The house is silent. It's gone ten at night, but I doubt the kids will be asleep yet. This house is so big that even if they were shouting for me, I probably wouldn't hear them.

Realising that, my anxiety spikes for a moment. Long gone are the days of using a baby monitor to keep an eye on them while they're asleep. Maybe there's a way of setting up some sort of panic alarm in their bedrooms. Perhaps that's a tad overkill. My kids rarely need me in the middle of the night and, if they did, they're both old enough to get up and come and find me.

Pulling my light cardigan around my body, I step out onto the small patio adjoined to the snug. Every main room in this place seems to have its own balcony, patio or a way outside. It's mind-boggling really, the sheer scale of it all. Even when George and I rented a holiday home over Christmas one year in the Lake District when the kids were small, it was nowhere near as big and grand as this.

The darkness is creeping closer, but the garden has lots of automatic lights that illuminate certain areas of the planting and paths. I have no idea how they turn off; perhaps they're on a timer. It's breathtakingly beautiful — the twinkly lights, the pops of colour in the borders. Plus, I can see to the edge of the garden where there's a . . .

Wait a second.

What *is* that?

I can see to where the large gazebo is. There's a fire pit in the middle and a pizza oven too, as well as plenty of seating areas, but that's not what's caught my attention.

An ominous dark shadow is hovering by the gazebo, highlighted even more by the cool lighting nearby. It almost looks like a . . .

Person.

The shadow is definitely humanoid in shape.

Instantly, my nerves tingle and I look behind me for no other reason than to double-check no one is standing there with a knife. How strange the human mind is when faced with a creepy shadow.

I squint my eyes, wondering if I perhaps have consumed too much wine this evening, but I've only had two glasses. The shadow remains and then it moves like lightning, running across the dark lawn to another area of lighting.

Yes! It's a person. I'm sure of it.

'George!' I screech.

But, of course, he doesn't hear me because this house is too big for sound to travel to wherever he is. Whoever it was, though, looked as if they were watching me, saw me watching them, then decided to flee across the garden. I'd caught them out and now they've made a quick getaway.

I grab the patio door handles, pull them closed and lock them.

A neighbour, perhaps?

Glory is our closest one and her husband is away, so the only other person it could be is her son, Ryan, but why would he be there?

I can't find George, so I head up to bed, no longer excited about tomorrow, but full of questions as to why someone is watching the house.

CHAPTER 11

I thought I'd sleep like a baby on the first night in our new home, but my mind races with endless questions, constant internal monologues and ridiculous, over-the-top visions of our future lives. I can't shut it out. In the end, somewhere around three in the morning, I give up trying to force my body to sleep and take a walk around the house, relishing the stillness and quiet. When I'm moving my body, my brain doesn't seem so loud.

I check on the kids first, a habit from when they were babies I've never been able to snap myself out of, then descend the spiral staircase to the ground floor, where the hallway tiles are cool under my bare feet. I'm restless, on edge. I shouldn't be. I should be safely tucked up in bed next to George, feeling the warmth of his body only inches from mine and listening to his incessant snoring that has, on more than one occasion, driven me to the brink of insanity.

Why do I feel like this? There's a foreboding sense of dread deep within my soul I can't explain. Yesterday's bubbles of happiness and excitement have popped, leaving me feeling deflated and anxious, like something bad is going to happen to take all this joy away, pull it out from under our feet. Someone, somewhere, is going to realise we (meaning I) don't deserve any of this luxury and will steal it away and give it to someone else. My family deserve it though. The kids deserve it because God knows George and I would never be able to afford this type of living, not even if we worked until we were a hundred and saved every penny.

I listen to the soothing hum of the house — the fridge-freezer in the kitchen, the ticking of a nearby ornate clock, the gurgle of the boiler. After several minutes of pacing the house, unsure where it is exactly I'm going, I arrive at the spa area, where the indoor swimming pool shimmers and glows under the nighttime lighting that always seems to be on. Bit of a waste if you ask me, but it is beautiful to look at.

Staring into the crystal-clear depths, my reflection stares back at me, but I don't look like myself. My face and body are twisted and distorted into some black, odd-looking creature. It sends a shiver of unease down my spine, so I crouch and reach out my hand, touching the still water with the tips of my outstretched fingers to diminish the beast I see staring back at me.

As soon as they dip into the coolness, a loud, long creak sounds behind me. I turn in a flash to look over my shoulder, but my feet slip out from under me. I lose balance, topple sideways and splash into the pool, sinking beneath the surface like a stone.

My arms flail about as if I'm drowning, my baggy pyjamas weighing me down. I claw my way to the surface, convinced there's someone standing poolside above me. I see the dark outline of a body, but as my face breaks the water and I wipe my eyes, there's no one there.

There's only me. Splashing in the indoor pool at half past three in the morning wearing my pyjamas.

I pull myself out of the water and sit panting on the edge. There was someone standing over me, I'm sure of it, and that loud creak wasn't my imagination. Cautiously, I get to my feet and fetch a towel from the pile in the spa area, drying myself as best I can before climbing the stairs back to the master suite. I undress and shower off the chlorine.

When I return to bed with damp hair, George is still snoring, lying on his back with his mouth wide open. I climb in beside him and pull the duvet up to my chin.

It's fine. I'm just exhausted. That's all.

* * *

Morning arrives, but I swear time has slowed down. Every time I look at my watch, it seems to be going backwards. I decide not to tell George about my nighttime swim because he'll think I'm crazy and most likely will laugh at me. The idea of someone being in the house at night without the external alarms blaring to life is laughable. George set them when he went to bed.

I should feel safe within these walls.

Then how come I don't?

I feed Boots, who seems to be settling in well and is already pawing at the door to be let out into the rest of the house. I close off a couple more rooms, including the kitchen, so he can come and explore while I'm sorting breakfast. As usual, he gets under my feet and attempts to push things off the side of the counter with his cute little paws, but eventually he gets bored of that and finds another sunny spot to stretch out in.

While I'm clearing up, I glance towards the bottom end of the garden where the gazebo is and get the same chill as I did last night, even though the sun is shining gloriously today. It's a perfect early summer heatwave and, after breakfast, the kids and George waste no time in getting dressed into their swimming things and cannonballing into the outdoor heated pool.

During the day, I take a leisurely walk around the grounds to see the vegetable plot and discover a delightful secret garden with a pond and a stone bridge. After that, I unpack my clothes into the walk-in wardrobe, eventually choosing the poshest items I own to wear for dinner at Glory and Victor's tonight.

I show George the wine cellar, which causes his eyes to bulge out of his head, and ask him to select a nice wine to take round to dinner tonight.

Eventually, the time arrives and I'm a bundle of nervous energy, checking and re-checking myself in the splendid hallway mirror.

'Why are you so nervous?' asks George.

And honestly, I can't give a real answer, so I smile and say that I'm not. I'm a bad liar.

Not that bad though, considering George doesn't know the truth about Heather . . .

We walk to Glory's house in the evening sunshine. Her house is beyond spectacular, very similar in layout and style to ours, but it's clear she's put her own stamp on the property, whereas ours is fairly standard and simply decorated with calming pastel colours. Glory, on the other hand, has very expensive taste and likes her bright, bold colours and patterns. Not on the walls, which are neutral in tone, but in the accessories, furniture and ornaments she uses to transform each area into its own delightful haven. A bright blue velvet sofa is situated opposite us in the hallway as we enter, complete with sunshine-yellow cushions.

'Welcome!' Glory says, spreading her arms wide before enveloping George in a tight hug.

The kids shrink back towards me. Heather gives me a look. I know that look well.

'And these two gorgeous people must be Heather and Liam! Ryan is so excited to meet you. Jess is gutted she's not here, but she'll be back for the summer holidays. Ryan, they're here!' Her voice booms around the entrance hall. Gosh, she's loud.

I hand her the bottle of wine. 'Here. Thank you so much for inviting us.'

'You're very welcome. Oooh, this one is lovely. I have several in my wine cellar.' She glances up the stairs. 'Hmm, I'm not sure where Ryan's got to. Perhaps you'll find him in the games room. Just through there on the left.' She points down the hall.

Liam sprints off, needing no further persuasion after hearing the words *games room*. I'm sure he's excited to see what they have in their house compared to ours.

Heather keeps her arms folded over her chest. She's guarded, not quite sure of this woman. I don't blame her.

'Do you want me to come with you?' I ask.

'No, Mum, I'm not a little kid.' She stomps off in Liam's wake.

Glory claps her hands together, jolting me out of my gaze. 'Right, let's go through to the kitchen. It's the perfect place to sit on an evening like this. Victor will be down in a moment. He only arrived back from work an hour ago and said he needed a shower and a nap first.'

I follow her into the kitchen, where she promptly places the bottle of wine I gave her on the side, then proceeds to open a nearby drawer, pulling out a bottle opener.

'Here. Allow me.' George picks up the bottle and the opener and pops out the cork like a pro.

'You have a lovely home,' I say, peering through the bi-fold doors leading out of the dining and kitchen area to the large expanse of lawn. At the bottom of the garden, there's a large tree with a tree-house hidden in the branches. I wonder how long Glory and Victor have lived here. The kids must have grown up in this house.

Glasses full, we turn and face each other in a semi-circle.

'Cheers!' Glory says, initiating the clinking of our glasses. 'Shall I give you a quick tour? Dinner's ready whenever we need it. Thought I'd do something light. Just a homemade salmon quiche.'

'Sounds lovely,' I reply, following her out of the kitchen.

Glory leads the way, gesturing wildly with her hands while holding her glass aloft. I wince every time she does it, scared she's about to slop wine out of her glass and onto the pale cream carpets. She doesn't. It can't be her first time. I sip as I walk, relishing the tangy taste. We enter the games room. Liam is playing on an arcade machine, but Heather and Ryan are nowhere to be seen.

'Hmm, perhaps he's taken her to his room,' says Glory with a mild shrug.

My insides clench. 'Um . . .'

'Oh, don't worry. My son is perfectly respectable,' adds Glory with a laugh.

'I'm sure he is, but . . .'

'Ah, here he is now.'

A teenage boy appears in front of us, having come from a different side room. He's tall and lanky with short, styled hair. Exactly the type of boy I know Heather likes. Even his clothes are smart, fitted and designer, just like his mother's. He freezes at the sight of us and looks straight down at the floor.

'Ryan, this is George and Fiona, our new neighbours.'

Ryan looks up and nods at each of us. 'Hey.'

'Hi, Ryan. Have you seen my daughter, Heather, around? She was supposed to have gone looking for you with Liam.'

Ryan shakes his head. 'No, not seen her yet. Sorry.' He steps up to the arcade game and starts chatting with Liam, giving him a couple of pointers for the controls.

Instant dread makes me almost double over. It feels as if all the air has been sucked out of the room. I turn to George, but he doesn't look even the least bit worried by the fact our daughter has wandered off in a stranger's home.

'I'm sure she's around here somewhere,' says Glory with a chuckle, although her voice cracks a little towards the end of her sentence. 'Come on, let's go through to the kitchen and get some nibbles. Ryan, can you perhaps go and look for her?'

Ryan looks up from the game. 'Sure.' He turns and strolls out of the room towards the garden.

'I'll be in the kitchen if you need me,' I say to Liam, but he doesn't appear to have heard.

Glory and George walk away, leaving me behind, wondering whether to join the search for Heather or pretend like everything's perfectly normal, as Glory and George seem to be doing.

I take out my phone and call Heather. Surprise, surprise, there's no answer.

Just as I'm about to go into meltdown mode, her voice comes from one of the rooms ahead. I jog down the hall a little to another doorway and peer round it. Heather and Ryan are standing near each other, chatting, the way normal teenagers who've just met do. Heads down, hands folded or in pockets and looking awkward, never making full eye contact.

But Heather's smiling too, a faint flush on her cheeks.

I back away and join Glory and George in the kitchen. They're standing close together, their hips almost touching. Should I be worried? He's laughing like I'm not standing right behind him, scowling.

I clear my throat. 'Found her.'

George turns and smiles. 'See. Nothing to worry about.' His eyes swivel straight back to Glory. She's dressed in another gorgeous outfit, a long chiffon skirt down to her ankles and another light top that accentuates her figure.

'How was your first night in the house?' asks Glory, finally dragging her attention off George and turning to me.

'Oh, it was fine, although I didn't sleep much.' Again, I feel the need to leave out my little nighttime dip.

'The beds are huge, aren't they?' she replies with a laugh.

'Yes, but . . . have you been inside the house, then? Into the bedrooms, I mean?'

'Oh yes,' she says, but doesn't expand. She stares at me, not blinking. I gulp back a large mouthful of wine and almost choke on it when my throat seems to close up, refusing to work properly. Red wine trickles out of my mouth and onto my cream top.

'Oh shit!' I mutter.

Glory leaps to my rescue. 'Oh gosh, you silly thing. Here, allow me.' She rushes to the sink, fetches a damp cloth and hands it to me.

I dab at the red stain, but it's no use. The damage has been done. My face burns.

'Well, that's ruined,' says Glory.

'I'll go back to the house and change,' I say, turning to leave.

'Nonsense! Let's head upstairs and you can choose anything you like from my collection.'

'Oh no, I couldn't possibly . . .'

'Tut, tut. I won't take no for an answer. Come with me. I'll show you the upstairs while I'm at it. Georgie, you'll be okay here, won't you?' She turns and bats her long eyelashes.

This time I almost choke on thin air at the use of her pet name for him. Is she being serious? I stare past her at George, hoping he'll have picked up on it, but no. He just smiles stupidly and holds up his wine glass.

'Don't worry about me,' he says. 'I'll be just fine.'

Glory giggles and beckons me to follow her. I glare at George for a moment before following her upstairs, using the gorgeous ornate wooden banister for support. Glory starts yammering on about all the various decorations and pieces of expensive furniture, all of which are exceptionally beautiful.

We reach the master suite, but just as she's about to open the door, she stops. 'Oh gosh, I forgot, I've got the bread warming in the oven. I don't want to burn it. You'll be okay from here, won't you? The layout is basically the same as your house. Don't worry about Victor. He has his own dressing room. You won't disturb him.'

'I . . . um . . . sure,' I stutter, but even if I'd begged her to stay, she wouldn't have heard me because she's already halfway down the hallway and gone before I can think of a straight answer.

I know what I should do. I should follow her and not enter the master bedroom by myself and spend the rest of the evening with a red wine stain on my top, but I don't do that because I'm slightly tipsy from inhaling a glass and a half of wine already and mildly curious as to what her bedroom looks like.

I cautiously push open the door and peer around it. 'Hello?'

There's no response. Feeling braver, I enter the bedroom, but as soon as the door swings closed behind me, a half-naked man steps out from the nearest doorway, a dark blue towel wrapped around his waist.

My whole body freezes, like I've been shocked with an electric current.

He stares at me. I stare back, as all words empty from my head.

'I-I am so sorry,' I gush stupidly. All my nerve endings are on edge, tingling, and I want nothing more than to sprint out of the room, down the corridor, grab George and the kids and speed back to our house, never to set foot in this one ever again.

This is not the kind of first impression I want to make. Seeing Glory's husband almost completely naked, having walked in on him in his own bedroom. What was I thinking coming in here? I did call out, but he can't have heard me. I didn't hear the shower going either. Glory said it would be okay because I wouldn't disturb him.

He's just as lost for words as I am.

'Um . . .' he says.

'I . . . I'm Fiona . . . from next door,' I say, my mouth as dry as a bone. I let out a breath, my heart hammering so hard in my chest, I'm sure it can be heard a mile away.

'Victor,' he replies. 'Sorry, I . . . What are you doing in here?'

'Oh God!' I shout, covering my mouth. 'I wasn't snooping or anything! Glory sent me in here to grab a clean top.' I look down at my flat chest. 'I spilled wine . . .'

'I can see that.' He's just as red in the face as I am. 'Give me a moment.'

Face still burning, I turn my gaze sideways, no longer looking at him. I wish the floor would open up and swallow me whole. This is mortifying.

Out of the corner of my eye, I watch as he grabs a shirt off the bed, turns his back on me and puts it on, but as he does I see something on his shoulder.

A tattoo.

My eyes focus on it, at the shape, the colour, the . . .

Holy shit.

I recognise that tattoo.

I know this man.

In that instant, my head swims as my world implodes around me.

Victor is Heather's biological father.

PART 2

CHAPTER 12

No. No. No. No.

This can't be happening. It's not possible. It *shouldn't* be possible, not in a million lifetimes. I cannot be staring at the man I slept with nearly seventeen years ago. The man who impregnated me during one night of pure passion. I never remembered his name. Hell, it was so long ago, I barely remember what he looked like, but I do recognise that tattoo.

I scratched his back so hard with my long nails I caused the skin to split and bleed. I apologised afterwards because I was afraid the tattoo would be ruined. It's him. I know it is. No one else would have that tattoo in the same place. The chances would be astronomical. Almost as astronomical as moving in next door to him all these years later . . .

I watch him get dressed, study his movements, his body, his . . .

He notices me looking at him.

I can't breathe . . .

'Are you okay? You don't look too good,' he says, taking a step towards me.

My immediate reaction is to jump back, as if him coming too close is going to ignite some sort of chain reaction or cause me to burst into flames. We stand awkwardly in front of each other, neither of us knowing quite how to react. I know how I *want* to react. I still have the overwhelming urge to turn and run from the room and hide under my duvet like a child having a strop, but I'm a grown woman. I can handle this . . .

'I . . . No, I . . . I'm a bit dizzy all of a sudden,' I say, raising my left hand to my head. My fingers brush against my hair and I instantly grab a strand and tug.

Victor quickly does up the flies on his trousers and gestures to a nearby chair. 'Please.'

I shake my head. 'No, I . . . I should go . . .'

'Do I know you from somewhere?' he asks as his eyes narrow like laser beams aimed directly at my soul. Now I'm the one who feels naked, like he's scanning me from head to toe, searching for something that sparks his memory.

Oh God . . .

For the first time in a long time, I want to cover my flat chest. It's never bothered me before, but the last time he saw me, I had bouncing C-cup breasts that were firm and perky. Not to mention I was much younger, not even a whiff of a wrinkle or grey hair. Everything was still tight and firm. I hate that my first thought is one of humiliation, like I feel insecure about surviving breast cancer. Why do I even care what he thinks about my body?

'I don't think so,' I say. I study him while he buttons up his shirt, eyes widening as I catch sight of his taut stomach muscles. He has only got better with age. My eyes snap away, making me dizzy as a memory pops into my head. One of me licking that same stomach. I can almost taste his sweat on my tongue and, out of the blue, I get a tingle between my legs.

I gasp. There I was, reprimanding George for ogling Glory and here I am doing the same thing to Victor. Even worse!

'I'm very good with faces,' he says. 'Names, not so much, but I'm sure I recognise you from somewhere.'

I attempt a light-hearted laugh, but it comes out as more of a snort. 'Hmm,' I say. 'Quite a mystery.'

'Indeed.'

The more he talks, the more I stare at him, the more I know without a shadow of a doubt that he's Heather's father. The man (although technically, he was an eighteen-year-old boy) all those years ago who shoved his tongue down my throat in the middle of the dancefloor without even asking. The man who led me by the hand to a corner of the club and fingered me in the shadows while dozens of sweaty bodies danced around us.

Then . . .

'Well, I guess I'll leave you to change your clothes in peace . . .' He leaves the sentence hanging. His eyes linger on my flat chest a little too long.

I bite my lip.

'Are you sure you're all right?' he asks.

My heart hammers wildly as if trying to break free from my chest. 'Yes, I'm fine, thanks. And, um . . . Don't worry, I didn't see anything.' My face flames with heat again.

'Of course you didn't,' he replies with a cheeky smirk. I stare at his mouth. The same mouth that caused me to nearly lose my mind when he swirled his tongue around my . . .

'See you downstairs,' he says.

He's standing beside me, about to walk past.

I nod overenthusiastically. 'My husband George will be down there.' What the hell did I say that for?

'I shall go and introduce myself, then.' He leaves with a polite nod.

Oh God.

I can picture it now. If he tells George and Glory that I walked in on him practically naked, tonight is going to be the most excruciatingly painful experience of my entire life. How can I ever look either of them in the face again after this? Glory will probably find it hilarious and be about as tactful as a galvanised nail, making a crude joke about it every time she sees me. But George . . . he'll take it the wrong way. I know he will. He's always been the jealous type, especially at the start of our relationship and marriage, but after I had the kids and I had my breasts removed, he lost his overprotectiveness.

But there are worse things George could find out about. Much worse things.

This is, quite possibly, the worst thing that could have ever happened to our family. Moving here was a mistake. I was dazzled by the glitz and glamour and now the universe is punishing me for my greed — by moving me in next door to the one man I never wanted to set eyes on again. Dear God, if George ever found out about Victor, about who he really is, I'm not sure what would happen. I can't risk it. I have to do whatever is necessary to stop this secret from getting out and destroying my family.

One thing is for certain.

I'm going to need a lot of wine to get through this evening.

A lot.

CHAPTER 13

Somehow, among the hundreds of tops that are designed to show off as much cleavage as possible, I manage to find a top that fits me and is suitably high-necked. I suppose Glory is an advocate of the age-old phrase 'If you've got it, flaunt it.'

Roughly five minutes later, I return downstairs without self-combusting or throwing up, even though it takes every effort imaginable not to escape out the nearest window and climb down the outside of the building to avoid spending the evening with the three people waiting for me downstairs.

I truly have no idea how I'm supposed to handle a shock of this magnitude. Stuff like this doesn't happen to me. Hell, even winning the house was a one-in-a-million chance, but add to that the chances of running into Heather's biological father next door is more or less impossible.

Yet here I am.

About to walk into a conversation between my husband of thirteen years who thinks he's the father of our daughter and the man who actually is her father.

The men are laughing as I step into the room.

Victor's told everyone. What a twat!

'Ah, there she is,' says George happily, halting his laughter to greet me. He opens his arms wide to beckon me to go to him.

Okay, he's clearly drunk. I shimmy across the kitchen tiles and take my place at his side, not daring to make eye contact with Victor, who is standing off to the left with a large glass of wine in his hand, holding it delicately by the thin stem. His damp hair is slicked back, the few grey hairs he has giving it a salt-and-pepper vibe. Why do men look so damn good with greying hair while women turn into old hags the moment one appears? How is that fair?

'That top looks gorgeous on you!' exclaims Glory, who of course doesn't have a grey hair in sight — her platinum-blonde locks could rival Sabrina Carpenter's (I only know about her because of Heather).

'Thank you,' I say. 'It's a very pretty top. You have so many beautiful things.'

Victor places his glass on the nearest countertop then claps his hands together once, immediately bringing the whole room to his attention. Something tells me he's very used to being the centre of attention, rather like his wife. 'Right, now we're all here, can I get anyone a top-up?' he asks.

It's safe to say in the few minutes Victor was downstairs while I was choosing a top, he didn't announce that I'd walked in on him in nothing but a towel. I've never been more relieved in my life, but it does nothing to quell the nausea and pure shock of seeing him again after so many years. Not to mention the inappropriate feelings I'm experiencing and the flashbacks that keep popping into my head like flipping daisies.

I was young, naive and very, very drunk, so I'm surprised I can recall any of the details regarding that night, but the more I quietly listen to him over the dinner table, the more I remember why I was drawn to him in the first place. He exudes a charismatic confidence I've rarely seen. Not arrogance per se, but calm, controlled confidence that sucks me in with every word he utters. Even his body language and mannerisms are hard to look away from, no matter how hard I try. He's truly captivating.

George seems enthralled by him too. They hit it off straight away, acting as if they've known each other for years by swapping jokes and regaling stories. If I didn't know any better, I'd say that George has a huge man crush on our new neighbour.

I don't talk a lot. I drink.

Too much.

Before I realise it, an hour has passed and I've had more than enough to send me staggering sideways as soon as I try and stand up to use the toilet.

'Whoops!' laughs George. 'Looks like my dear wife has had a little too much this evening.'

Everyone laughs. He's been putting it away too, but George can handle his drink a lot better than I can. I haven't overlooked the extra empty wine bottles in the recycling bin over the past few months.

My cheeks heat as I straighten myself up.

'I'm fine. Just need to pop to the loo!' I say the last four words excitedly, like I'm a child about to visit a sweet shop. I walk away mentally kicking myself.

After splashing water on my face, I stare at myself in the huge mirror above the sink in the downstairs bathroom. My cheeks are flushed, my make-up is slightly smudged and my eyes are glassy. The room spins and a wave of dizziness threatens to flatten me. I've drunk too much. It's blatantly obvious.

A knock at the door makes me jump.

'Just checking you're all right.' Victor's deep voice sends my nerves sky-rocketing again.

'Fine!' I take a breath and open the door, hoping to find that he's heading back to the party, but he isn't. He's leaning against the wall, waiting for me, the sleeves on his shirt now rolled up, revealing tanned forearms covered in dark hair. His molten-chocolate eyes bore into me and my belly does a little flip.

'Um, I think I'd better head home. The kids must be tired.'

'They're all watching a film in the snug.'

'Yes, well . . .'

'Listen, I don't mean to overstep the mark here, but . . . I think I may have remembered where I know you from.'

If Victor can hear my rapid breathing, he does a good job of hiding it. 'Oh?' I say, as calmly as I can.

'Leicester University, right?'

Shit. Shit. Shit.

There's no point trying to deny it. He's hit the nail on the head. I may as well make a joke about it.

'Oh my God!' I say with a fake laugh. 'Freshers week . . .'

Victor laughs out loud. 'Holy fucking shit, it is you! Sorry, excuse my language.' He waves off his remark. 'Uh, we . . . had a rather intense night together, right?'

I relax my jaw, turning my laughing smile into a sterner expression. 'Yes, I suppose we did. Gosh.'

'I'm sorry I didn't recognise you when you first walked in, but I was rather distracted.'

'So was I,' I answer with a chuckle, then instantly realise how that must sound.

Victor actually blushes, his usual confident demeanour faulting.

Oh God . . . I'm inadvertently flirting with him.

'It's fine. Honestly. It was my fault. I shouldn't have even been in there, but Glory said . . . Doesn't matter. I just . . . I appreciate that you haven't told anyone I walked in on you, and maybe we could keep the fact that we knew each other back then . . . to ourselves.' I talk fast, out of breath by the time I finish. I seem to have forgotten how to breathe.

Victor's chin raises ever so slightly. 'Of course. I understand. I think Glory would find it hilarious, but I get the impression from George that he'd . . . well, he wouldn't take it well.'

'I think you're right. There's no need to dredge up the past.'

'Right . . .'

We stand in silence for a few moments until he says, 'It was a pretty epic night though, wasn't it?'

My head swims, as if all the blood from my head has drained to my feet. 'Y-Yes, from what I can remember. I was . . . very drunk.'

'Right,' he says again.

I give him a small smile then go to walk past him.

'Fiona,' he says, stopping me in my tracks. It's the first time he's ever spoken my name and it sends a jolt of adrenaline straight into my heart. I summon all my courage and look up at him, into those deep cocoa eyes. 'I tried to find out your name after that night. I had no idea who you were. I know we barely talked or even told each other our names, but . . . I did try and find you. I just want you to know that.'

My mouth opens but nothing comes out because the truth is, I tried to find him too.

* * *

When I return to George and Glory, they're doing shots. Oh God. Not shots. I can't drink any more or I'm going to end up spewing my guts up and humiliating myself even more. It's creeping closer to midnight. I need to get the kids home. One of us has to be the sensible parent here.

'Um, George . . . I'm going to take the kids home.'

'Aww, yeah. Yeah, we should . . .' He stops with a shot glass close to his lips.

'You stay,' I say. 'It's fine. I'll walk them back.'

'Can't Heather just walk back with Liam? She's old enough.'

'I don't . . .' I sigh, unable to say what I really want to say — that I don't want to stay here any longer and risk saying something stupid. 'You stay. Honestly. Enjoy yourself. I can't drink shots, you know that,' I add with a hint of humour, hoping it will break the slight tension. I feel like a party pooper.

I'm not stopping him. I've not seen him connect with people the way he's connected with Victor and Glory. There's a hint of jealousy within me at how flirty he is with Glory, but it's nothing I haven't seen before from him. He's a chatty, fun guy when he's had a few drinks and it hasn't slipped my attention that he's a magnet to certain women.

I trust him, but I don't trust myself right now. Not around Victor.

Almost on cue, Heather walks through the door, and my heart stops as I see her and Victor side by side. The kids didn't join us earlier for dinner — they ate in the other room — but now I see her standing next to her father, the resemblance is uncanny.

My stomach lurches as Victor approaches Heather. 'My, my,' he says. 'You can tell she's your daughter straight away.' He glances back at me and winks. 'You've got your mother's eyes.'

Heather curls her top lip at him in disgust. 'Er, yeah, thanks. Mum, can we go now? The movie's over.'

She looks straight past him, urging me with her firm stare. For once, I'm not embarrassed by her brash, rude nature. 'Yes, let's go.'

I turn to Glory and say goodbye, not even attempting to soothe Victor's hurt feelings at the fact I didn't acknowledge his compliment. He does look a little shocked to have been blatantly ignored by Heather too.

I usher the kids out the door, finally able to take a calming breath when I step outside into the cool air. All evening, even before I came face to face with Victor for the first time in almost seventeen years, I've felt heat searing in my chest. Like heartburn, but something different, like my body has been sending me a warning that I don't belong here.

The kids run on ahead, but I can just about see them in the darkness.

'Fiona, wait up,' comes a voice from behind me. My insides clench as Victor jogs to catch up. 'I thought I'd make sure you got home okay.'

'I only live five minutes away.'

'But still, you can never be too careful, even out here in a beautiful place like this.'

'True,' I say. I fold my arms across my chest and we continue to walk towards my house, our feet crunching across the gravel. 'I was going to ask Glory, but I forgot earlier,' I say, deciding to initiate small talk rather than spend the time in awkward silence. 'Do you know if the house comes with a cleaner or gardener or anything? It's just . . . I'm used to living in a tiny rented house, so . . .' My face burns hot and I'm glad the cover of darkness hides my embarrassment.

'Yes, I believe it does.'

'Do you know who lived here before? The radio station hasn't really provided much information, like . . . I'm not even sure why it was used as a giveaway house. It's all a bit . . .' I stop, feeling stupid.

'Much,' Victor finishes for me.

I breathe out. 'Yes. It's a bit much.'

'It's been empty a while, but the cleaners and gardeners still keep on top of the work. I'm not too sure who officially owned it before you, but . . . it's yours now.'

'I guess it is. It's just a bit . . . odd.'

'What's odd?'

'Did you ever meet the previous owners?' I'm not ready to let this go yet.

'Not really. It was their second home. I think they spent most of their time in France.'

'Right.' I want to keep asking him questions, but we've reached my front door. Heather has already opened it with her set of keys and disabled the alarm, and she and Liam have disappeared upstairs to bed, leaving me and Victor standing outside at the bottom of the stone steps, the wisteria emitting its beautiful fragrance around us.

'Thank you for walking me back,' I say, feeling like a teenage girl at the end of a first date.

'Even though you didn't really want me to,' he adds.

I gulp. 'Was it that obvious?'

'Hey, listen, I know running into each other like this all these years later wasn't exactly planned, but . . . I'm glad we did. I still think about that night.'

'Y-You do?'

'You don't?'

'It . . . It was a drunken fling.' Victor's face falls slightly, not by a lot, but enough for me to realise I've hurt his feelings. 'I'm sorry, but . . . it was a long time ago. Yes, it was a great night, but I don't lie awake at night thinking about it.'

'Right. Not long enough for me, I guess.' He looks at the ground, kicking the gravel with his foot.

Oh God. What does that mean?

'Fiona, I . . .' He looks up, locking eyes with me.

I'm breathless. He can't possibly be trying to say what I think he's trying to say. Can he?

'I'm sorry. This is all coming out wrong. I was just so surprised to see you and . . . Glory and I have been having problems and . . . Shit, what am I saying? I've had too much to drink. I apologise.' He shakes his head, backing away from me.

Without thinking, I reach out and grab his arm, stopping him from walking away into the darkness. I didn't want him to walk me home, but now I don't want him to leave. Not yet. What's wrong with me? What's going on between us? This can't be happening . . .

My fingers clench around his forearm, merely wanting him to not walk away, but he reacts suddenly, stepping close, pressing himself against me and crashing his lips against mine.

My whole body freezes. I can't breathe. I can't . . .

Then, I sink into his warmth, his hard body and let out a small moan as he lightly bites my bottom lip. No. No. No. This is wrong . . .

Stop it. Stop it now.

I back away, pushing him gently. 'No.'

'I'm sorry . . . I shouldn't . . . Fuck.'

We stand in silence.

'Goodnight, Fiona.' His deep, soothing voice almost makes me melt into a puddle on the floor.

'Goodnight, Victor.'

He turns and walks away, disappearing into the dark beyond.

I spend a few seconds gazing after him. My drunken brain is fighting against my body, which is responding very explicitly.

Fuck. Fuck. Fuck.

I didn't mean to make him think that I wanted to kiss him. I just didn't want him walking home feeling bad. That's all. Why did he kiss me? Why didn't I stop it sooner? Why am I still standing out here in the dark gazing after him like a lovesick puppy?

CHAPTER 14

George doesn't come home that night. Either that, or he decided to crash in one of the spare bedrooms to avoid waking me up, but something tells me he didn't. He spent the night at Victor and Glory's house.

The next morning, despite a heavy night and limited sleep, I'm still up before the kids. Boots meows and paces up and down the kitchen like he's never been fed a day in his life. He squawks at me when I enter the kitchen wearing my dressing gown and swerves in and around my ankles, almost sending me off balance.

'Yeah, yeah, I'm getting it.'

I feed the damn cat, then switch the coffee monstrosity on. While I wait for it to warm up, I stand at the set of bi-fold doors, looking out across the garden. The sun has been up for hours, but the air hasn't quite warmed up yet. It's nice. Quiet.

Then, like a herd of elephants, the memories from last night stampede through my head, jostling for top position, but I'm not sure which one should get that honour.

Perhaps the one when I walked in on Victor while he was changing, the man I haven't seen for nearly seventeen years.

Or maybe the one where he, unknowingly, set eyes on his daughter for the first time.

Or . . . the one where he kissed me.

Shit.

How am I ever going to face him again without wanting to throw up or run away?

I thump my forehead with the palm of my hand. What was I thinking? I'm not a cheater. I've never, not in my wildest dreams, considered cheating on George. He's my person. Then, just like on the first night we met, Victor sweeps me off my bloody feet and shoves his tongue down my throat. I didn't want that, despite how my body responded. I don't want it to happen again. It can't. It was a stupid mistake and it shouldn't have happened. I pushed him away and hopefully he got the message. Hands off.

Footsteps sound behind me, knocking me out of my spiralling thoughts.

Heather enters the kitchen, looking much fresher than I do.

'Morning,' I say.

'Uh huh.'

'I'm sorry about last night — I got a bit drunk and forgot the time.'

Heather shuffles to the cereal cupboard (yes, we have a whole cupboard for cereal now) and removes a box of cornflakes. 'I don't care.'

'Okay, well . . .'

'Where's Dad?'

'He . . . uh . . . I think he slept in one of the spare rooms.'

Heather fetches a spoon from the cutlery drawer. 'Pretty sure he didn't. He was wasted.'

'Maybe Glory and Victor put him up in one of their spare rooms.'

'Glory was all over him.'

'Yes, well . . .' I squirm in my seat. The fact she noticed their behaviour, despite barely spending any time with the grownups last night, goes to show how blatant Glory and George were being. 'Anyway, how was your night? Was Ryan nice? What's he like?' The fact Ryan's her half-brother isn't lost on me, but I can't tell her the truth. Yet more lies I must tell. They seem to be growing lately and getting harder to keep track.

She shrugs. 'Ryan's okay, I guess. He's into video games. He also knows a lot about electronics. Liam asked him like a billion questions. I barely got a word in edgeways.'

'Oh, that's nice.'

'Yeah, like he's super into his tech.'

'Hmm, maybe he can teach me how to turn the oven on properly, then.'

Heather and I sit in the kitchen while she eats cereal and I sip coffee. It's the first time in ages that we've talked. I don't quite understand what's going on with her, but to hear her using words and full sentences is completely bewildering. For the past year or so, she's barely made eye contact with me. Perhaps this is the start of our new journey as mother and daughter. We have to adapt to our ever-growing relationship, learn how the other responds to the other's comments and mannerisms.

I find myself staring at her while she's talking, marvelling at my beautiful daughter and how proud I am of her, even if she does hate my guts sometimes. Heather tells me she likes the house, but is worried about starting a new school in the middle of her GCSEs. She's got lots of studying to catch up on and will miss a week of lessons. I reassure her that her new teachers will understand her predicament and I'll do whatever I can to support her.

She smiles at me, and then footsteps sound. George appears at the doorway, having come from the entrance hall. I turn and look at him, refusing to speak first. He's dressed in the same clothes he wore last night, a clear five o'clock shadow across his jawline and cheeks.

George clears his throat. 'Heather, would you mind giving me and your mum a moment to talk, please?'

Heather glances sideways at me. 'Good luck,' she mutters before hopping off the kitchen stool, taking her bowl of cereal with her. I'm momentarily taken back to when she was a child and used to walk around with a bowl of cereal while eating it. The amount of times she spilled it got beyond a joke, but whenever I see her with a bowl in her hand, I look fondly back on those memories.

I can't say the same about the sporadic and blurry memories from last night, which have been plaguing my head since I woke up this morning. Now, seeing George in the doorway, I realise me kissing Victor is the least of my problems.

Does he want to talk to me alone because he has something to confess, or has he somehow found out about me and Victor? Oh God. There are security cameras everywhere in this house. Did he see us? Has he logged into the online security system yet? The thought didn't even occur to me until just this second.

I've left the coffee machine on, mostly because I was planning on having a second cup, quite possibly a third later on, but I think George needs one more than I need another right now.

He shuffles to the machine and starts to sort out his cup, but his movements are all jerky and his legs are visibly shaking. I get up and take the cup from his hand.

'I'll make it. Go and sit down.'

'Thanks,' he mumbles, too ashamed to look me in the eyes.

I'm not feeling my best either. I haven't felt this bad since my early university days. I can't drink like I used to back then and, to be honest, I haven't tried to for the past couple of decades. Yet last night the wine was going down as easily as water and I couldn't seem to stop.

It seems George had the same problem.

I hand him a freshly brewed cup, then sit down nearby and wait.

'Fiona . . . we need to talk about last night,' he says.

'Y-Yes, okay,' I say. 'Um . . . did you spend the night there?'

'Yes, but this isn't about my behaviour. It's about yours.'

'Mine?' I search my foggy brain. Yes, I was drunk, but I didn't say or do anything inappropriate, not in front of him anyway. Shit . . . he knows. How? Did Victor tell him?

'Yes. Yours. You embarrassed me.'

My mouth drops open. 'George, I . . . I'm so sorry. It was an accident, I swear.'

'What was an accident?'

'Walking in on Victor naked and—'

'Wait, what! You walked in on Victor naked?'

'Yes, right at the start of the night, but—'

George jumps to his feet, the coffee cup crashing to the floor. The black liquid splashes everywhere, but neither of us make a move to clean it up. 'Jesus Christ,' he mutters. 'I was talking about your behaviour at dinner.'

'What behaviour?'

'What behaviour! Seriously? You're going to sit there and deny what you said and did in front of our new neighbours?'

'W-What?' Okay, I really am flummoxed now. I have no idea what he's talking about.

George laughs and runs his hands through his messy hair. He smells ripe, like warm, gone-off fruit.

'Look,' I say, palms facing towards him. 'I know I got drunk, but I don't remember saying or doing anything inappropriate . . .' *Except for the fact I kissed Victor at the end of the evening outside our house while the kids had only just run upstairs.*

George scoffs. 'You wouldn't.'

'What's that supposed to mean?'

'You don't think I haven't seen you drinking more lately?'

'Okay, hang on a second, I might like an extra drink now and then, but I'm no alcoholic. You're the one who was doing shots with our attractive new neighbour and spent the night God only knows where. Also, since you're accusing me of drinking more, what about the empty wine bottles I kept finding in the recycling at our old house?'

'I slept in a spare room,' he snaps back. The fact he's glossed over my accusation isn't lost on me.

'Yes, and I slept in our new home, under the same roof as our children.'

George's eyes blaze and his nostrils flare.

'Walking in on Victor was an accident, okay? But I'm not going to stand here and let you gaslight me into thinking I said and did things that I know for a fact I didn't say or do.' Inside, I feel like a complete and utter hypocrite, but if I admit what happened on the front steps, then George will never forgive me. He's still drunk. He's never usually like this. I've never seen or heard him be so horrible towards me. 'I think you need to go upstairs and sleep it off. Let's talk again when both of us are feeling better,' I say, bending to pick up the broken pieces of the coffee cup.

George sighs. 'You're right . . .' I look up, slightly surprised that he isn't fighting back. 'I'm sorry.'

I frown. What's with his sudden change of tone? I can't keep up. 'Me too,' I mutter, even though I'm not.

'I'm going to take a shower and go to bed.'

'Fine.'

'But we're going to need to do some damage control over last night. With Victor and Glory. I need you to apologise to them.'

I keep hold of a broken piece of cup as I stand, facing George squarely. 'I already apologised to Victor for walking in on him. Tell me exactly what it is you think I did . . .'

'You said my body was nothing compared to Victor's. Last night I had no idea how you'd even know that, but now it all makes sense. You've already seen him naked, haven't you?'

'I . . . I told you it was an accident. And I didn't even see anything.'

'Sure you didn't.' George turns his back on me and stomps up the stairs.

I stare after him, squeezing the broken piece of pottery in my palm, tighter and tighter until the sting of pain appears. Does George know about me and Victor? Did Victor tell him after I left? I know I let Victor kiss me, but that was an accident too.

I feel like George has somehow got his wires crossed on a lot of things, yet he also knows more than he realises. It's like a tornado has crashed into our marriage and torn it apart. We've only been here two days and already, it feels like everything is turning against us.

Blood trickles out from between my clenched fist and drips into the puddle of black coffee still oozing across the tiled floor.

The doorbell sounds and I jump. I'm not expecting anyone, so that means it can only be . . .

CHAPTER 15

The volume of the doorbell surprises me. It must be linked to speakers throughout the house, which makes sense since there's no way we'd be able to hear it otherwise.

The palm of my left hand throbs, but I ignore it and head to the door, praying to any God who will listen that it's not Victor standing on the other side. I'm not in the mood, nor am I dressed to receive company right now.

I open the door. There's no one there.

Frowning, I stick my head out and glance left and right. I didn't race to get here from the kitchen, but if they'd turned around and walked away, I would still be able to see them on the long driveway. Unless they're now hiding somewhere . . .

I step out onto the large porch, the morning sun almost blinding me. I raise my hand and block out the rays, scanning the area ahead.

There's no one around.

Maybe I should check the security cameras, although I have no idea how to use any of it. I need to log in to all the gadgets and systems around the house and connect them to my smartphone, but I'm useless with technology. A year ago, when I got a new phone, it almost killed me having to log into every bloody app. I don't know how to save my passwords securely or even remember any of them, so I had to change every single one. It's safe to say that me and technology are not friends, but this house is full of it and, if I want to feel safe, and if I want to be able to use my oven, then I'm going to need to learn how to use it.

I head back into the house and close the door. I look down at my palm, a thin slice straight through the middle. Blood is still trickling through my fingers. I need to get this cleaned up. There are droplets of blood from where I walked to the door just now.

George is right about one thing. I do need to do some damage control with Victor and Glory, find out exactly what happened last night, especially after I left. I don't know why George thinks I need to apologise to them for my actions, but maybe he's trying to cover up for something he did.

It's Saturday, so I know Victor will be around all weekend before he goes back to work in London early Monday morning. I'm not ready to face him yet though, or Glory, not feeling the way I do — hungover and sick to my stomach.

'Mum!' The sound of my son's voice booms from above me.

'Coming!' I call back, reaching for the banister and pulling myself up the stairs, one step at a time. I head to his room and knock, but he doesn't answer. 'Liam? Everything okay?'

'He's not in there, Mum,' says Heather, walking up behind me.

'Where's he gone? He just called me.'

'Uh, I don't know. What did Dad have to say for himself, then?'

I sigh. 'He's not feeling too good. I'm sure he'll make more sense after a nap and a shower.'

Heather clicks her tongue and folds her arms. If I didn't know any better, I'd say she was the parent around here. 'Ryan texted me this morning. Apparently, he saw Dad and his mum getting mega close last night after we left.'

My face flushes with heat. 'What? He did?'

'Yeah.'

I clench my jaw, grinding my teeth. What the hell is George playing at? How dare he! I'm mortified that Heather has found out like this.

'I'm sorry, Heather. You shouldn't have to put up with this. We all had a little too much to drink and . . . it's no excuse. I'm going to talk to him when he's feeling better.'

Heather shrugs and walks away, leaving me standing in the hallway not knowing what the hell to do next. Where is Liam? Why did he call me and then run away?

I head to the bathroom and find some antiseptic and plasters, tend to my split palm and then walk downstairs and clear up the spilled coffee.

* * *

By midday, George hasn't emerged from the master suite, Heather has asked if she can go round to see Ryan, who has offered to show her around the area, and Liam is playing online games with his friends from back home. When I eventually found him and asked him what he wanted earlier, he looked at me like I was mad.

I tell him I'm taking over some vegetables for next door and that his dad is asleep upstairs. He nods, barely taking his eyes off the screen.

I take a trug from the greenhouse and pick a selection of vegetables and the ripest tomatoes from the vines. I know Glory has her own greenhouse, but I need some sort of peace offering before I head over there and question them about what happened last night.

There are a lot of blanks to fill in.

I have no idea how Glory is going to react to me visiting, and how on earth I'm going to speak to Victor without my face matching the colour of the tomatoes, but I need to try. We're neighbours. I can't ignore them forever. I hate confrontation and awkwardness, and I especially hate when my husband accuses me of something I haven't the slightest recollection of doing.

The handle of the trug hooked over my arm, I make my way down the driveway, turn left at the bottom and walk the one hundred yards or so to the entrance of their property. I stop short as I see Victor, who is closing the gate behind him. It looks as if he's had the same idea as me, because he's carrying a bouquet of freshly cut flowers, most likely from his own garden.

'Ah,' he says when he sees me. He nods at the trug. 'A peace offering?'

'And also a form of bribery,' I add.

'Bribery?' He lifts his bouquet. 'I only brought these, I'm afraid.'

I smile. 'They're beautiful.'

'Glory chose them.' He steps forwards. 'Listen, about last night . . . I'm hoping we can start again. Forget you walked in on me, forget we all got drunk, forget I walked you home and kissed you. Forget what I said about me and Glory . . . I'm sorry.'

'I'll accept your apology on one condition.'

'Name it.'

'You accept mine.'

'Done.'

'And answer a few questions.'

'About what?'

I shift the trug on my arm and allow the silence to linger for a few more seconds. 'What happened with George when me and the kids went home? Ryan told Heather that . . . Well . . .'

'Glory is like that with everyone. I wouldn't read too much into it. Trust me, I'm used to it by now. She's an attractive woman.'

'Right, but I'm not used to it. Should I be worried?'

'I don't know . . . Should you be?'

We lock eyes and I can't look away. 'I trust my husband,' I say sounding more confident than I feel. That's a complete lie.

I don't trust him, but if I said that then Victor might get the wrong end of the stick and think it's an open invitation to revisit our kiss.

Victor nods. 'Okay then . . . Good. I don't trust Glory, but we have an understanding.'

'Are you saying you have an open marriage?'

'Something like that.'

'Well . . . I don't. George and I. We're not open. We're very much closed.'

Victor nods, and I feel stupid.

'What happened over dinner?' I ask, deciding a change of topic is in order.

'What? You were there. Don't you remember?'

'George said that I said some inappropriate things.'

'Not that I can remember.'

'That's what I thought.' I bite my lip, thinking.

'What's going on?' asks Victor. 'What did George say?'

I shake my head. 'It's not so much what he said, but the way he said it. He was . . . mean and angry. It almost felt like he was trying to gaslight me into thinking it was my fault that last night was such a disaster.'

'I think we all had a part to play in how last night went, but the fact he's blaming you for it isn't fair. Are you busy? Would you like to come over for coffee? I'm sure Glory would like to see you. Heather's out with Ryan somewhere, I believe.'

I nod and walk with him through the gate, which he holds open for me. 'Thank you, yes. And thanks for being so understanding.'

'What are new neighbours and old flames for, right?'

'I wouldn't call us old flames,' I reply with a laugh.

Victor chuckles. 'Fair enough. We might not have caught fire long enough to be a flame, but we certainly sparked, right?'

* * *

I spend the next couple of hours with Glory and Victor, chatting out on their patio, drinking coffee and eating pastries. Heather and Ryan return from their trip, and that's my cue to follow her home and check on Liam.

I've had such a lovely afternoon with Glory and Victor that last night feels like a blurry, distant memory. Glory holds no ill will towards me and she apologises for being a bit overly touchy with George.

'Although,' she adds when the conversation drifts that way, 'he wasn't exactly making any effort to push me away either.'

Victor and I share a look, which I quickly break by standing up.

'What did you do to your palm?' asks Victor.

'Oh, nothing. I just cut it on a broken coffee cup.'

His eyes darken.

'Thank you so much for the coffee and pastries,' I say, picking up the bouquet. 'I best get these back home and in some water.'

Victor leaps to his feet, moves in close and gives me a kiss on the cheek to say goodbye, but as he pulls away, he whispers something in my ear — words that send goosebumps bristling over the surface of my skin.

'If George ever hurts you, I'll kill him.'

* * *

As I walk home, the bouquet of flowers in my arms, my mind buzzes with what Victor has just said to me about George. He clearly took the injury on my hand completely the wrong way. It brought out a darker side of him, one I haven't seen until now.

I head into the kitchen and begin to arrange the flowers in a glass vase I find on one of the kitchen shelves. The light is beaming through the French doors, highlighting the sparkles in the quartz worktops. It really is a beautiful room.

'Hey,' says a familiar voice.

I look up, holding the stem of a pink flower, to see George standing in the doorway.

'Hey,' I respond. 'How are you feeling?' He does look a little better after a shower and a rest. Smells better too.

He chuckles. 'Better, thanks.' He steps forwards, keeping his head bowed, like he's ashamed to look me in the eyes. 'I . . . I was still drunk earlier when I came home. It's no excuse, but . . . I'm so sorry about what I said. I didn't mean any of it. I just . . . got jealous of Victor. The way you kept looking at him.'

'I-I wasn't . . . I mean . . . Yes, but . . .'

He cracks a smile. 'I guess we both got a bit swept away by our new neighbours, huh?'

I smile back, tucking a strand of hair behind my ear, wanting more than anything to tug at it instead. 'I guess so.' I can't quite get a read on him. Does he still think I said inappropriate things over dinner? 'I went to visit Victor and Glory while you were asleep.'

'Oh?'

'Everything's fine. I smoothed things over.'

George nods. 'Good. Thank you. Again, I'm sorry. I think I just got the wrong end of the stick. Are we okay?'

His question catches me a little off guard because no, we're not okay. Not quite.

'I think we need to spend some time together,' he says gently. 'Just us.' I turn back to the flowers and stick one in the vase. 'Perhaps we can take a weekend away somewhere together.'

'What about the kids?' I ask.

'Heather's old enough to look after Liam overnight.'

My breath catches in my throat and my body tenses. She's not quite sixteen yet. I don't like the idea of leaving them home alone in such a big house, especially one we've only just moved into.

'Victor and Glory can look after them instead, then,' says George, clearly taking my silence to mean I don't like the idea.

'I'm not sure,' I say. 'We've only just met them.'

George doesn't respond. He stares at me without blinking. 'I thought this would be a way for us to make a fresh start. You have to leave the kids one day, Fiona.'

'I just don't think now is the right time.'

'It never is with you, is it?' George exits the room before I get a chance to explain or provide an alternative suggestion.

I finish the flower arrangement and plonk it in the middle of the breakfast bar. It seems that whatever I say or do around here isn't good enough for anyone.

All I can do is hope that, over time, things start to improve. Maybe no more boozy dinner parties for a while.

CHAPTER 16

The following two weeks whizz by like a speeding car, and I can barely acknowledge what's happened one day before the next arrives and I'm forced to change direction. It keeps me occupied, which is both a good and a bad thing. On the one hand, I like being busy because it stops my brain from overthinking every tiny detail. I don't have time to worry about Victor and the kiss we shared. I don't have time to worry about whether or not George saw us on the CCTV, nor do I have time to worry about the snide comments George keeps dropping in front of the kids, causing me to look foolish.

I find new things around the house that I haven't seen before, like the laundry room and its drying rack, perfect for rainy, cold days, or the wine fridge in the kitchen. I also manage to drag the kids away from their screens at the weekends and take them out to explore the local area. There's a gorgeous nature walk around our house, with a public footpath. I meet a few of the other locals, but none of them seem to know anything about the previous owners of the house, which I find increasingly odd. But again, it's one of those small, insignificant details that I don't have time to dwell on.

Our cleaner and gardener arrived a few days after we moved in and, I have to admit, I could have hugged them; they're both lifesavers. I barely even see them to speak to, but I want to make the effort to make sure they know how valued they are.

Clive, the gardener, pops his head into the house from time to time to double-check a few things, but otherwise he just potters about, mowing the grass, trimming the hedges and pruning the plants. One day, I go out and join him in the grounds. He regales me with everything he knows about plants and flowers and I find myself completely absorbed.

George tuts at me and questions why I want to learn about gardening when we have a gardener, but it's not about putting Clive out of a job. I've always wanted to know how to grow vegetables and look after rose bushes, but I've never had the time before now.

Lily, the cleaner, arrives every morning at nine and stays till twelve, but I barely see her either. She's my own magical cleaning fairy, exactly what I used to be at our previous house. When I go to dust the shelves or hoover the carpet, I discover it's already been done. I have new-found respect for cleaners.

Lily has, apparently, been cleaning the house for a year or so, whereas Clive is a recent addition. She doesn't say a lot, keeps herself to herself, but does an excellent job. I can't fault a single thing she does. She even cleans the tops of the kitchen cabinets and moves the ornaments to dust underneath, not just skim around them.

Heather and Liam start at their new school and, I must admit, I'm a nervous wreck as I wave them goodbye at the bus stop at the end of the road and wish them good luck. No more school pick-ups and drop-offs! I realise that uprooting them from their routine and tearing them away from the friends they've known since primary school is hard for them, but I'm hoping our new lifestyle makes up for it. A new school near the end of the academic year is hard too, but as far as I know, they're both enjoying the house and Heather has spent a lot of time with Ryan, which I'm not overly thrilled about. He's her half-brother. She hasn't mentioned that she likes him, but how can she not? He's charming and polite. Even Liam likes him, but mainly because he has a cool drone that he lets him fly around the grounds. I'm going to have to have 'the talk' with her soon, or risk a very inappropriate and awkward conversation.

Victor isn't home during the week. We haven't seen each other since the afternoon tea in the garden the night after the dinner party and I'm quite glad about that.

George has been extra affectionate and attentive at times, attempting to make up for his behaviour. He's mostly been working from home. I thought he would have more free time considering he's part-time now, but he says there's a lot of work on, and his company needs him. He has always been a hard, dedicated worker, so I leave him to it.

Luckily, George hasn't brought up the dinner party again and, the few times I've seen Glory, she hasn't either, preferring to talk about the latest online shopping spree she's done or how well her roses are doing this year.

I thought I'd enjoy the free time I have now, but it turns out owning an enormous home and walking around it during the day without the need to clean anything gets quite tedious after a while. I'm not sure how Glory copes. What does she do all day? That's why I join Clive in the garden sometimes, and I'm considering starting an online course to get myself a qualification, but I don't know what it is I want to study.

I find myself at a crossroads. There are numerous options open to me, but I'm still lost, a little unsure of where I need to go next. I suppose there are worse things in life to complain about. Maybe I should revisit my plan of being a fashion designer. I asked George for his input one evening while we sat around the fire pit in the garden and he laughed at me and said, 'Why the hell would you want to design clothes?' He made me feel rather silly, to be honest.

I use the pool and the gym and look up new recipes to try each evening, but it's exhausting. The good thing is that I've lost four pounds and have developed a decent tan thanks to tending to the garden when the sun is out. The height of the summer is fast approaching and I'm looking forward to having the kids home for a few weeks. I've already started looking at all-inclusive holidays abroad. It's so nice not to have to worry about getting the cheapest deal available.

I'm thinking Greece or Turkey, two countries I've always wanted to visit.

* * *

Exactly two weeks after we moved in, I decide to try and initiate a conversation with Lily. There are still questions about this house that I need answers to, and since she's worked here for a year, she'll surely have the information I need.

'Can I get you a drink?' I ask her, as she dusts the library shelves in the snug. It's where I spend a lot of my time reading, especially in the evenings.

'Oh, no thank you, Mrs Howden. I'm fine.'

'Please, call me Fiona.'

Lily nods and smiles, then gets straight back to work. She's dressed in a simple black uniform of knee-length skirt and t-shirt with a white apron tied around her waist, her hair piled high on her head. She's quite young. Late twenties, I'd say.

'Have you ever worked for Mrs and Mrs Hamilton, next door?' I ask.

'Um, I'm not supposed to talk to you . . .'

I open my mouth to laugh, thinking she's making a joke, but then it hits me. Why would she joke about something like that? Maybe she's a little nervous. I'm not her boss though. I have no idea who pays her.

'It's fine,' I say casually. 'I won't tell if you don't. Can I just ask though . . . Who employs you?'

'You do, ma'am.'

'No, I mean . . . Who pays your salary?'

Lily glances sideways, her eyes darting all over the place. 'Um . . . you do, ma'am.'

'Okay, enough with the ma'am thing. It makes me sound old. But no, I don't pay you . . . Does the radio station pay you?'

Lily clenches the duster between both hands, twisting and squeezing. 'I'm just a contractor,' she says, stuttering over the last word.

'But . . .'

A crash from above us makes her dart out of the room. I look up at the ceiling, expecting it to collapse on top of me, considering the noise that's erupting up there. The hanging light on the ceiling shakes. I race out of the snug and take the stairs two at a time, pausing for a moment at the top to catch my breath.

The house is so big that I struggle to remember which room is located above the snug. I think it's one of the guest rooms. I run down the nearest hallway and yank open the first door, finding only an empty room.

I check every door on this side of the house, but nothing in any of the rooms looks out of place. It sounded like a wardrobe fell over, but all of the wardrobes are built into the walls, custom-made.

Confused, I walk back down the hallway and stop on the landing at the top of the stairs, looking over the banisters to the entrance hall below. The front door is wide open. It wasn't open when I ran past it just now.

Has Lily finished for the day and forgotten to shut it properly behind her? Using the wooden banister to steady my shaking legs, I descend the stairs and close the front door. The house is silent.

'Lily?' I wait several seconds for an answer, but none comes.

What did she mean earlier when she said that I pay her salary? I most certainly don't. I didn't hire her. Victor said that a cleaner and gardener came with the house, but what does that mean? I'm mildly annoyed that the radio station has remained silent too. No one has contacted me or responded to my emails and the number I used to speak to Julia goes straight to voicemail.

* * *

That evening, I plan on speaking to George about it, but the kids distract me by arriving home from school in foul moods. Liam runs straight up to his room and slams the door, and Heather screams as she dumps her bag on the floor and kicks off her shoes.

The school bus drops them at the end of the road, which saves me a job of collecting them, but now I don't work, I find I'm missing picking them up, even if they never used to talk to me when I did. I don't know any of the other parents, even to look at.

'What's wrong?' I ask Heather before she stomps into the kitchen for her usual after-school cupboard raid.

'I hate my new school!' she shrieks, slamming a cabinet door.

'Okay . . .'

'Everyone hates me there. I'm just the weird new girl who's turned up at the end of GCSEs. Everyone is talking about prom and have dates and people to go with. No one talks to me. They keep whispering . . .' Her voice drops off as she fights back floods of tears.

My heart goes out to her. I know how hard it is to be an outsider, and now she's looking to me to say something to make her feel better. It's what any good mum would do, but what do I say? The fact is, she *has* turned up at her new school at the worst possible time. I didn't even think about her prom.

'I'm so sorry,' I say, reaching out my hand to stroke her gorgeous long hair. She lets me curl my fingers through it, straightening out a small knot.

'Do you think Ryan would take me?' she asks, looking up at me through long, water-logged eyelashes laden with mascara. 'He's a bit older, so it would be so cool if he did. Plus, he's really good-looking, so all the other girls will be jealous. Maybe we could even ask his dad to borrow his cool Jaguar?'

'Oh, um . . .' God, how do I explain this? This is the moment I've been dreading. There's no way I want to ask Victor a favour for anything to do with his biological daughter. Not to mention Ryan is her half-brother and the thought of them getting drunk and close at the prom is sickening. 'I'm not sure that's such a good idea, sweetie,' I say, attempting to keep my tone light.

'Of course you'd say that,' Heather says, flinching away from me. 'You never care about what I want, do you? You don't even care if I fail my GCSEs.'

Before I can defend myself, Heather takes off and runs up the stairs.

I close my eyes and count to ten, slowly lifting my hand to my hair and tugging at a few strands, feeling instant relief as they snap.

* * *

George is away with work for two days and over the weekend, so I have no idea what I'm supposed to do to keep myself busy. I ask the kids if they want to take a trip into town to do some shopping, but that gets shot down. Liam, it turns out, is taking part in an online gaming battle that's due to last all weekend, and Heather snorts as she tells me she'd rather be dead than go shopping with me. She also has a lot of studying to do to make up for lost time because apparently I was too selfish to think of how it would affect her before moving the family out here.

Friday evening, I take a bottle of wine and a glass to the patio and set up camp under the large parasol. I switch on the bug zapper lamp then take a seat. I close my eyes and listen to the evening sounds. The wind rustling through the trees, the birds singing, the bugs electrocuting themselves on the zapper. I can just about pick out the shouts and whoops from my son in the gaming room.

'Penny for your thoughts?' comes a nearby deep voice.

CHAPTER 17

My eyes fling open to see Victor standing over me, his hair slightly damp, wearing a light-blue shirt that's open at the collar. My hand flies to cover my heart, hoping it won't leap out of my chest.

'Bloody hell, you scared me half to death!'

'I'm so sorry, I didn't know how to announce myself,' he says, a faint blush appearing on his cheeks.

He must have sneaked up on me, but in order to get into the back garden, he would have had to walk through the front door and then through the kitchen area or round the side of the conservatory.

I look behind me at the house. The back door is closed to keep the cat in. I didn't hear it open.

'Sorry,' he says, 'Heather let me in.'

'Uh . . . she did?'

'She's a great kid.'

'Yeah . . .' My brain frantically scrambles to change the subject. Talking about my daughter in front of him feels wrong, like I'm stepping foot into dangerous territory that I have no right to be in.

Back away. Back away now.

Victor's holding a bottle of wine. I nod at it. 'Is that for me?'

'It was, but I can see you've beat me to it.' His eyes linger on the bottle on the table.

He's hinting for an invite to sit down and join me, but even I know that's a terrible idea. He hasn't sat down yet and is shifting his weight from foot to foot. Uneasy. He knows it's wrong too.

'I guess it would be rude to turn down a gift.' I gesture to the empty chair ahead. 'Please.'

'Thank you,' he says.

'I'll fetch you a glass.' I go to stand, but he puts his hand out.

'Please, allow me.' He turns and strides through the doors behind me. I notice he didn't ask where the glasses were in the kitchen. He returns only moments later, takes a seat, tops up my glass and pours one for himself.

'So, what's the real reason you're over here?' I ask with a sigh. There's no point being polite about it, dodging round the huge elephant on the patio.

'I uh . . . just thought you might fancy a drink and a chat. George is away this weekend, right?'

'Yes, and you're back from London and should be spending the weekend with your wife and son, not hanging out drinking wine with your next-door neighbour. What would Glory think if she found out?'

'Aren't you more concerned with what George would think?'

Victor's words from two weeks ago still echo in my ears. His threat to kill George if he ever hurt me. He didn't specify whether he meant physically or mentally, but even so, what gives him the right to say that to me? Does he think I'm going to swoon over him like he's a knight in shining armour rescuing me from my abusive husband? George isn't abusive. Yes, he got drunk the other week and said some nasty things to me, but before that, he's never said anything that could be considered verbally abusive. Hell, most of the time he barely says a word to me, which is just as bad.

I honestly don't know how to feel about Victor being here. He looks good. Too good. Tantalizingly good. But despite not being able to take my eyes off the broadness of his chest and shoulders, my brain is telling me to send him away. It doesn't feel right, having a drink with him. Even if we didn't have history, even if he wasn't Heather's real father, I still wouldn't feel right having a quiet, romantic drink with my hunky new neighbour.

'Listen, if you want me to go, then . . .'

'It's not that. It's just . . .'

'Mum?'

My eyes swivel to the back door, where Heather is now standing, a frown across her face. She's looking from me to Victor and back to me, like she's trying to work out what's going on. She sees the bottle of wine and the two glasses. Oh God. I can only imagine what she's thinking.

But surely she knew he was here. She was the one who let him in.

Right?

'Hi, love. Everything okay?' I ask.

'I heard a man's voice, so I thought it was Dad . . .'

Her words send an icy bullet straight to my heart.

I thought it was Dad . . .

'Um, no, Victor just dropped by to . . .' Victor catches my eye. He's lied to me and he's been caught out. Heather didn't let him in. He walked straight in through the front door, letting himself in as if it was his own house.

I stand up. 'Thanks so much for dropping by, Victor.'

He doesn't stand up, not right away. Not as fast as he should. He locks eyes with me, slowly rising, then flicks his eyes to Heather.

'How old are you, Heather?'

I don't like his tone of voice or the way he's directed his attention to my daughter.

'Almost sixteen,' she replies bluntly.

I swallow the saliva building in my mouth.

'Sixteen, huh?' His eyes focus back on mine.

Oh God . . .

Does he . . .

Is he doing the maths in his head right now?

My body betrays me as my face floods with heat. I turn to Heather and quickly slap on a smile. 'Could you go and check on Liam for me?'

'Why?'

'I thought I heard him calling me.'

'I didn't hear him . . .'

'Please.' I widen my eyes at her, hoping she gets the message. She gives me her trademark solemn stare, then huffs and walks back into the house.

The second she's out of earshot, I round on Victor. 'Heather never let you in. How did you get into my house?'

Victor's facial expression changes as if I've just slapped him. 'What are you accusing me of exactly? The front door was open.'

'So you just decided to walk on in?'

'I called out, but no one answered.'

I narrow my eyes. 'Please leave.' I pull my cardigan tighter around my body and resist the urge to tug at the hair that's blowing around my face in the light breeze.

Victor lowers his head like a scolded puppy. He leaves the bottle of wine he brought on the table and goes to walk past. He stops right next to me, our shoulders almost touching. I'm not sure if it's the tension buzzing through the air or the lamp that's zapping bugs nearby, but something is causing the tiny hairs on my arms to tingle. Something is setting the air around us alight.

'So Heather was born nearly seventeen years ago,' he says. 'That's not long after we spent the night together, if I'm not mistaken.'

My mouth drops open, but then I clench it shut. He doesn't say anything else as he walks away, back through the house. I hear the front door close and only then do I let out a long breath, the air whooshing from my lungs.

I bend over double, clutching my heart.

Whether it's a wild guess or a thinly veiled threat, I don't know, but Victor's demeanour has changed. I've made it clear I'm not interested in starting up an affair or spending any time with him, and now he's, what, threatening me?

Is he just trying to make me nervous? If so, then he's well and truly succeeded. I grab my glass of wine and down the rest of it in two large gulps. The fact he let himself into my house sets me on edge too. I'm not sure who he thinks he is, but this isn't his house. He may have known the previous owners, but that doesn't give him the right to enter unannounced.

I need to ensure the front door is always locked, but because this house is so large, there are multiple points of entry all over the building and various cut-throughs from the main driveway through the gardens.

Maybe it's time I get to grips with the CCTV set-up and the security systems around here.

I should have done it straight away.

CHAPTER 18

I stuff both empty bottles of wine into the recycling box, regretting finishing off the second bottle. I've never drunk as much as this before and it's something I'm noticing more and more. The plan had been to move here and be happy with my new and improved life, but all that's happened is my mental health has taken a nosedive, and I've been retreating to the bottom of a bottle instead of facing up to the issues in both my marriage and life.

I check in with Liam at ten o'clock and give him a fifteen-minute warning before the Wi-Fi turns off, something George and I put in place last week, otherwise Liam would stay up all night if he could.

He grunts, signalling he's heard me, so I traipse up to bed, stopping at Heather's room on the way. I knock and wait for her to allow entry.

'Yeah.'

I push the door open and pop my head around. 'I'm going to bed,' I say. 'Everything okay?'

'Finished your date, have you?'

I step all the way into the room, sighing. I'd been hoping she wouldn't bring it up, but who am I kidding? 'It wasn't a date. Victor just popped round to make sure I was all right, that's all.'

'Uh huh.'

'I promise you, nothing is going on.'

'I don't like him, Mum.'

This piques my interest. 'Why's that?' I ask. Could it be that Heather is picking up the same eerie vibes as I am? I can't quite put my finger on what it is exactly that sets my teeth on edge when it comes to Victor, but his close attention is unwanted. My daughter feeling the same way can't be a coincidence. At first, he'd had an alluring air about him, but the fact he turned up announced and somehow found his way into the house is raising all the red flags.

'He keeps staring at you,' she says.

'Ah. Well . . .' I'm not sure what to say to that.

'Dad wouldn't be happy.'

'No, I guess not, but your dad and I are very happy and I have no feelings towards Victor, so there's no need to worry, okay?'

'How did he get in?' she asks, bypassing my comment.

'I left the front door open. It won't happen again.' Of that, I'm sure, once I've got to grips with the security system and memorised the codes. Heather nods and goes back to looking at her phone. 'You won't . . . tell your dad about Victor's visit today, will you?'

'Bit late for that. He probably already knows.'

'How? Did you tell him?'

Heather swivels her eyes at me and rolls them. 'Gee, thanks for your trust there, Mum. No, I didn't tell him. He hooked up to that Ring doorbell app thing the day after we moved in, didn't he? Gets a notification every time there's movement by the front door.'

An icy shiver floods my body. 'He . . . he does?'

'Yeah. He did it so he'd know whenever me and Liam came home.'

'Right.' He didn't tell me he was doing that. Why hadn't he hooked my phone up to the app at the same time? The day after we moved in was . . .

Oh, fuck.

That means . . .

'Mum, what's wrong?'

'Nothing . . .' I back away towards her bedroom door, feeling hot and flustered at the thought of George receiving a notification on his phone that night Victor walked me back from the dinner party. The night we . . .

There's a chance George didn't look at his phone that night. He was wasted and happily enjoying Glory's company. But if he has known all this time, then no wonder he was in such a foul mood the next morning. If he saw the video footage, then what the hell happened when Victor came back? Did George confront him? Did they have it out?

'Goodnight, darling,' I say before swiftly exiting the room.

I close the door, leaning against it, taking a deep breath, but my lungs won't expand properly. There's a vice locked around my chest, squeezing tighter. I use the wall for support, touching it with my fingers, finding comfort in its firmness as I stumble towards the master suite. My bed is calling my name. The wine is making my head spin and my eyes lose focus; my mind is foggy, warped.

I get to the en-suite and splash cold water on my face, then stare at my tired, dark eyes in the mirror. Something doesn't feel right. I'm not sure what to believe or who to trust. Does George know about my kiss with Victor or doesn't he? If he does, why hasn't he confronted me about it?

After our bust-up the following morning, we made up and things have been relatively back to normal ever since. A little icy, perhaps, but nothing new there. Granted, he's been busy and his plans to work from home have fallen by the wayside, and he's had to go away on longer work trips, but I hadn't thought anything of it until now.

Is he avoiding me because he's disappointed and ashamed of me? Or angry?

To quieten my mind, I try and sleep, but it doesn't come.

Not for several hours.

I listen to the sounds of the house instead. The nearest bedroom window is cracked open, allowing a light, cool breeze to blow the curtains. The calls of foxes and owls linger in the background as the late night creeps into the early morning.

Did I set the exterior alarm?

Did I get the chicken out of the freezer to defrost for tomorrow's dinner?

My mind won't stop with the multitude of questions. Swirling. Round and round. I roll over, kicking off the thick covers that feel as if they're trying to suffocate me, but as I do, a loud bang erupts nearby, like a firework has exploded behind me.

My body jerks in shock, turning towards the noise just as a body throws itself towards me.

'Mum!'

'Jesus Christ, Heather!'

My little girl leaps into bed beside me, grabs the duvet and pulls it up to her chin. She's shaking all over.

'What's wrong, darling?' I ask, my heart rate still not showing any signs of decreasing. It's pounding like a drum, hard in my chest.

'Mum, there was someone in my room.'

My stomach lurches. 'What?'

'I swear. I'm not making it up. There was someone in my room. It looked like a man.'

I reach over to the side table and switch on the lamp. It throws the whole room into yellow light, burning my eyes. The surrounding shadows instantly disappear. I rub my dry eyes, which fight to stay open. 'Are you sure it wasn't a dream?'

'Mum, I know the difference between a dream and reality.'

'Okay, but . . . remember when you were little and you used to have those nightmares about the man in your room?'

'This wasn't like that,' she says, her voice full of panic.

God, I can't remember the last time she had one of those nightmares, but it's been at least eight or nine years. We took her to a child therapist, who asked us all sorts of awkward questions, ones I had no idea how to answer. Eventually, she was diagnosed with a type of sleep disorder, which we were told she'd eventually grow out of. She did, thankfully, but it scared me every time it happened. She'd race into our room in the middle of the night, convinced a man was standing in the corner of her room, watching her sleep. It was impossible. We knew that. I even set up her old baby monitor in the room, but it never caught anything, even on the nights when she woke up and screamed for us to come quick because he was there. He wasn't. There was no one there.

But it's happened now.

Again.

Does that mean anything or is it only because of the change of routine, the uprooting of her life? The therapist did say to watch out for anything like this in the future. We were warned about any changes in mood as she grew up, but it's been difficult to separate her usual hormonal mood swings from the not so usual changes of late.

Heather settles herself under the duvet and lays her head on the pillow that George usually uses. 'Can I sleep in here tonight?'

'Of course you can,' I reply, pushing back the covers. 'I'm just going to go and double-check your room and the alarm system, okay?'

She nods. 'Okay.'

I leave Heather in bed, grab my fluffy dressing gown from the hook on the back of the door, then pad out into the hall, my feet a little chilly without my slippers or thick socks on. I creep towards Heather's room. Her door yawns wide, flung open in a hurry. The light isn't on, but I leave it off as I take a step over the threshold, eyes peeled for any dark shadows that shouldn't be there.

Damn it, I should have brought a weapon.

George always sleeps with a baton under the mattress on his side. He has done ever since we had a break-in when Heather was still a baby. It shook us both up. I didn't think to grab the baton though.

I search all over her room, using the light from the moon and the outside lights that illuminate the garden . . .

Wait. The garden lights have sensors, only activating when they've detected motion.

I rush to the window and peer out, sweeping back the curtains. The lights are on for a few seconds as I scan the green grass below, and then turn off.

Perhaps a rabbit or a fox has run across the turf.

Yeah, or perhaps someone is running away from the house after somehow appearing in my daughter's bedroom.

It makes no sense. How would they get down from up here? Using the light of the moon, I unlatch the window and poke my head outside, the coolness of the night air sending a ripple of goosebumps across my body.

There's no drainpipe or anything that could be used to climb up or down from this window. Feeling a little less tense, I duck back inside and close the window before returning to the comfort of my bed and the warm body of my daughter, who has fallen asleep since I left her.

I slide in next to her, pulling the duvet up to my chin.

And stay awake all night, my mind and body on high alert.

CHAPTER 19

I leave Heather asleep early the next morning and traipse down the hallway to check on Liam, who is snoring soundly, in the clothes he wore yesterday, his headphones still on his head. I roll my eyes and back away, heading downstairs to put on the coffee machine.

There's some mail on the kitchen worktop. I don't remember putting it there last night, even if I was half cut. Frowning, I pick up the pile of envelopes and flick through them, assuming one of the kids put them here yesterday and I just didn't notice.

That reminds me. I need to change our address at the bank, car insurance and all of that malarky. I should have done it already, but it's one of those things that keep slipping my mind. Finding nothing of interest, I walk to the hidden bin behind the nearby cupboard, ready to chuck the envelopes into the recycling, when a name catches my eye on a business-looking envelope.

Victory Enterprises.

In the address window it says: *To the Owner.*

Hang on . . .

I don't recall Victor ever telling me the name of his business before now, but what are the chances of it being a play on his name?

If it is his business, then . . . was *Victor* the owner of this house before me?

My fingers stop as I'm about to tear into the letter. No. I have my limits . . .

Don't I?

No.

Screw it.

I tear into the envelope like a woman possessed, eagerly absorbing the words on the single sheet of paper inside. It's a reminder regarding house insurance. It doesn't mention Victor by name. As I read it, I realise I may have been too hasty.

I recheck the address.

Yep. I've fucked up.

The address is Poppy Field View, whereas we live at Poppy Field Close.

Who the hell names two identical houses almost the exact same name?

Great. Now I have to explain to Victor why I ripped open his private mail.

Sighing, I shove all the other envelopes into the bin and leave the one addressed to Victor on the side. I'll drop it round to him at some point or give it to him the next time I see him, but I could kick myself for what I've just done.

The coffee machine whirs and gurgles in the background, so I head to the front door where the CCTV set-up box is located. I flip it open and check the various readouts on the screen. It all may as well be in a different language. I need someone to explain it to me in a way I can understand.

I turn as Heather walks down the stairs.

'Hey,' I say.

'Hey, Mum.' She rubs her head and fluffs out her hair, which is tangled and sticking up. 'Thanks for letting me sleep in your bed last night. Sorry.'

'Don't be sorry. There's no need. Are you all right?'

'Yeah. Now that I think about it, I guess you were right. It probably is like those nightmares I used to have.'

'Hmm,' is all I say in response. 'Is everything okay? Why do you think you're getting them again?'

'Probably just under a bit of stress at school. Did you ask Ryan's dad about using his Jaguar for the prom?'

'Um, no, not yet. Have you asked Ryan?'

'He said he'd love to.'

'Ah.'

Shit.

'You couldn't do me a favour, could you?'

She tilts her head. 'What?'

'Could you invite Ryan round here later to go over a few things with the CCTV and some other gadgets around the house I know nothing about?'

Heather smirks. 'Sure. I'll text him now.'

'Thanks, darling.'

I might be able to kill two birds with one stone.

* * *

Two hours later, Ryan knocks on the door. Heather lets him in and they chat and laugh for a bit before joining me in the kitchen, where I've taken to baking bread. It's one of those things I've always fancied trying, but never got around to doing. Plus, I have a fancy bread maker now. So far, I've made a granary loaf and half a dozen seeded rolls. I'm not quite ready to apply to *Bake Off* yet, but I'm happy with my efforts.

'Hi, Ryan. Thanks so much for coming round,' I say when he walks in.

'What can I help you with, Mrs Howden?' he asks with an awkward smile. He looks so much like his father. It scares me a little as I look at him and Heather, who are half-brother and sister.

It's icky, making a thick lump form at the back of my throat. Somehow, I need to convince him not to take my little girl to prom, thereby destroying her happiness and cementing the fact she'll never talk to me again.

'Could you explain how to use the CCTV and check something for me on the playback, if there is such a thing?'

'Sure.'

Ryan spends a few minutes familiarising himself with the CCTV system, pressing buttons and checking a few things. Then he talks me through it, explaining how to turn it off and on, start a timer, check playback and more. He also shows me all the various camera angles that are set up. There are twenty-two cameras situated around the house and grounds, which cover most of the angles, including all exits, entrances and windows.

He sets up the app on my phone, which means I'll get notifications every time there's unwanted movement around the property, especially between the hours of ten at night and six in the morning.

It settles my stomach a little, but I still can't stop thinking about George and how he may have seen what Victor and I did that night . . .

Ryan explains it's programmed to delete the footage every week, which means the camera feed from that night has already gone. I thank him, then, when he turns to rejoin Heather, I navigate to the playback setting, searching for last night's footage of the front of the house where Heather's window is and the angles across the garden where the lights came on.

I can't recall the exact time she jumped into bed next to me, but I know it was after one. I press fast-forward, but because it's night, it looks as if the footage isn't even playing. Every now and then, a gust of wind causes the nearby tree to rustle.

There . . .

A fox darts across the garden like a dark lightning bolt. The lights flash on and the whole area is plunged into bright light. I replay it back a couple of times to be sure.

So . . . it was a fox.

But . . . what made the fox run across the garden so fast? Was it frightened of something? Usually, foxes like to scavenge, don't they? Potter around and search for something to eat. But it launched itself from one side of the lawn to the other as if it were being chased by a predator or it had been spooked by something . . . or *someone*.

Convinced there's nothing else to see on the camera footage, I reset it the way Ryan showed me and head back into the kitchen to continue making loaves of bread.

* * *

An hour later, Ryan pops his head round the door as I'm finishing the last dozen rolls.

'Thanks for having me round, Mrs H. Bye.'

'Oh, Ryan, before you go, may I speak with you for a moment?'

Ryan steps all the way into the kitchen. 'Sure thing.'

'Um, it's about Heather and her prom that's coming up. I'd love for you to take her, but I'm a little worried that . . . Well, she's a bit younger than you and . . .'

Ryan holds his hands out in surrender. 'Relax, Mrs H. I'll make sure she's safe, and don't worry about me. I don't think of her like that.'

'You don't?'

'I mean . . . she's a great girl and all, but . . . we're just friends.'

'Oh.' His answer is enough to render me speechless.

'Bye, Mrs H,' he says with a wave.

'Bye, Ryan,' I reply as he turns and walks out of the kitchen.

Instead of feeling relieved, I now feel sorry for my daughter, who is going to be crushed if she ever finds out that Ryan doesn't fancy her. This is too complicated to think about, but at least I don't have to worry about them getting too close at prom.

* * *

George arrives home from his work trip away, kisses me lightly on the cheek and then goes in search of the kids. I serve dinner at six, happy to have the whole family back together, but there's an unsettled ache in my stomach as I sit across from my husband while he eats.

Liam fills him in on his gaming weekend. Then, he suddenly blurts out, 'Oh, shit!'

'What?' I ask, stunned by Liam's outburst.

'I was supposed to do something for school tomorrow, but I forgot.'

I sigh. 'I asked you outright on Friday if you had homework to do over the weekend and you said no. Did you lie to me just so you could play online all weekend?'

'No, I swear. I honestly forgot. Sorry, Mum.' Liam looks down at his dinner.

I look up at George, wondering how I should play this. George doesn't seem to care either way. 'It's fine,' I say. 'What is it you have to do?'

Thankfully, long gone are the days where I have to hand-make an arts and crafts project from scratch or come up with a fancy dress outfit overnight, but I hope to God it's not a long report.

'On Friday, we learned about blood types, and I had to find out what everyone's blood type is, then make some sort of diagram.' Liam gets up from the dinner table and we listen in silence while he runs upstairs.

Heather hasn't eaten much. She's staring at her plate of food as if she's disgusted by it.

'Not hungry?' I ask.

'No. Just . . . never mind.'

'You sure?'

'It was something Ryan said earlier . . .'

I open my mouth to ask her to continue, but Liam disrupts my train of thought as he comes barrelling back into the room, holding a few pieces of paper and a pen. He sets them out on the table next to his half-eaten plate of food.

'Right,' he says. 'Dad, what's your blood type?'

George sips from a beer bottle. 'Gosh, it's been a while since I've given blood. AB positive, I think.'

'Mum?'

'I'm B positive.'

'What am I?' Liam asks, jotting the information down on the page.

'Same as your dad.'

'And Heather?'

'O negative,' I reply without missing a beat.

A long silence follows.

'Are you sure?' asks Liam.

I look up at him. 'Of course, I'm sure. Why?'

'Because . . . from what I learned at school, a person can't have O negative type blood if both their parents are AB and B positive.'

And it's at that moment that I realise I've made a life-changing, monumental mistake.

CHAPTER 20

Every pair of eyes around the table focuses directly on me. I freeze like a rabbit caught in headlights, unable to form a single syllable or move a muscle, hoping that by staying completely still, I can somehow erase what's happened. What I've just said. But I can't, can I? Once words are spoken, it's impossible to take them back, no matter how hard you try. That's why I always try to teach my children that they need to think before they speak. I wish I'd taken my own damn advice because I've no one to blame but myself for whatever is about to happen next.

Shit. Shit. Shit.

Say something, Fiona! *Anything.*

'Um . . . I must have remembered wrong, then,' I say, slowly reaching to pick up my glass of water, which has a trickle of condensation down the side. Damn it, I wish it were wine. I take a sip, soothing my dry-as-the-Sahara mouth, and put it down with a trembling hand. 'She must be AB negative or . . . something.'

I wish someone else would speak because all I can hear is the blood pounding in my ears like a heartbeat. My head swims as I risk a glance at George, who has his mouth open, a piece of unchewed food still inside it.

'Sorry,' I say to Liam. 'I can't remember what blood type Heather is. I'll have to . . . look it up.'

Liam crosses out the note he made on the paper. 'Mrs Philips said . . .'

'Well, maybe she's wrong,' says George, finally finding his voice after swallowing the food in his mouth. He clears his throat, snapping out of his initial shock. 'Maybe Heather is one of those unique blood types or . . . whatever.' He says the words confidently enough, but I can hear past them, to what he's really saying. He's making excuses for me, covering up my slip of the tongue to protect the children. He doesn't want to have this conversation in front of them.

'Mum . . .' says Heather.

Shit. She hasn't said anything yet. I hoped she was paying more attention to her plate than listening to what her brother was saying.

'I must have misremembered your blood type,' I say. Even as I say it, the blood rushes to my face. Am I on fire? I feel like I'm on fire.

Liam flips his notebook open, scrolling back a few pages. I need him to stop looking for the answer. Everyone just needs to stop.

Stop. Stop. Stop.

I stand up, shoving my chair backwards. It scrapes against the tiled floor, sending a ripple of unease straight through me. 'Right, well . . . I better start loading the dishwasher.'

I pick up my plate, which still has leftover roast potato on it with puddles of thick gravy, and carry it to the kitchen bin, all the while trying not to drop it. My hands are numb, shaking as I scrape the food into the bin.

'Liam, take your homework and do it in another room, please,' says George.

I close my eyes, silently praying as I open the dishwasher; a luxury I'm still relishing every time I clear the table. I focus on loading plates and cutlery rather than the scraping of chair legs and shuffling of papers behind me. No one is facing up to what my slip-up may mean. Something I'm grateful for, but I can already feel the storm approaching. The air has changed in the house. It's colder, thicker, darker.

Shuffling footsteps fading into the distance tell me the kids are out of the room. I remain at the dishwasher, focusing on lining up the plates so everything fits. I know where George is without checking. He's still sitting at the head of the table — watching me, waiting for me to say something.

The tension is so thick I want to choke on it.

Several minutes pass while I finish wiping down the surfaces, waiting for George to speak to me. Eventually, I turn my head and look over my shoulder.

He's not there.

I'm not sure when he left. A ripple of goosebumps brush across my skin, making me shudder as I turn back to the kitchen side, tears brimming behind my eyes.

* * *

That evening, I'm sitting in the snug in the oversized chair, reading my Kindle. The door is open, showing anyone that they can enter if they wish. George walks in and closes the door slowly. Too slowly. Like he's deliberately moving at a glacial pace to cause my blood pressure to rise. He wants me to suffer.

It works.

'Hi,' I say. 'The kids okay?' My tone is light, cheery, but inside I know we're about to have the conversation, the one I've been dreading for so long.

'They're fine,' he says.

The door finally clicks closed.

Time stops dead.

He turns, but doesn't look at me, keeping his eyes roaming around the room, anywhere but at me. He walks past, towards the double doors that lead out onto the patio. I've kept them closed because the cool evening air is a little too brisk tonight. I have a blanket over my legs as it is. Comfy. Cosy. Or, at least I was, until George walked in. Now, I'm somewhere between sweating and shivering and my body can't make up its mind which one it wants to do the most.

'So, uh . . . Liam has decided that he believes your little story when you said you made a mistake about Heather's blood type, but me . . . not so much. I decided to do a little research of my own to clear some things up.'

My palms are wet, so I wipe them on the blanket, attempting to hide the fact they're shaking. I put my Kindle down.

'Turns out . . .' continues George. 'Turns out that his teacher is correct, a child can't have O negative blood if both their parents are A or AB positive.' He stares out of the patio doors, then grabs the curtains, dragging them closed, blocking out the last of the evening sun. I'm trapped like a caged bird.

'George, I—'

'Oh, I think it's best you don't say anything just yet,' he replies coolly with a hint of a smile. His calmness is making things worse, winding me up like an old-school alarm clock.

He carries on, never once making eye contact, but studying the library books, touching the shelves and picking up random objects, studying them.

'Of course, the research always says that sometimes a child can be born with a different blood type. It's one of those rare, one-in-a-million type cases, which is obviously possible, but . . . something tells me that Heather isn't one in a million.' He pauses for a long time. 'Is she?' This time, when he finishes, he stares straight at me, eyes blazing. 'Now,' he says, 'I suggest you start talking.'

CHAPTER 21

My breath is running away from me like a freight train gathering speed down a steep hill. I eventually gasp like a dying fish, sucking in gulps of air.

'George, I . . . I don't know what to say.' I really don't. Words have lost all meaning. Is there really any point in continuing to deny it? I've made a huge mistake and he knows it. There's no way he'll forget about this and sweep it under a rug, laugh it off like an awkward slip of the tongue. Whatever happens next is my fault and I have to accept that, accept the consequences.

'How about you tell me the truth?'

Tears flood my eyes. Somehow, I've been able to hold them back until now, stunned into silence, but the emotions are too overwhelming, too powerful to keep at bay.

'Sh-she's not yours.'

I stay where I am on the large corner sofa. I don't risk getting to my feet, approaching him, because I'm not sure my legs can support my weight and I very much doubt George wants me anywhere near him. He turns his back on me, but not before I catch a glimpse of disgust and disappointment on his face.

Oh God . . . What have I done?

I wish I could take it all back, just suck the words out of the air. But I can't. They're out now. They may be invisible, but they hurt.

I've done more damage by saying those three little words than I have done in the whole of our marriage, even when I called him a fucking selfish twat once because he wouldn't do the washing-up when I asked him because I had a hundred and one other things to do.

George's body is shaking, but as he turns around, I realise it's not from crying, but from pure anger. His fists are clenched at his sides, his arms ram-rod straight. I've never seen him this angry. I've never seen anyone this furious in real life. In movies, yes, but not like this.

I can't keep sitting still. My body needs to move. I push the blanket off my legs and get to my feet. George doesn't move a muscle, but I don't get too close for fear of him retaliating or lashing out. He's unpredictable right now.

'Who? Who's her father?' he says, his jaw clenches, teeth grinding.

'You are! You're her father. You always have been, I just . . .'

'You just what, Fiona? Huh! You just . . . *what*?'

A huge sob erupts, and the excess saliva in my mouth almost makes me choke. 'I was young. I didn't know what to do. I was scared! I met you only a few weeks after I fell pregnant, but I didn't know at the time. Then, we slept together and a few weeks later, I found out. I thought she was yours, but then the dates didn't add up and . . .' I stop, rethinking my words.

Does he even want to hear any of this? There's nothing I can say that will make this any better, not even a little bit. I know that, but the truth spills from my mouth before I can stop it. If I'm not careful, then I could tell him the one thing that could push him over the edge . . .

George laughs, but it's a menacing laugh, one that sends creepy tingles up my spine. 'So, you thought, "I know what I'll do, I'll lie to a man, tell him the baby's his, so he'll marry me and we get to live happily ever after." Is that what you did, Fiona?'

'I . . . I didn't think that. I just . . . reacted in the spur of the moment. I was afraid you'd leave me. I'd fallen in love with you, but I was afraid you wouldn't want me, wouldn't want us, so I . . .' I can't say it. It's too horrible.

'So you let me believe she was mine,' George finishes. 'Oh, you were clever, Fi. I'll give you that. You were fucking clever. You never said explicitly that she was mine. You just never denied it. You let me come to that conclusion on my own because I had no reason to not trust you. Is that about the gist of it?'

I blink, allowing several large teardrops to escape from between my lashes, and nod once. 'I-I'm sorry,' I squeak, my voice as quiet as a mouse.

'I'm afraid it's a little too late for *sorry*.' His voice is venomous. I hate it. I hate that it's my fault I've made him this angry, this horrible. I barely recognise the man in front of me. We've had spats before, all married couples do, but this has the power to do irreparable damage, damage that will never heal properly, no matter how much time passes or how hard I try to fix it.

'P-Please,' I whisper. 'Please don't tell Heather.'

'Oh, you'd like that, wouldn't you?'

'Please,' I say again. 'I . . . I will tell her, but . . . you can't just blurt this out to her. It'll destroy her.'

'No. It will destroy *you*.' He points a stiff finger at me, his whole body rigid, vibrating.

'Please.'

A long silence stretches between us. I don't know whether to keep begging, get down on my knees and clasp my hands together in prayer or just wait it out. Let him decide. Because it is in his hands, after all. He has to decide whether he's more angry at me or more concerned for Heather's well-being. Does he want to punish me enough to risk her mental health?

This will break her and she will hate me. Hell, she may even hate George, but she'll blame me. Of course she will. And I'll deserve every bit of her hatred, but I want to be the one to tell her when the time is right. Not now. Not like this.

'You know,' says George, his voice calmer now, 'she may already be suspicious after the whole blood type thing with Liam at the table. You really fucked up there,' he adds with a chuckle, although I know it's hardly a laughing matter.

'I know,' I say.

'She may have questions, and if she does, I'm not going to be the one to answer them. You got that?'

I nod fast, all words evaporating.

'Fine. I won't tell her, but you need to do it soon.'

'I will. I promise. W-What about us?'

George places his hands on his hips. 'I'm not ready to have that conversation. I need time. I need space.' He turns and heads towards the door.

'A-Are you leaving?' What I really want to ask is, Are you leaving *me?* but I don't add the last word. This can't be about me right now.

'Yes,' he says. 'I'm going to stay in the cottage.'

'O-Okay,' I manage to get out. He leaves the snug, slamming the door behind him.

My legs finally give out. I sink to the floor and allow my emotions to take over. My body shakes, the tears flow and I only get up hours later when I'm too exhausted to keep my eyes open. I've never in my life felt this hopeless or guilty, knowing I've destroyed my family.

I stumble upstairs to bed, checking on the kids before I do. Liam is fast asleep with the light still on, so I switch it off and pull the duvet over his skinny body. His homework is lying on the floor next to the bed. I pick it up.

It's rushed, but he's drawn a messy diagram with all the blood types and circled the ones relating to George and me, and then him. But Heather has a question mark next to her name. I'm hoping there aren't any awkward questions from his teacher tomorrow.

Not everyone knows their kids' blood types. It's only because I had them both tested when they were babies. This was during my phase when I was convinced something bad was going to happen to them, so I needed to know everything, including their blood types. Just in case.

Heather's bedroom door is ajar and there's a faint glow emanating from within. I knock gently, but there's no answer, so I push the door open, only to find her also asleep, tucked up in bed, clutching her favourite stuffed toy: a pink elephant called Pinky, which she's had since she was four.

I smile as I watch her slow, steady breaths. She's so beautiful, so peaceful. It sickens me that I've kept such a huge secret her whole life. I should have handled it differently. I should have trusted George.

It's too late to take it back now.

I have to accept that whatever comes next is all my fault, but I can't lose Heather. I can't. And I'll do anything to keep hold of my daughter a little longer.

Just a little longer.

CHAPTER 22

Monday morning arrives and, with it, a growing sense of unease that means I can barely catch my breath as I go about the daily chores. The kids get off to school on time, but there's no sign of George. I assume he'll be working from home today. He hasn't mentioned there being any work trips on the horizon, but I don't expect to see him. He'll be in the cottage, staying as far away from me as possible.

I've never felt more alone. The house is too big; there are too many doors, too many empty rooms, too many hiding places. I walk around it, eventually ending up back in the snug. My sanctuary. The wine cellar beneath the floor calls my name.

It's eleven in the morning. I should find something to keep myself occupied, but the next thing I know, I've descended the staircase and I'm standing in front of the huge array of wine bottles, debating which one to open. Maybe a nice crisp white would go well with a fresh salad for lunch . . .

A creaking noise makes me look up.

I watch in horror as the glass roof slides closed above me.

'No!' I scream, as I stumble towards the narrow, steep steps. But I'm not fast enough. The roof closes and the lights switch off, plunging me into a dark, sealed tomb.

What the hell has just happened? Why did it close by itself? It's supposed to have a failsafe to stop anyone getting trapped down here. The only way to make the floor slide closed is to press the button on the control panel in the snug and keep it pressed.

Which means . . .

Someone has trapped me in here. On purpose.

I can't focus on that though because there's a more pressing matter to worry about.

There's no oxygen down here.

No way of letting myself out. There must be some sort of release catch somewhere that will re-open the ceiling so I can get out.

I take a few deep breaths, then panic I may be using up all the oxygen. How long will it take for me to run out of air?

Shit.

Pure body-rattling fear claws its way up my throat. I let out a garbled cry as I desperately search around the wine-laden shelves for a hidden door release. There isn't one. What kind of idiotic installation company thought it was a good idea to not include an exit button on the inside of the wine cellar, an actual death-trap?

The room is small and cramped enough as it is, but now the circular walls feel as if they're edging closer and closer, squeezing. Oh my God, I'm going to be crushed to death by hundreds of bottles of wine. I'd laugh if I wasn't so terrified right now.

'Help!' I bellow as I bang on the underside of the glass ceiling. The glass is thick, reinforced to withstand people walking across it, so I highly doubt anyone will be able to hear me.

I'm well and truly trapped, and all because I thought it would be a good idea to start drinking wine at eleven o'clock on a Monday morning. To make matters worse, like rubbing salt in an already sore wound, not one of the bottles down here is a screw top, meaning I can't even drink myself into a stupor to stave off the rising panic.

Someone will come and find me. The kids are due back from school in roughly four and a half hours. George is working in the cottage, but . . . he has no reason to come into the house, especially since our confrontation last night.

I sit on the bottom step of the spiral staircase and blink back the tears threatening to spill. My right hand reaches up to my hair and I start to tug. Over and over. Twirl and pull. Twirl and pull.

Snap. Snap. Snap.

All I need to do is stay calm for the next four and a half hours, then the kids will arrive home, notice I'm missing and come searching for me in my favourite room of the house.

But then a little voice pops into my head. My voice.

Will they even notice you're not around? They never have before.

Let's face it. They barely pay attention to me as it is. I could be down here longer. When it gets to six in the evening and they notice dinner hasn't magically appeared on the table, *then* maybe they'll start to worry. *Then*, they'll go and find their dad and ask them where dinner is. I expect they'll be more concerned about the lack of food than the whereabouts of their mum.

Six o'clock is over six and a half hours away.

Is there enough air to keep me alive that long?

* * *

Five hours later, I'm still breathing, but the panic has well and truly rendered me incapable of moving or speaking for fear I may use up the last of the oxygen. I haven't heard the kids come back from school, but then the ceiling is soundproof, so I stay as still as I can, conserving oxygen.

Another hour passes and I've now accepted I may die down here surrounded by bottles of wine I can't drink. My mouth is dry, my eyes are sore and it's getting harder and harder to take a full breath.

Just as I'm deciding whether or not to lie down on the floor and sleep, a shadow passes overhead, then a loud whirring noise makes me jump.

The roof is moving!

Gasping for fresh air, I clamber up the steps just as the roof slides away.

'Mum?'

I throw my arms around my daughter, trying to hold back sobs of relief and joy. 'Oh, thank God!'

'What the hell?' says Heather. She doesn't push me away or flinch when I hug her tight. 'How long have you been down there?'

'Since eleven this morning,' I say, letting her go and composing myself.

'What . . . How did . . . I don't understand,' she says, frowning, giving me a look like I've lost the plot. I probably have since being trapped down there. The strands of hair surrounding my face are practically non-existent now I've yanked them all out.

'Someone trapped me inside,' I say. I walk over to the control panel on the wall. 'Look . . . it only closes if someone presses the button.' I demonstrate by pushing the button — the glass floor springs to life, slowly moving across — and letting go after two seconds. It stops as soon as I let go. I hold it down again, allowing it to close fully before turning to face Heather.

'Shit,' she says. 'Are you all right?'

'Other than being afraid I was going to die, yes. Where's your dad?'

'In the cottage still. Liam went to get him when we . . .' Her face turns red.

'When you realised there was no dinner on the table,' I finish. She blushes further and nods. 'It's fine,' I say. 'Let me go and put something quickly in the oven.'

Heather follows me out. 'Who trapped you down there?'

'I have no idea.'

'By the way, Mum, why is Dad living in the cottage?'

I reach the kitchen and turn on the oven to allow it to heat up. 'We . . . had a fight,' I say.

'About last night at dinner?'

I attempt to act nonchalant as I open the fridge and peer inside to check what there is to eat. Luckily, there's leftover chicken pie that's still edible. I bring it out and place it on a baking tray.

'No, about something else,' I say.

'About Mr Hamilton?'

I stop for a moment and look at my daughter. The thought of losing her, of breaking her heart, is too much to bear. I could stand to lose George if push came to shove, but I couldn't lose Heather or Liam. I'd rather have one of my arms chopped off with a rusty axe.

'It was just a silly thing really,' I say with a weak smile. 'I'm sure everything will be back to normal soon.'

Heather doesn't reply. She sits down at the kitchen table, watching me prepare dinner. Liam enters and joins us.

'Is your father coming?' I ask him.

'No,' says Liam. 'I couldn't find him.'

'He wasn't at the cottage?'

'No.'

I place the chicken pie in the oven and close the door.

If George hasn't been at the cottage, then where the hell has he been all day while I've been trapped inside the wine cellar?

Rather than dwell on the fact my husband has done a disappearing act, I make sure the kids are fed and happy, then attempt to call George on his mobile. It goes straight to voicemail. I even make the short trip across the yard and knock on the door of the cottage, peering through the windows, but Liam is right. George isn't there. He clearly has been there at some point because his things are inside, including his laptop, which he never goes anywhere without.

Perhaps he's popped to the shops. His car is still here though. I'm not really sure what to make of the situation, but I'm not about to call over to next door and ask them if they've seen him.

Stuff it. He's a grown man. He can take care of himself.

I traipse back to the house and hastily eat my dinner, even though I'm not hungry, despite missing out on lunch. I do gulp down a pint of water though. Being stuck in that cellar has really rattled me, and now I'm worried I'll never summon the strength to go down there again to fetch a bottle of wine.

I check the CCTV footage once the kids have gone upstairs, wondering if there's a shot of the snug or even the hallway outside of it, but there isn't.

That's convenient.

CHAPTER 23

George eventually shows up the day after Heather rescued me from the wine cellar. I attempt to fill him in on what happened, but he barely says two words to me in response, not even bothering to explain his absence. He won't look me in the eyes, and while I understand his anger, he's showing no tact when it comes to the kids. He makes snide remarks towards me when they're around and refuses to explain why he's sleeping in the cottage. I know I'm supposed to be the one to tell them, but I can't seem to find the words. It's easier with George out of the house and the kids at school because whenever they're nearby, I want to hide. Hiding from my own family because of my shame is a new low for me.

I pop round to see Glory during the week to ask her about her wine cellar, knowing Victor is out of the house, and she tells me that, while it hasn't happened to her specifically, she has heard of this happening before. It's a glitch that can sometimes happen and she's told me in order to stop it happening again, I need to press the lock button after I've opened the glass floor, which keeps it from sliding back across. It doesn't answer my initial question though because she hasn't provided me with an answer as to how it could have slid across on its own in the first place when it's designed to have the button held down the whole time. The only explanation is that someone kept the button depressed and locked me in there intentionally.

A little voice in my head says it was George, that it was a form of punishment for what I've done to him, but would he really do that to me? Trap me like that? I could have suffocated. My children could have found my dead body the next day . . .

George sleeps over at the cottage the whole week. He does come over for dinner so he can see the kids. Apparently, his anger at me doesn't outweigh the chore of having to cook his own meals. As the week goes on, he does start talking to me more, but his answers are short and sharp.

Friday evening arrives and I get the place to myself. Heather is sleeping over at her new friend's house. A girl called Melody. I did meet Melody's mum briefly the other day when I drove over to pick Heather up. She seemed polite, friendly, happy to have Heather stay over after school to study for the last few exams she has coming up. I'm so glad that Heather has made a new friend. Her prom is next week and I've promised to take her dress shopping this weekend in London. She did have a dress she planned to wear, but that was before we won the house and became wealthy, so now she has her heart set on a very expensive designer piece.

Liam is sleeping over at a new friend's house as well, so it's just me alone in the big house tonight, but after the incident last weekend, I'm a little apprehensive about spending time in the snug, so I take up residence in the conservatory instead, which is an ambient space with big green plants in pots and wicker furniture.

I pour myself a glass of wine, which I asked Heather to fetch for me from the wine cellar before she left. I opened the floor for her and stood near the top of the hole while she went down and chose one of the bottles. I take my wine to the far corner and settle down on the small corner sofa.

The sun is setting and everything is so still, so quiet. I'm completely absorbed by the heavy smut scene I'm reading on my Kindle, so when the house alarms blare to life at full volume, I leap in fright, slopping wine over my lap and dropping the Kindle in the process. It clatters to the floor.

The alarm is so loud it takes my breath away. I cover my ears, attempting to dull the sound so that I can think rationally.

It's not turning off.

I rush to the front door where the control panel is, quicky typing in the alarm code, but I'm in such a hurry that I keep pressing the wrong numbers. It takes three attempts to input the correct one, but it doesn't work. The sound continues on and on.

I try again. Nothing works.

Has George changed the alarm code and failed to tell me?

I try a third time. A warning flashes up saying I only have one attempt left to enter the correct code or the police will be notified. Damn it.

I fumble for my phone, which is in my pocket, but the noise is disorientating and it drops to the floor. Grabbing it again, I call George, but there's no answer. Of course there isn't because my husband has decided I no longer exist.

I scream in frustration as I rush to the front door, grab the handle and pull.

It's locked.

Why the hell is the front door locked? What's going on? There's a smart alarm and locking system in this house. Maybe the system has triggered the locks on all the doors because it thinks there's an intruder.

Tripping over my feet, I race to the nearest door, which happens to be the one in the kitchen leading out to the patio, but that's locked too. The noise is making my head spin. I can't think straight. I cover both ears with each hand and take a deep breath. Maybe I should try one of the windows.

I grab a latch and give it a tug, but it doesn't budge.

I'm trapped in my own house.

Then, before I can freak out even more and have a full-on mental breakdown, the alarm switches off. A solid ringing still sounds in my ears, but the silence is utter bliss.

Why did it turn off on its own?

Returning to the front door, I take a look at the control panel. It looks like it's been disarmed, but . . . to do that, someone would have had to enter the correct code, and I'm the only person in the house. Aren't I?

'George?' I call out, popping my head round the nearest door leading to the games room and the hallway beyond.

I turn around and bump straight into Victor.

'Woah!' He backs away from me, holding his hands up to show he's no threat.

'Victor? How did you get in here?' I ask, my ears still vibrating from the shrill alarm.

'I heard the alarm from my house. What's going on? Are you all right?'

'No, I'm not all right. You almost gave me a heart attack.'

'I'm sorry, I didn't mean . . . I wanted to check everything was okay. That's all.'

I place a hand on my heart, attempting to steady it, but it's galloping away at full speed, showing no signs of calming down.

'The bloody alarm went off and my code wasn't working, so I couldn't switch it off. Plus, all the doors and windows locked. I was trapped inside, but then it suddenly turned off and . . .'

I stop, realising the meaning of my words. Hang on . . . Victor is *inside* my house. How did he get in if all the doors and windows were locked?

'Did you turn the alarm off?' I ask.

'No. Why would you think that?'

'Then how did you get inside?'

Victors frowns at me. 'The front door was open. Well, not open, but it was unlocked. The alarm turned off seconds before I reached the front door.'

'It's funny how you keep letting yourself into my house,' I say, narrowing my eyes at him. I don't like this. It keeps happening. 'I think you need to back off.'

Victor raises his eyebrows. He steps in front of me. 'Fiona, I swear, I came running when I heard the alarm. That's all. Where's George?'

My eyes flick sideways, searching for something to use as a shield or a weapon should he decide to lunge at me, but the idea is laughable. Victor wouldn't hurt me, would he? He said himself that if George hurt me, he'd kill him. He is dangerous, but not towards me.

'I . . . He's . . .'

'Fiona, I don't know what you're implying here, but maybe you should think about it before you start accusing people of things they haven't done. I don't mean any harm. I care about you . . . and the kids.' His tone of voice is calm, but it's doing nothing to alleviate my rising blood pressure. The way he said *kids* was weird too.

'Look, I've had a bit of a fright, okay? I'd like you to leave now.'

'What were you and George arguing about last weekend?'

I take a step back because he's dangerously close to invading my personal space. 'How do you even know we were arguing? Don't tell me — you could hear it from your house?' It comes out as a joke, but it doesn't quite land the way I intend.

'George came round straight after and we had a drink.'

'He . . . What? Why would he do that?' His comment throws me completely. Why the hell would George visit Victor straight after our argument and have a friendly drink with him? It's not like they're best friends. They barely know each other.

'Well, perhaps George needs some male friends to vent to.'

'To *vent* to?'

'I'm sure you're not the easiest person to live with.'

How dare he!

'Hang on a minute,' I say, interrupting him just as he's about to say something else. 'What gives you the right to assume you know anything about me and my marriage?'

'I know a lot more than you think I do,' replies Victor coolly.

I fold my arms across my chest. 'Like what?' Now I sound like my teenage daughter.

Victor smiles. 'Like . . . I know *why* you argued. It's amazing how much a guy will talk when he's pissed off at his wife and had a few drinks.'

No . . .

I'm stunned. Too stunned to form a coherent thought, let alone any words to fire back at him. I want to shout, deny everything. He's bluffing, surely? He doesn't know anything. Why would George tell a complete stranger our personal business like that? It makes no sense.

Victor continues to stare at me, waiting for me to speak, but I dare not open my mouth in case I say the wrong thing or he reads too much into it.

'I know Heather's mine,' he says.

Rather than allowing my silence to make me look guilty, I take a defensive stance. 'How dare you,' I say, seething. 'I don't know what the hell George told you, but . . .'

'Oh, fucking stop it, will you?' he snaps back. 'Don't even bother to try and deny it. The timings match up perfectly.'

Tears fill my eyes, but I'm too angry, too shaken to wipe them away. I don't care if he sees them. 'How did . . . Did George tell you this last weekend?'

Victor doesn't reply, not at first. He waits, allowing the silence to stretch between us, prolonging the torture. 'No, not last weekend.'

'I don't care when he told you,' I reply, almost biting my own lip in the process. 'You have no right to . . .' I stop, play his words back over in my mind. 'If he didn't tell you last weekend when he found out, then when *did* he tell you?'

'I've known for a while.'

'Define *a while*.'

'A year. George told me a year ago.'

'He . . . he told you . . .'

My head spins. The room tilts sideways.

George has known that Heather isn't his daughter for *an entire year*?

And Victor has known about her too . . .

What. The. Fuck.

PART 3

CHAPTER 24

Victor stands in front of me, but his body is distorted, blurry around the edges. I'm dangerously close to passing out if I don't take a breath in soon, but my lungs seem to have lost the ability to function. How can he be telling the truth? How can George have known about Heather not being his biological daughter for a whole year and never let on, never given me even a whiff of doubt that he was hiding the truth. Either Victor is lying to throw me off track, or I don't know my husband at all.

'Why would you say that?' I ask, stumbling sideways against the wall like I've had way more than the one glass of wine.

'Because it's true,' replies Victor. He's made no move to help me, no gesture to ensure I don't collapse to the floor, which is a real possibility at the moment, considering my legs feel like soggy bread. 'I'm sorry it came out like that, but . . . there's a lot you don't know about George.'

His words make no sense. A lot *I* don't know about George? I'm his wife. We've been together for most of our adult lives. I know he has a small freckle on his backside. I know he prefers using sweetener in his tea but proper sugar in his coffee. When he's sick, he likes to listen to Bon Jovi songs on repeat. I know a hell of a lot about my husband, but this practical stranger thinks he knows more.

'No, he wouldn't . . . he found out last weekend,' I repeat, but I'm now questioning my own words, my own beliefs. 'Wait . . . how do you and George know each other?'

'Maybe you should speak to your *husband*.' His emphasis on the word drips with condescension.

'This isn't over, Victor. I swear to God, if you tell Heather or I find you in my house again without an invite, I'll call the police.'

Victor nods. 'I want a relationship with her, Fiona. I deserve to know my daughter.'

'Get out.' I thrust a finger towards the front door of the house.

He walks slowly past me. 'This isn't over. I could very easily take all of this away.'

I don't understand what he means, but the second he's out of sight, I sink to the floor and weep like a child who's lost its mother. My whole world is falling apart, crumbling around me like a dilapidated building. I want to reach out and grab all the broken parts, try and keep them together, but it's impossible. I'm not strong enough. I've managed to do it for nearly seventeen years, but now it's out of my control.

One way or another, Heather will eventually know I've betrayed her.

But now I realise George may have been lying to me as well. Perhaps not for as long as I've been lying to him, but . . . if Victor is right and George has known about Heather for a year, then why has he waited until now to reveal his hand?

And how did he and Victor meet?

* * *

A few minutes later, I push myself to my feet and stumble towards the front door. I need to speak to George, yet I have no idea what I'm supposed to say. My whole body is vibrating with nervous energy. I only make it halfway across the yard before I see him walking up the driveway, coming from the direction of Victor's house.

I stop and wait for him to join me.

'Were you just over at Victor's?'

'I heard the alarm. What happened?' The fact he didn't answer my question doesn't go unnoticed. It's interesting how Victor made it over here first.

'Nothing, It . . . It went off and the code wouldn't work. I found Victor in the house, but I don't know how he got in there.'

'Victor was in our house?' George's whole body bristles and he stands up a little straighter.

'Yes, but . . . George, he said some things that I need you to explain.'

'Like what?'

'Like . . . did you know about Heather before last weekend?'

George stares at me, his jaw clenched. He clearly doesn't like talking about this subject, but tough luck. I can't keep my mouth shut about this. I need to know if my husband has been keeping things from me. Pot calling the kettle black.

'You honestly think I would have been able to keep it together if I found out before then? I lost it, Fiona. My whole world collapsed in the blink of an eye the other night.'

'I know, but . . . Victor said you told him a year ago.'

George laughs, which makes me feel as if I'm a silly little girl making up stories. 'We've only known Victor like two weeks.'

'But . . .'

'Are you actually saying you believe some random bloke over me? Your husband of over sixteen years?'

I don't know what to think. Is George trying to gaslight me again? What is he playing at? I decide to test my theory. It's risky, but I need to know for sure.

'He's not a random bloke,' I say.

'Oh?'

'He . . . He's Heather's real father.'

George makes no movement. I'm not sure if he's even breathing. 'You're lying. Why would you say that? How could you!'

'Because it's true.'

He storms past me, shoving my shoulder in the process. 'I don't believe you.'

'George, I'm telling you the truth. He and I had a one-night stand a few weeks before you and I met and . . . I never told him I got pregnant. I never saw or spoke to him after that until two weeks ago when he just happened to be our new next-door neighbour.'

George stops in his tracks, keeps his back to me. 'What are you saying?'

'I think he might have planned this whole thing. Something doesn't add up. I don't know what or who to believe, but I don't feel safe around him. This house . . . I think it belongs to him and . . .'

George bursts out laughing, spins around to face me. 'Are you hearing yourself, Fiona? You sound deluded. You won this house fair and square, right?'

'Yes, but . . .' I stop, reconsidering what I'm about to say. I don't have the energy to try and convince him of my insecurities. 'I think we need to sell this house and move. It was wrong to come here.'

'It was your fucking idea to move here!' bellows George.

'I know, but . . .'

'No,' he snaps. 'No, we're not moving. You made your bed, Fiona, so now you need to fucking well lie in it.' George stomps towards the cottage, slamming the door behind him.

I pull my cardigan tighter around my trembling body. A part of me wants to run after him, beg him to support me, to believe me, but I'd only be wasting my breath. I'm not sure who to trust, so how do I expect him to trust me? I've betrayed him, but do I believe him? He says he didn't know about Heather before last weekend, but why would Victor say that if it weren't true?

At the end of the day, it comes down to whether I believe my husband or the guy I had a one-night stand with nearly seventeen years ago. They both have reason to hate my guts right now, but the idea of George knowing about Heather for a year is too far-fetched. Maybe Victor has known for that length of time, but there's no way George could have told him. He must have found out another way, but there's no one else in the world who knows, so how is it possible?

I expected George to react worse to the news that Victor is Heather's father, but he barely blinked. He doesn't believe me.

I walk back to the house, defeated and exhausted. I shut and lock the doors and set the alarm. This time, the code works, which begs the question as to why it wasn't working before when I tried to use it to turn the alarm off.

I should go to bed and try and sleep, to get through the hideousness of tonight, but climbing into bed and pulling the duvet over me does nothing to alleviate my anxiety or racing heart. I'm alone in this huge house with a top-of-the-range security system, built-in CCTV cameras, yet it feels as if there's a monster out there roaming the halls, stalking me.

I turn on my side and stare at the crack of moonlight on the wall next to the bed. When I next open my eyes, the sliver of light is gone.

Did I fall asleep?

My nerve endings explode with mind-numbing terror as I realise someone is standing next to my bed, blocking out the moonlight.

CHAPTER 25

A blood-curdling scream catches in my throat as the dark shadow lunges at me. A hard, strong hand clamps over my mouth before I can utter another sound. A whimper escapes as the pressure increases against my jaw.

I kick out with both my legs, but they're trapped beneath the duvet. Whoever the intruder is, they're strong, so I assume it's a man, but it's difficult to tell because they're dressed all in black. Even their face has no discernible shape to it, covered with a balaclava.

I keep trying to scream as I fight and claw with my hands. My head thrashes from side to side against the pillow, attempting to loosen their grip over my mouth. They don't say a word or make a single sound.

One of my legs springs free from the duvet and I manage to land a solid blow, which knocks them backwards. They take off for the door and sprint down the hallway.

I throw back the covers and leap out of bed, scrambling for my phone on the side table. I can barely hold it steady as I input my password, which I get wrong twice before it opens. I call the police.

'I was just attacked in my home while I was sleeping!' My tongue sticks to the roof of my mouth as I scream.

The operator asks me several questions, which I answer, but I keep tripping over the words, repeating myself. Eventually, they tell me officers are on their way and to stay inside and hide somewhere safe. They offer to stay on the line, but I decline.

I hang up, then crawl into my walk-in wardrobe and manoeuvre myself with my back up against the wall, my knees pulled up to my chest. I have no idea how long the police will take to arrive, but I'm going to need to let them in, which means leaving the safety of this position at some point.

That's when I remember that Ryan showed me how to control the security system from my phone, but when I go to disable it, I realise it's already been deactivated.

Somehow, the intruder knew the code.

There are only three people who know the security code.

George, Heather and Liam.

But there is one person who has managed to get round it before.

Victor said the alarm deactivated before he arrived only a few hours ago, allowing him entry, but he's a technology expert, isn't he? It's probably child's play to him to hack a security system.

The police knock on the door and enter. Their voices carry up the stairs.

'I'm in here!' I call out.

I can't move. I don't want to move. My mouth and jaw ache from the attack, from where the intruder clamped down hard, but otherwise I'm unhurt.

The wardrobe door opens. A female officer with dark brown hair tied in a bun kneels in front of me. It's the middle of the night, but she looks surprisingly fresh.

'I'm PC Watkins. What's your name?' she asks me.

'Fiona,' I whisper.

'Okay, Fiona. Is there anyone else in the house?'

I shake my head. 'My children are sleeping over at friends' houses.'

'Do you know who attacked you? Did you see their face?'

Another head shake.

'Are you hurt? Do I need to call an ambulance?'

'No, I'm okay. Just a little shaken up, that's all.'

'We're going to search the house, okay? Why don't you come downstairs and I'll make you a nice cup of sugary tea. You have a lovely kitchen by the looks of it.'

I know what she's trying to do and I'm grateful, so I gingerly get to my feet and follow her out of the wardrobe, then through the bedroom and down the stairs. When I reach the bottom, George bursts his way through the front door. PC Watkins immediately steps in front of me and holds up her hand to stop George taking another step closer.

'Hey! What the fuck? I live here!'

I nod at her when she looks over at me. 'It's okay. He's my husband. George.'

'And where was George during the attack?' asks PC Watkins, squaring up to him.

'Wait . . . you were attacked? By who?' George pushes past the officer and directs his attention to me, despite the fact PC Watkins is giving him the evil eye, like she wants to cuff him.

'I don't know, but I'm guessing it was Victor,' I say, even though George is a close second guess.

'And Victor is?' asks PC Watkins.

'Our next-door neighbour,' says George. 'I want him questioned immediately.'

'There seems to be no sign of a break-in, which begs the question — how did Victor enter your home? Does he have the security code or a spare key?'

'No, he doesn't, but I . . .' I stop when George blushes red. 'What?' I ask him.

He scratches the back of his neck, a sure tell he's hiding something. 'I may have given him a spare key.'

PC Watkins and I hold our breaths.

'You what! When?' I explode at him.

'A few days after we moved in. Everyone gives their neighbours a spare key, right? I have a spare key to *their* house. You know, in case of emergencies.'

PC Watkins and I stand with hands on our hips, staring at George, who has the decency to blush an even deeper shade of red. It's like we're ganging up on him. Good. He deserves it. What kind of idiot gives a spare key to someone they just met?

'I can't believe this,' I say. 'I've been worried he's been breaking into our house and he's had a spare key this whole time. Did you tell him the security code too? He's been in here without permission, George. He keeps showing up unannounced.'

'Is this true?' asks PC Watkins.

'I . . . Yes, I gave him the code. Well, actually, I gave him a different one to ours so I can see when it's used, but I'm not sure about him entering unannounced because I haven't seen him here when he hasn't been invited. My wife . . . she . . . she's been under a lot of stress lately and . . .'

'Don't you dare try and gaslight me again!'

George continues speaking to PC Watkins as if I'm not standing right next to him, fuming.

'She spends all her time in this big house, day in and day out and . . . I think she's been drinking during the day. You need help, Fiona.' He turns and speaks to me directly for the last bit.

I clench my jaw so hard that I clamp down on my tongue. It hurts.

'Okay,' says PC Watkins. 'I'll go and have a word with Mr . . .'

'Hamilton. Victor Hamilton,' answers George.

'. . . with Mr Hamilton. In the meantime, Mrs Howden, are you happy for us to leave now that we've finished our search?' At this point another officer, this one male, enters from the kitchen. I hadn't realised there was a second officer in the house.

I glance from PC Watkins to the male officer, to George and back to PC Watkins. I don't know what to say to make this situation any better and, to be honest, I want the police to leave so I can punch my husband in the face, so I nod and thank them for arriving so quickly. I'm a little put out that I didn't get my cup of sugary tea either, thanks to George barging in and announcing that he's the biggest idiot in the world.

'What will happen now?' I ask.

'Once we've spoken to Mr Hamilton and got a better understanding of what's going on, then we'll be in contact, but I think the best idea is to change your security code, and if you're not happy with Mr Hamilton having a spare key, I suggest you ask for it back.'

I nod, happy with her suggestion. Victor never should have had it anyway. Funny how he never mentioned it either, just made me feel as if I was crazy that he kept appearing randomly in my house even though the doors were supposed to be locked.

Why the hell would George do that without speaking to me first? Plus, he said he gave Victor the key a couple of days after we moved in. We were strangers to them! It's not normal. When we lived in our old house, the neighbours never had a spare key, so why start that tradition now?

I say goodbye to the police at the door and find George loitering behind me when I close it.

'Now do you believe me that Victor is dangerous? He told me he knows about Heather. He can get into our house whenever he wants. I was attacked in my sleep. What the hell possessed you to give him unfettered access our house? A complete stranger!'

'Not a stranger to you though, is he?'

'What's that supposed to mean?'

We lapse into silence, neither of us knowing how to proceed with this conversation.

'You know what I think?' he finally asks me.

'What?'

'I think you're fabricating this whole thing.'

His words knock the breath from my lungs. 'Excuse me?'

'You heard me.'

'Why would I make something like this up? I swear, he's been watching this house, and now I find out he can walk in any time he likes because you gave him a key.'

George tilts his head back and stares at the ceiling, something he always does when he's about to explode in anger. He's thinking about his options, how he's going to play his next move.

'How do you expect me to react, huh? You've lied to my face for years. What makes you think I'll believe a word you say ever again?'

Tears flood my eyes. I deserve that. I do, but he has to believe me. I'm not crazy. Victor is punishing me for never telling him about Heather. I don't feel safe in this house.

'I'm your wife,' I whisper.

George scoffs. 'Yeah, unfortunately for me.'

With that, he walks out of the front door and slams it behind him, leaving me to crumple to the floor in pieces.

* * *

The next morning, Liam and Heather arrive home at roughly the same time after being dropped off by their friends' parents. Thankfully, they don't stick around for small talk. We just swap a few pleasantries and I wave them goodbye. Liam immediately asks if he can go to visit Ryan, who apparently has a cool new gadget to show him.

'No, you can't. Neither of you are allowed to go there anymore. You are not to speak to Ryan either. I don't want you even to message him.'

'What?' they both shout at the same time.

'Why?' asks Heather, dropping her overnight bag on the floor. 'He's taking me to prom in two days!'

'Not anymore, he's not.'

'This is bullshit!' She stomps her foot.

'You told me you didn't like Victor. He gives you the creeps. I'm just trying—'

'I'm not going to prom with Mr Hamilton, am I? I'm going with Ryan.'

'I don't care.'

Heather makes an angry, cat-like hiss between her teeth, then turns and stomps up the stairs, leaving her bag on the floor. Liam stays where he is, staring at me.

'Not cool, Mum. Not cool.' He shakes his head and follows Heather up the stairs, albeit much more quietly. A door slams above.

Heather and I had plans to travel into London today for her dress shopping, but something tells me that's not going to happen now. I've just ruined one of the most magical nights of my daughter's life. But how do I tell her to stop seeing a cute boy she has a crush on without telling her the truth, that he's her half-brother and that I'm worried his father attacked me last night?

I climb the stairs, head to her room and lightly knock.

'Go away!'

'Darling, I'm really sorry, but . . . there are things that have happened and . . . I'm afraid . . .' I open my mouth, then close it and open it again. The words keep getting stuck. I clear my throat to try again.

The door opens and Heather stares at me, eyes blazing. 'What are you afraid of, Mum?'

'I don't trust any of them. Ryan included.'

'Ryan's never done anything to make you not trust him.'

'I know, but . . .'

'This is so typical of you. You don't like someone or do you something to fuck things up and then punish me in the process. Thanks a lot, Mum. Oh, and don't bother about my new dress. I'm not going to prom.'

She slams the door in my face.

Fuck.

CHAPTER 26

I spend several minutes begging and pleading with her, telling her she'll have a lovely time without him, but it makes no difference. For the rest of the day, she refuses to utter a single syllable in my direction, barely makes eye contact, and uses Liam to send me messages back and forth like a carrier pigeon.

Without her knowing, I buy her the most expensive designer prom dress I can find online and get it expedited next-day delivery. It arrives in a beautiful see-through bag by courier all sparkly and pressed. The morning of the prom arrives and it breaks my heart to hear her crying in her room. I hang the dress on the outside of her door, then I call round to Victor's house, knowing he's not there. He'll still be at work in London.

Glory answers the door. She still exudes grace and elegance and, despite my less than civil opinion of her husband, I have to do this for Heather.

'Hi, Glory,' I say.

'Fiona! This is a surprise. Lovely to see you. Would you like to come in?' She's only being polite, but I fold and step over the threshold anyway.

'Thank you. Is Ryan around?'

'Is this to do with Heather's prom?'

'Yes.'

'He was so broken up that she cancelled. Is she still going?'

'No, not unless I can fix things.'

'Well, I'm afraid he's not here now. His father took him into London for some work experience.'

Fuck.

My face falls. 'Oh, that's okay,' I say, even though it most certainly isn't, but I have no one to blame but myself. 'Thank you anyway.' I say my goodbyes and walk back home, feeling deflated and hopeless.

The thought occurs to me that Victor may have taken Ryan away on purpose, almost like he knew Heather would turn against me because of it, but I can't blame this on Victor. It's all my doing and I hate myself for it. I'm only trying to protect her, but in doing so I'm ruining our relationship.

The next time I walk past her room, the dress is gone, but she doesn't come out. I knock on her door, providing a peace offering in the form of smores over the barbecue later, but she tells me to go away. I have no idea how I'm going to fix this. I'm losing the plot, trapped between a rock and a hard place. If I allow her to continue to see Ryan, then there's a risk of them becoming close, and if they get close, then she'll potentially be scarred for life when she finds out they're related.

Yet, if I tell her the truth, then there's no going back and she's likely to never forgive me for lying to her all her life. Our family will never be the same again.

We have to move. There's no doubt about it. I can't stay in this house any longer, knowing that Victor lives only at the end of the driveway, watching, waiting. I don't know what he wants, but I can barely take a deep breath without feeling sick, knowing he's there.

Every day I spend in this house, I feel more and more like a caged animal. George won't speak to me. Luckily, I haven't seen or heard from Victor since the incident the other night. I didn't tell the kids about the intruder. I don't know why, but I think it's because I'm doing whatever I can to protect them. It's all I've ever done. It's why I've spent so many years hiding the truth from them, from George.

That night, I'm getting ready to go to bed. Heather is in her room and Liam is already asleep. I sink into my pillow, groggy from drinking another bottle of wine. It's become a staple part of my routine these past few days, the only thing that will knock me out enough to get a decent night's sleep. I changed the alarm code so even George doesn't know it, so I feel relatively safe to fall asleep tonight.

* * *

Hours later, my body jolts violently, like I've plummeted off the edge of a cliff. It's the scariest feeling, thinking you're falling, then waking up in bed covered in sweat, very much alive, but not knowing where you are or what's happened. The weightless sensation is both elating and terrifying. I've never been a fan of rollercoasters, but it's the same type of feeling when you're at the top and then plummet down to earth. Except this time, I don't come back up.

I keep falling. Falling.

But it's not a dream anymore, more like a nightmare that I can't wake up from.

My heart pounds frantically against my ribcage, like a prisoner rattling its cage. I fight to catch my breath, my body and brain too slow to catch up with the fact that I'm not falling, but lying in my double-queen-sized bed under my duvet, safe and sound.

The darkness around me envelops me like a warm blanket, but I know something isn't right even before I reach out my arm, feeling for the warm body of my husband beside me, and find nothing but empty space, cold sheets.

I forgot. He's not here.

The walls echo with the sound of silence, and it's not one I relish.

I'm wide awake now, my falling nightmare far behind me. I don't even remember it. There's no chance of me drifting back to dreamland. Letting out a long sigh, I roll onto my back, but as I do, my nose tickles with a foreign smell.

What *is* that?

Pushing myself up to sitting, I take a longer breath. It smells like . . .

I sneeze as it tickles my nostrils again.

Smoke.

Before I even realise what I'm doing, I fling the bedcovers back and stand up, quick as lightning, a massive head rush almost sending me toppling sideways.

'Liam! Heather!' My voice screeches so loud that I cough with the effort as the smoke catches in the back of my throat. I stumble towards the bedroom door.

'Lights on!' I shout at the intelligent lighting system, but the only light that appears is the white glow from the full moon outside.

I grasp the handle and yank the door open. A wall of smoke hits me like a slap in the face. My body instantly rejects it, culminating in a full-blown coughing fit that sucks the breath from my lungs. The taste of it makes me retch, but I fight against all my bodily reflexes and throw myself towards the landing.

'Liam!'

His room is the closest to the master suite, just down the corridor, third door on the left. I plough onwards, almost tripping over my feet.

This house was supposed to bring us all together as a family, reignite the connection we've lost over the years. Instead, it's burning down around us, trapping me and my children within its walls. It's blinded and tricked us with its vast and many rooms, fancy decorations and expensive furniture, into thinking it could change our lives, but now it's threatening to take everything away.

I won't let it win. Nothing will stop me from saving my children.

Nothing.

CHAPTER 27

'George!' The instant I open my mouth, fumes and smoke are sucked into my lungs and I erupt into a coughing fit that rattles my whole body. I don't know why I'm calling for my husband. He's sleeping in the cottage. Unless he has a window open, I doubt he'll be woken by the smell of smoke or the sound of my terrified voice.

The smoke alarms aren't sounding. Why isn't the smart system activating and the sprinklers turning on? The police and fire brigade should have been called already, but I have no way of knowing for sure, especially since the fire alarm isn't working properly. This house is broken. I'm broken.

It's up to me to get the kids out.

I reach Liam's room first and burst through the door only to find it empty.

'Liam!' More coughing follows as I retrace my steps to the landing.

'Mum!'

I spin to face the direction of his scared voice, then collapse to the floor with relief when I see him running towards me, cradling Boots in his arms. Of course, he had to risk his life to go in search of the damn cat.

'Liam,' I gasp.

He coughs in my face, attempting to cover his mouth with his arm while holding onto Boots, whose eyes are as round as saucers, but he's keeping still. Probably too scared to move.

'Where's Heather?' I ask. I can barely keep my eyes open, but Liam looks so small and helpless dressed in his Pokémon pyjamas, reminding me he's still just a little boy.

'I don't know,' he says, coughing again.

The flames are blazing at the end of the hall. I point to the stairs leading down. 'Get outside. Go and wake your father. Get him to call the fire brigade.' I turn to run in the opposite direction, down the hallway towards Heather's room.

'Wait!' he shouts. 'Don't leave me.'

I crouch to his level and take hold of him, forcing him to face me. Boots lays trembling in his skinny arms. 'Listen to me. You need to be brave, okay? I need to go and find your sister. You need to rescue Boots. Can you do that? He needs you.'

Liam nods, tears and snot streaming from his eyes and nose. He wipes his face with his arm, then turns and heads towards the stairs. I watch him until he disappears, then run down the corridor, screaming Heather's name.

The fire seems to be hotter, stronger down this end, and when I reach her bedroom door, I understand why. Crackling flames lick the walls nearby. I push my whole weight against the door as I fling it open. Her room is also empty.

It fills me with both dread and relief.

Where the hell is she? Has she already escaped?

My lungs are full of smoke and I can barely see in front of me. My body is reacting to the lack of oxygen, and if I don't get out soon, I'm going to pass out. But I can't leave without Heather. What if she's trapped somewhere?

'Mum!'

I rush out of the room and back down the corridor, following the sound of my daughter's voice. When I reach the stairs, I call her name, but get no response. The smoke is so thick now I can't see more than a few feet in front of me. My head spins as I go to take a step and I sink down to the ground, collapsing at the top of the stairs.

Closer to the floor, I find it a little easier to breathe, but I'm still in danger of suffocating if I don't move soon. I start sliding and crawling down the stairs as fast as possible. Behind me, the fire crackles and spits. The heat chases me as I tumble the rest of the way down the steps, landing in an awkward heap at the bottom.

'Mum!' Liam is screaming from outside. At least I know he's safe, but I haven't been able to find Heather. I thought I heard her voice, but maybe it was Liam's voice and I heard what I wanted to hear.

Where the hell is George? Has Liam found him? Why isn't he in here searching for Heather? Surely he wouldn't let her die? I can't leave without her.

In the distance, sirens get louder and louder.

The fire brigade are on their way. They'll help search. I can't stop searching though. I'm all she has. By the time I stagger to my feet, a firefighter bursts through the front door, dressed in safety gear, goggles and a helmet.

'I can't find my daughter!' I scream at her.

'Ma'am, your daughter is outside. She's safe. Is there anyone else in the house?'

Her words make no sense. How can she be outside already? 'No, it's just me.'

The firefighter grabs my arm and pulls me towards the door. I struggle to keep up with her. She's strong, but I'm glad she's leading the way because my vision is now almost completely gone and I'm too disorientated to think straight.

When I see my two babies huddled together, Boots still clutched tight in Liam's arms, I yank my arm away from my rescuer and race towards them.

'Mum!' Heather and Liam run towards me, crying. I wrap my arms around both of them, sinking to my knees. My body starts convulsing with coughs and sobs as I hug my children tighter than I've ever hugged them in my life.

My back is turned to the house, so I have no idea how bad it is, but I couldn't care less about the bricks and mortar. My children are all I care about. It's not till I hear George's voice bellowing across the yard that I pull away from them and look up through stinging, puffy eyes.

A paramedic starts trying to put an oxygen mask on me, but I wave it away, immediately rounding on my husband, who's come running from the cottage.

'Where the hell were you!' I lunge at him, wanting to pummel my fists against his chest, but my legs instantly collapse and he catches me, holding me close.

'I'm sorry. I'm so sorry,' he says, gasping for breath after his sprint.

'She really needs to wear this,' says the paramedic, pushing the mask towards me again.

George lifts me off his chest and turns me around. 'Fi, please. Get yourself checked over.'

'The kids . . .'

'They're fine.'

'No, I have to . . .' I turn to face them.

'Mum, we're fine,' says Heather. 'I arrived just as Liam ran out of the house.'

I allow the paramedic to put the mask over my mouth and nose and take a few breaths. I still feel as if the whole world is spinning, and my throat and airways burn. But staring into the faces of my children is all I can focus on. It's enough to take away the pain.

'Where were you?' I ask Heather from behind the mask.

'I was . . .' She looks at the ground and kicks a pebble. 'I was just sneaking back from seeing Ryan. He was back from London with his dad. I'm sorry. I know you told me to stay away from him, but he's really a decent guy, Mum.'

'Oh, God. You didn't . . .'

'Not that it's any of your business, but no. We haven't done anything. I just like hanging out with him. That's all.'

'Actually, it is my business, Heather. You're not even sixteen years old.'

Heather rolls her eyes. 'Trust you to ruin the moment, Mum. You should be glad I disobeyed you, otherwise I could be dead right now.'

Her words cut deep. Too deep. She's right.

'I didn't mean—'

'This is all your fault anyway.'

'Excuse me?'

'If you hadn't moved us all here, then none of this would have happened.'

I want to argue, but my logical brain stops me. She's in shock. We all are, so there's no reason to squabble with each other. We're alive. That's all that matters.

But she's also right about that too. She just doesn't realise how right she is.

At that moment, I turn to look behind me at the house. The firefighters have been working on getting the blaze under control, shouting in the background, but I've barely noticed them. Despite knowing I need to be mad at Heather for going against my wishes and seeing Ryan in the dead of the night, I've actually never been more relieved she decided to defy me. Her room had been the one closest to the fire. She may not have made it out. She could have easily been trapped behind the wall of flames and smoke, which makes my brain start thinking the worst.

Did someone deliberately start the fire to trap her? Was my daughter the intended target or was I? Were we all targets? Someone must have started it and disabled the fire alarm. If it had been active, then it would have alerted me to the danger a lot sooner, waking me up long before I woke up naturally. It was a miracle I woke up at all.

I glance at George, who's speaking with the police who have also turned up without me noticing. The firefighters have managed to extinguish the fire, but the air is thick with smoke. I stand in a trance, looking around at the scene. Everything that's happened over the past couple of weeks has culminated in this disaster, but the gnawing feeling in my gut tells me this was no accident.

The security system not working.

Me getting trapped in the wine cellar.

My midnight attacker.

The intruder in Heather's room.

Now a house fire . . .

George leaves the police and jogs to my side. 'They can't go inside until the firefighters have completed their checks, but they're saying there's no structural damage. Due to the smart design of the house, the fire managed to stay in one area upstairs.'

'Near Heather's room,' I say.

'Yes. She's lucky she wasn't in there when it started.'

I squeeze my lips together. 'Hmm, lucky,' I murmur. 'Seems this family is having a lot of *luck* lately.'

'What's that supposed to mean?'

'Nothing. Why didn't the fire alarm activate?'

'They don't know yet. They'll look into it as soon as they can.' George sighs. 'You're more than welcome to all stay in the cottage until the house is safe to enter again.'

'Oh, how nice of you to offer.'

George tuts at my snippy sarcasm and marches back towards the police. I fold my arms across my chest and glance across the driveway towards the neighbours' house. They must have seen and heard the racket going on. And Victor is now back from London.

Would Victor really go as far as to set fire to our house? Heather could have been killed. Any of us could have been trapped inside. George may not believe Victor is dangerous, but I do. Besides, George seems to go against anything I say at the moment. I could tell him that the sky is blue and he'd argue that it's a dusky pink. Victor's casual comment about George spilling the beans a year ago has thrown everything I ever thought into chaos.

Too many things have happened lately for this to be an accident. I need to speak to the police alone. They may not have taken me seriously the other night when I was attacked in my sleep by an unknown intruder, but this fire is proof that someone is after me and my family.

We're not safe here.

But where else are we supposed to go?

CHAPTER 28

A few minutes later, once they've been cleared by the paramedics, George takes the kids (and Boots who is also unharmed, if perhaps a little freaked out) into the cottage to get away from the commotion and try and get some sleep. It's just after two in the morning, but even though I feel like a walking zombie and would kill to follow them and collapse into a bed, I still haven't been given the all-clear by the paramedics. They've been trying to convince me for the past twenty minutes to go to hospital to be put on a ventilator, but I can't. I won't leave my children alone. I barely want them to be alone with George. He feels like a stranger to me.

When the paramedics finally get off my back, I spy PC Watkins, the female officer who visited the house before. She and a couple of other officers have managed to go inside the house to check out the scene. Like George said, the house is structurally intact, but Heather's room, along with the corridor outside it and one of the other spare bedrooms, is burnt and in ruins. Heather is going to be devastated when she learns that all her prized possessions are gone.

'Do you suspect arson?' I ask PC Watkins.

'Why do you say that?' she asks.

'Well, considering we had a break-in the other night and I was attacked in my sleep and my daughter has been seeing strange men in her room in the middle of the night, this must be connected somehow, don't you think?' My patience is wearing so thin it's practically see-through. I'm astonished and irritated it's got this far. Maybe I should have pressed harder for the police to take it more seriously. They assumed that because George had given our neighbour the spare key, there was no reason to suspect foul play. I changed the code, but somehow, they still found a way in and started a fire that could have wiped out my whole family.

'We still have a few checks to do, but the fire does look as if it started outside your daughter's bedroom door.'

My blood runs cold. Someone tried to kill my daughter. There's no doubt about it, even if the police are taking their sweet time to reach that conclusion. I know more than they do regarding Victor's background and his interest in Heather.

'What happens now?' I ask, shuddering against the cool night air. I've been running on adrenaline up until now. It's still buzzing through my body, keeping my nerve endings tingling, but the initial jolt has lessened, leaving me trembling and cold. I want to sleep for a week.

'The house will need to be unoccupied for a few days while we go through our investigations. Once complete, you can begin the repairs. Was the alarm system set?'

'Yes, but as you know, we've had a bit of trouble with it lately. I did change the code though. Even my husband doesn't know the new one.'

'But you said your daughter was out at the neighbour's house. Is that right?'

'Yes, she snuck out, apparently around eleven last night. When I went to bed, she was in her room. I set the alarm beforehand.'

'Did she reset the code? Did she go out the front door?'

'I . . . I don't know.'

'We'll need to question her about that and take her statement.'

'Can it wait until the morning? She's just gone to get some rest. We're all a little shaken up.'

'Yes, of course. We'll be back at nine tomorrow morning to speak to your daughter.'

'I suggest you speak to next door while you're at it. What did Victor say when you questioned him about entering my house?'

PC Watkins looks at me and sighs. She glances over her shoulder at her male colleague, then leans closer, keeping her voice low. 'I understand your apprehension. Your husband's explanation about the key seemed plausible, but after reviewing the timeline and alarm logs from the other night, something isn't adding up. We're taking your comments about Mr Hamilton very seriously.'

'Thank you.'

'But we will be taking this further, don't you worry.' I'm glad to find she's on my side. I'm not sure the male officers agree.

But I do worry. How can I not? Someone tried to kill my daughter tonight.

George was right. She was lucky.

But luck can only get you so far in life before it runs out.

* * *

I sleep on the sofa in the cottage. The kids and George are asleep in each of the rooms upstairs. I lay on my side, facing the front door, like a guard dog. My mind is all over the place and it takes over an hour before my eyes flicker closed. They spring open at first light. I wake up feeling more exhausted than if I hadn't slept. I dreamed of falling off a cliff again, jolting awake every few minutes.

It's just gone seven.

The kids are sound asleep. I check on them as soon as I can summon the strength to stand and walk up the wooden stairs. One of the rooms has twin beds. As soon as I peer my head round the door, I smell smoke, and my insides clench. It must be from Liam's clothes though, or maybe mine.

I'm going to need to get into the house at some point to grab us some basic items. Yet the thought of Heather's belongings being burned to a crisp brings tears to my eyes. She doesn't deserve this. It's my fault this has happened.

I gently close the door to avoid waking them and pad down the short hallway to the main bedroom, where I assume George is sleeping, but when I push open the door after a quick knock, I find it empty. I didn't hear him leave and I'm a light sleeper, especially lately.

I decide to visit the house to gather some items and clothes for the three of us. Heather will have to borrow some of my clothes for the time being.

As soon as I step outside the cottage and head towards the main house across the yard, my nostrils pick up the smoke still lingering in the air. Yellow tape has been stretched across the front steps, making it look like a crime scene.

Victor stands in front of the house, hands on hips, staring up at it. He must hear my footsteps crunching across the gravel because he turns and watches me as I get closer.

'What are you doing here?' I ask. My hackles are up, like a mother cat defending her young.

'I wanted to make sure you were all okay. I heard the sirens and the commotion last night.'

'Oh gosh, I'm so sorry our house burning down disturbed you.'

Victor's jaw clenches. 'That's not what I meant.'

I ignore his comment. 'Did you know Heather was at your house last night?'

'I had no idea. Not until Ryan told me this morning. Thank goodness she was though, right?'

My eyes narrow like laser beams.

We stand in silence for a few moments, then anger bubbles up from within, starting off as a simmer, but within seconds erupting like a volcano. I can't hold back any longer. Every part of me is screaming that this man tried to kill Heather last night, and he's doing his utmost to rile me up. I don't know what his plan is or why he's doing these things to me, but it has to stop. Surely, he realises that he can't keep getting away with it.

'You need to back off, Victor. Heather isn't your daughter. She may be biologically yours, but that's it. Why are you doing this to us?' I could say more, but I'm not going to give him the satisfaction of watching me beg.

Victor glances past me at the cottage, then his eyes flick to me. They're dark, unreadable. 'I suggest you start looking closer to home, Fiona.'

'If you're suggesting George would try and burn his own daughter alive, as well as risk the lives of his son and wife, then you're seriously mistaken. George isn't perfect. He's angry with me, yes, but he wouldn't do this.'

Victor's face remains impassive. He then sighs as he goes to walk back down the driveway. 'I'll back off,' he says. 'But a word of warning . . . sometimes the truth hurts.'

He's already walking away and I feel as if the rug has been pulled out from underneath me.

I'm flailing.

No. *Failing.*

I'm failing my family and I don't know how to fix it.

CHAPTER 29

The kids are too rattled and exhausted to go to school the next morning, and I don't force the subject. They've been through enough and the police are due at nine to speak to us anyway. I do think it will be better for them to be away from the house though, so I'm planning to send them in for the rest of the week, as it's only a few days until they break up for the summer. I can't protect them while they're at school, but it seems I can't protect them while they're here either. Maybe they'd be safer as far away from me as possible; for all I know, it's me who Victor is after, and by being close to me, I'm putting them in danger.

The kids are quietly eating breakfast. I've never known them to be so silent, heads down, neither of them on their phones. Heather is wearing some leggings and a t-shirt of mine and I'm taken straight back to when I was her age. She looks exactly like me, all down to the hair colour and dusting of freckles across her nose. She eats a spoonful of cereal, then pushes her bowl away. Liam, on the other hand, scoffs toast and cereal down like he's never eaten a morsel in his life. Even a near-death experience doesn't take away his ravenous appetite. Boots is sleeping upstairs on George's bed. We'll have to keep him inside if possible, as I don't want him running away or trespassing into the smoky house.

George turns up after his early morning absence and starts work, acting as if nothing has happened. I watch him while he sips his coffee, types on his laptop and takes phone calls. He's not acting like a worried father, whereas I'm pacing up and down the hallway of the cottage, unable to settle, unable to form any rational thoughts. I don't know what to do with myself.

Do we have home insurance? The radio station told me all bills would be paid for the next year. I'm assuming that includes home insurance, so to make myself useful, I look up the number for the radio station again and give them a call. They'll want to know about the fire. I'm sure it won't be too long before it's all over the news. In fact, now I think about it, why isn't it already? Have the police released a statement yet?

'I'm sorry, but the number you have dialled is no longer in service.'

I check the paperwork with the contact details for Radio West and dial again.

'I'm sorry, but the number you have dialled is no longer in service.'

That's odd. The number is correct. I scroll through the email I received from the radio station, looking for any other numbers, but there are none. So I hit reply on the email and send Julia, the lady I spoke to over the radio, a quick message, informing them of the fire and asking if someone could contact me soon.

Within seconds of sending the email, I get a reply.

I hastily open it, my breath hitching in my throat.

Unable to deliver email. Address no longer in use.

What the hell? I slump back in my chair, unsure what to do next. This wasn't a big radio station like Heart or Capital, who run lots of competitions all the time where listeners can win vast sums of money or dream holidays.

This was a smaller one, a station I'd never heard of before . . .

A sickening dread starts clawing its way up my throat. Oh God.

It hits me like a sledgehammer.

What if I was lured here on purpose? What if Victor knew about Heather all along, and tricked me and my family into moving next door?

Victor's name was on the letter I received a few days ago . . .

Maybe it's not a mistake, delivered to the wrong house. What if he *owns* this house too?

What if . . .

I take my phone and use Google to search Victor's name. I reach up to my hair and snap some strands as the results pop up on screen.

Victor is the Victor!

Victor Hamilton expands his multi-million-pound company.

Millionaire homes in on his victory.

There are dozens more online articles and posts like this with similar headlines. The more I read, the more my stomach twists and turns. My eyes scan the small screen, eagerly soaking up the information at lightning speed, hungry to learn the truth that will no doubt jump out at me any second. There must be something here . . .

The articles talk about Victor expanding the company, but there's nothing about radio stations or anything like that, so perhaps I'm barking up the wrong tree on that idea. What I really need is an article about his personal life. Where he works. His family. *Something.*

But there's nothing. He keeps his private life very, well, private.

I'm reading another article about his business, which involves technology and the use of AI, when my eyes pick up a name nestled among the several dozen others who Victor has recently hired as part of his close network. I search the page for the date of the article. Roughly a year ago.

I stare at the name.

My husband's name.

George is working for Victor's company, and has done for the past year.

And I had no idea.

CHAPTER 30

My whole life comes crashing down around me. Blood rushes around my body, pounding in my head like a heartbeat. I've got this all wrong. Somehow, I've overlooked everything. I was swept away in the sudden glitz and glamour of my new life in the country, completely disregarding all the warning signs. Because there have been signs. Right?

I need answers. *Real* answers, but Victor is refusing to tell me. He told me to look closer to home. I assumed he was trying to confuse me, throw me off course, but what if he wasn't? What if he's been trying to warn me? He even told me that George told him about Heather being his daughter a year ago and I ignored it!

George has known who Victor is for the past year, has worked for his company, and now our family is living next door to him. That's no coincidence.

Victor must have wanted us to be here, but why? To get closer to us? To me? To Heather?

And George has allowed it. Or is he being manipulated by Victor? How did he orchestrate me winning the house? How would he know I would enter the radio competition?

It's all too much — the questions, the theories, the betrayal.

I stagger to my feet, wanting — no, *needing* — to speak to George. I haven't heard him leave. He's still in the dining area of the cottage, working on his laptop.

On wobbly legs, I keep the tab open on my phone, stride up to him and place the phone on his laptop keyboard, so he has no choice but to look at it. I stand back and wait for the gears to click into place.

'Fi, what the hell . . . I'm working.' He pushes the phone off the keyboard.

'No, you don't get to push me aside anymore, George. I know you're working for Victor Hamilton and have done for the past year. Give me one good reason why I shouldn't put the kids in the car right now and walk out on you.'

George flicks his eyes up from the laptop screen. 'Because if you did, I would ruin you.' His voice is full of seething rage, similar to how he sounded when he found out about Heather, but now I know that was all an act. At least, at the time it was. He's a good liar, I'll give him that.

'I suggest you start talking, George. I didn't win this house in a radio competition, did I?'

'Of course you did.' George laughs as if I'm completely bonkers. I know what he's doing. He's doing what he's always done. Gaslighting me into thinking I'm the one in the wrong, that I'm the crazy one who has their wires crossed and needs to apologise.

Now I think about it, he's done that for our entire marriage, but up until the past few weeks, I've not realised it. That's the thing about a skilled liar and manipulator like my husband; he can keep his motives under the radar, simmering beneath the surface until it suits him. But then . . . I've been doing the same to him, haven't I? Am I as bad as he is? I had my reasons for keeping my secret, that Heather wasn't his biological child, but what's his reason for lying to me now, for controlling me for so long?

'You're working for Victor, aren't you?'

'What are you talking about, Fiona?'

'I'm talking about the fact you've been working for Victor for the past year and you never told me. Hell, you didn't even tell me you'd changed jobs. What happened to your other job? The one with . . .' Shit. I can't remember the name of the security firm he worked for.

'Ha! That's exactly my point, Fi. You don't even take the time to learn about what I do. I changed jobs and you didn't care enough to notice.'

'Stop turning this around on me!' I bellow, clenching my fists. 'It's not my fault you didn't tell me you changed jobs. I'm not a fucking mind reader, like this whole family seems to think I am. You've known who Victor is all this time, and I want to know why you never confronted me about it. Why are we living next door to him?'

George blows out his cheeks and drags both his hands through his hair. 'I didn't know the whole time, okay? I was headhunted by him over a year ago. He says he didn't know who I was. He approached me because he wanted me to work for him because I'd be a great fit for his company and he liked my work ethic. It was a complete fluke that we happened to meet, but we hit it off, started chatting. I told him your name and then he started probing and asking questions. It wasn't long before we figured out we had a connection. You.'

A lump forms in my throat, but my mouth is so dry, I can't dislodge it with merely swallowing. I lick my lips and cough. 'Okay, so . . . what did he say about me?'

'Nothing, not at first. But then he told me how you two *knew* each other. It felt a bit weird, knowing my boss had shagged my wife before me, but then, when he told me *when* you'd had your brief encounter, I started putting two and two together. He told me he'd tried to find you, but—'

'Hang on,' I say. 'You said he only started asking questions about me *after* you told him my name?'

'Yeah, so?'

'So . . . we never swapped names. I never gave him my name.'

'Classy,' he scoffs.

'Oh, shut up, George. I know all about your random one-night stands from your university days. You don't remember half of the women you slept with back then.'

'I'm a bloke. It's different.'

This time I scoff. 'Talk about double standards.'

'Whatever, Fiona. The point is, I never knocked anyone up.'

'And you're one-hundred-percent certain about that, are you?' George opens his mouth, ready to argue back, but then he stops and his face blushes pink. 'Yeah, that's what I thought,' I continue. 'What happened next? After you started figuring out the timeline.'

George rolls his eyes. 'Nothing. I didn't believe it. I couldn't believe it. I kept talking myself out of it, convincing myself that my darling wife would never lie to me for so long, never lie to our daughter for her whole life, but no matter how hard I tried, I couldn't get it out of my head. I had to know for sure, so I stole some of Victor's DNA by grabbing a glass of water he'd used, then took some of Heather's hair from her hairbrush.'

I think back to a year ago to see if I can remember George acting different around me or Heather, but I can't recall anything out of the ordinary. He hid it well. But then, I'm guilty of not always paying attention to him either, or the kids. Yes, I did everything for them, attempted to be a part of their lives, but I allowed them all to brush me aside.

'I'm so sorry you had to find out that way,' I say quietly.

'Oh, please. You never had any intention of telling me, did you? You would have taken it to your grave.' His voice is bitter, harsh. It makes me shudder.

'I . . . I guess not,' I say. 'I was afraid it would ruin us.'

'No, you were afraid of ending up alone, having alienated your whole family.'

'Yes, you're right. I was selfish, but I was selfish for the right reasons.'

George laughs, shaking his head. 'You're deluded.'

'What happened next?' I ask, ignoring his dig.

'I had solid proof that Heather wasn't my daughter. She was Victor's. I approached him one week while we were away at a work event and told him. He was . . . shocked. Angry. I didn't blame him. He wanted to meet her, get to know her, but I said no, not yet. I had a different plan.'

At the word *plan*, my heart leaps in my chest.

'So you planned for me to win the house next door to his so he could get to know his daughter?'

'No, of course not.'

'Then why—'

'We planned to get our revenge on the person who'd lied to us for almost seventeen years.'

CHAPTER 31

Revenge.

A small word with a lot of meaning behind it.

My husband and Victor have made it their mission to seek revenge on me for keeping the truth from them for so long. But how is me moving into my dream home part of their revenge plan? What's the end goal here?

I stare at George, hoping he'll continue his story, but it seems he's done talking.

'I don't understand,' I say. 'Did Victor already own our house?'

'No, he paid off the family who was living in it, had them move out and sign the deeds to hand over ownership to him. The deeds you signed were fake. The house belongs to Victor.'

'And you knew this the whole time, that he had access to our home, to our children, and you didn't care, you didn't think he might be dangerous? What the hell is wrong with you?'

George shrugs. 'What can I say? He wanted his revenge too, Fiona. I let him do whatever he wanted, as long as he kept the kids out of it. I thought he might take his time, maybe even try and seduce you, but as soon as he set eyes on you, on Heather, the coward backed out of the whole thing.'

'He *what*? I thought you just said . . .'

George shakes his head, a smirk across his face. 'I knew I shouldn't have trusted him, but I needed him, needed his money, his power, so I took over the plan myself. Went solo . . . in a matter of speaking.'

I can't believe this. Victor backed out? Is this George's plan to lie to me again? But everything fits. Victor was turning up randomly. He attacked me in my sleep. He was watching the house and letting himself in whenever he wanted. Wasn't he?

'I don't believe you,' I say. 'He can't have changed his mind. Victor attacked me during the night.'

'No, stupid, it was me,' George spits. 'Did you even listen to what I just said?'

'But why?' I cry out, my voice cracking and breaking.

George sighs. 'Seriously, Fiona. The amount of thriller books you read. It's always the husband, remember?'

'I don't read thrillers, George. I read spicy dark romance books.'

George curls his top lip in disgust. 'Whatever. The point is, for me, it went past just mere revenge. It wasn't enough for me.'

'Let me guess . . . you wanted what Victor had. His power, his money, his influence. You always did have an inferiority complex.'

George winks. He's enjoying this! He is loving the fact he's got one over on me and everyone else. 'Got it in one, love. Of course I wanted what Victor has. I've worked my fucking fingers to the bone for years and got nowhere, so when he approached me, offered me a job, I started to see a way out.'

'You mean a way *up*.'

'Right. I didn't see why he should have all the wealth and fame and glory. I wanted my piece too. As I said, the plan became much more than just revenge. That was merely the cherry on top of the cake for me.'

'What about the fire . . . that was you? You could have killed us! What the hell were you thinking!' Pure unfiltered anger is pulsing through my veins. The man in front of me is no longer my husband, the man I've slept next to for over sixteen years, who's comforted me when I needed it the most, who has raised our children alongside me.

I don't know this man.

But I do know one thing. He's a danger to me and my children, and he has no idea just how far I will go to protect them.

He's still talking. 'Heather was out. Liam's room was the furthest room away from the fire. Stop being so dramatic.'

'You're not going to get away with this, George.'

'I already have, Fiona. The police are going to find Victor's DNA all over our house once the investigation starts. He's going down for arson. I've got it all planned out. He made a mistake by bailing on me. He thought he could play happy families with my wife and kids. Not a chance. We had a deal and he broke it and if you say a word, then you'll never see Heather or Liam ever again. I can promise you that.'

'You can't do that!'

'Watch me,' he growls.

I couldn't care less if George threatens me. He can take away everything I own, I won't mind. He can have everything. Everything except my children. The fear of losing them ignites something in me I've always known I have.

A mother's instinct is to protect her young, no matter the cost to her own life, but this is different. A primal urge to kill those who would do them harm. It's not even a question. No doubt in my mind. I'd kill George if he ever did anything to them.

I'd push him in front of a car to protect them. Hell, *I'd* jump in front of a car to protect them.

I don't know what to do next. Do I call the police and tell them my husband has admitted to everything? If I do, then I'll risk Heather and Liam being taken away. I have no idea how much planning George has done behind the scenes. He's been clever enough to frame Victor. Surely, he doesn't think I'll roll over and let him take my children away from me?

'What happens now, George?' I ask. 'How do you expect to keep getting away with this? How do you see this playing out? I'm not staying quiet about this.'

At these words, George clamps his eyes on me. 'You're going to stay quiet, Fiona, and do you know how I know that? You've always stayed quiet. That's your best quality, right?'

His words land like a fist to my chest, leaving me breathless. 'You're right,' I say, tears brimming in my eyes. 'I have stayed quiet. I should have ended our marriage a long time ago.'

George laughs. 'I had the same thought. That's why I've been sleeping around behind your back.'

His words should hurt, but they don't. It's like my brain has disengaged from him and all his drama. I don't care anymore. I just want my children.

'Who?'

At this point, the cottage door bursts opens and Glory rushes in, red in the face with tears streaming down her cheeks. There's terror in her eyes.

'He's dead!' she shrieks.

I'm still trying to absorb George's revelation, and it takes me a couple of seconds to understand what she's said.

George rushes to Glory. She collapses into his arms, sobbing. 'He's dead!' she screams again.

'Who's dead?' I ask, matching her tone.

Glory shoves herself away from George, eyes blazing at me. 'Who do you think, you evil bitch? Victor! Victor's dead!'

CHAPTER 32

Her words echo around my head.

Victor. Victor's dead.

'How can he be dead? I've only just spoken to him, barely an hour ago. He was standing outside on my drive staring at the house. How is it possible he's now dead?'

Glory puffs and pants, turning red in the face while I stand motionless, trying to process what's happening. I replay her words in my mind, over and over, but the more I do, the less they make sense.

'What happened? Should we call an ambulance?'

'I think a coroner would be more appropriate,' Glory replies frantically.

My eyes study George, scanning him. His eyes are wide and he's standing very close to Glory — too close.

Wait a minute . . .

His big reveal a moment ago slots into place.

'Oh my God! You've been sleeping with Victor's wife. To get back at him, like you said.'

Glory throws her head back and laughs. Actually, it's more of a witch's cackle. It makes my skin crawl. 'Oh, please. I'm not Victor's wife.'

The room lapses into silence.

'You're *not*?'

Another laugh. 'No! Honestly, Georgie, I thought you said she was smart.'

I stare open-mouthed at George, who's keeping his mouth shut for once.

'Don't you recognise my voice?' she continues, smiling at me with perfect teeth. Then her voice changes tone. '*Hi, this is Julia from Radio West. Congratulations, you've won the Cotswolds multi-million-pound house draw!*'

Holy shit.

'It was you!'

'Yes, it was me. And it was very clever, if I do say so myself. It was my idea, but Victor handled all the technical side of things. He set up a temporary broadcast signal just for your area, and created a ghost website that was only live for twenty-four hours. By the time anyone got suspicious, Radio West had vanished.'

'But . . . why have you been pretending to be married to Victor? What about Jess and Ryan?'

'Well, Jess doesn't even exist and Ryan's a paid actor. We hired him a few weeks ago. Part-time, of course. He hasn't been staying with us for the whole time.'

Oh my God . . .

That means Ryan and Heather *aren't* related. I don't know whether to feel more relief over that fact or shock that the whole thing has been a set-up from the start. Was it all a ploy to drive a wedge between me and Heather? I kept telling her to stay away from Ryan and all she did was push back, defy me.

'Why would Victor go along with that?' I ask. 'Why did he need a fake family?'

Glory shrugs. 'Because family men are more trustworthy. He's an ageing millionaire playboy who likes to fuck around. Hardly an advertisement for trust, is it? He was fine with it at first.'

'How long has this been going on?' I point at the two of them, feeling slightly sick.

'I met Georgie at a work function only a few days after he started working for Victor. I work for him too.' Her pet name for George makes me want to retch. She side-steps closer to George and slips her hand into his. The sight sends a jolt of repulsion through me, but I find I don't actually care about any of it. The only thing I care about is making sure my children are safe.

'And what . . . you just thought it would be fun to fuck with his wife too?'

Glory shrugs nonchalantly. 'Hey, if it meant Georgie would be free from you eventually and be mine, then who was I to say no?'

'Will you stop calling him Georgie!'

'Make me, bitch.'

At this point, George steps in front of Glory. It's a good job he does because Glory was about to get bitch-slapped across the face. Hard.

'Right, we don't have time for this,' says George. He turns his back on me, facing Glory square on. 'We need to report Victor's death immediately.'

'You killed him,' I say in a whisper. I step backwards towards the stairs leading up to the bedroom where I know my children are.

George shakes his head slowly. 'No, my darling wife. *You* killed him.'

That's his plan. He's planning on framing me for Victor's murder, then taking the kids.

My eyes drift to the ceiling, and George reads my mind. 'If you're wondering where the kids are, then don't worry.'

'They're not upstairs?'

'No.'

I clench my fists at my sides. 'Where are my children?' I step closer to the door, ready to sprint if need be, but Glory shuffles to stand in front of me.

'They're safe,' she says.

'I wasn't talking to you,' I reply through gritted teeth. I stare directly at George. 'What have you done with them?'

'Now who's gaslighting who? I haven't done anything with them.'

I can barely breathe. I need to know they're safe, need to see them with my own eyes. I don't believe a word that comes out of my husband's mouth anymore. My focus is on Glory, who's standing in front of me with a grin across her perfectly plumped lips. I want nothing more than to punch her beautiful face.

I don't see George come up behind me.

The next thing I know, white-hot pain erupts from the back of my head and the whole room goes dark.

CHAPTER 33

The moment I come to, pain crashes into me — the worst I've ever felt in my life. Worse than any hangover. It's a full-bodied, pulsing ache that pounds through my skull and over my eyes, forcing them to stay shut. But I need to open them and see what's going on. It's a monumental effort, but when I do, I see nothing but darkness.

My side aches too, and my ankle. What's that about? It's possible when George struck me on the head that I collapsed awkwardly to the floor, twisting my ankle and landing on my side.

But I can't dwell on the pain.

All I can think about is the kids. What is George going to do with them? He was using them to punish me. Now I'm going down for Victor's murder and I'll lose them altogether. George wanted revenge. Well, he's bloody well got it.

I'm done for. I'm locked in some sort of pantry or cold storage room. Every cell in my body is urging me to get out, escape, run, find the kids and hide, but what will that accomplish? George is always going to come after me, isn't he? There's clearly a lot of things I've overlooked when it comes to my husband, but one thing I know for sure is that he doesn't like to be made a fool of, and I've committed the ultimate betrayal in his eyes.

He wants to take the kids away from me, to teach me a lesson. I reckon he doesn't even care that Heather isn't his. This is all about me and what I've done to him. The worst thing is that if he gave them the option of choosing between us, they'd choose him over me every time. It would be like asking them to choose between their favourite ice cream flavour — vanilla or chocolate. Vanilla wouldn't even get a look in. And to be perfectly honest, I don't blame them. I love chocolate ice cream more too.

Has George been slowly turning them against me for the past year? Was that his plan?

Is that why he always gave them whatever they wanted when they asked for it and I ended up looking like the bad guy when I said no? He's always been the less strict parent, the more fun one, especially lately, but I never realised it was all because he was buttering them up.

I've been blind about so many things.

But I can't sit on my bum and sulk. It's never solved anything. That's what I always tell my children. I don't see a way out of this though. Not where everyone wins. Someone has to lose.

I grope around in the dark, feeling my way around the walls with my fingertips until I find a door handle. Yes! I give it a shake then start pummelling my fists against it.

'Help! Anyone!'

Damn it. I shouldn't have shouted so loud. It feels as if my skull is splitting open at the back. Cautiously, I reach behind my head and assess the damage. My fingers come away wet and sticky; there's definitely a deep wound buried beneath the matted mess of my hair.

Impulsively, I reach for a loose strand and tug.

No.

Stop.

Breathe . . .

There's not even a whisper of sound around me. George must have taken the kids already and disappeared. Am I to be left here to be found by the police? Has he even called them? If he's expecting me to go down for Victor's murder, then how is me being locked in a cupboard going to prove my guilt?

I have no idea how much time has passed.

My watch has been removed from my wrist. Clever. He's thought of everything. My body is showing all the signs of dehydration, exhaustion and hunger, but I can't afford to think about how awful I feel right now. I need to get out of here and find my children.

God knows where he's taken them, or how far away they are now.

Slowly, I continue to explore the dark area around me, but I find nothing in the way of an exit or even a weapon to defend myself should George make a return. I sit in the dark and take some deep breaths, deciding not to freak out like the last time I was trapped in a small room with no air.

He planned to trap me inside the wine cellar. He knew I was down there for all that time, probably laughing to himself on a job well done. Or maybe it was Glory who did it. I feel bad for Victor. He played his part in this, but he didn't deserve to die. Little did he know just how ruthless and vindictive my husband could be. Little did I know.

All my nerve endings stand to attention as I hear a scuffling noise from behind the door. I don't know who's out there, but it's the only noise I've heard for what feels like hours.

'Hello?' I call out in a whisper, too scared to shout louder in case my head splits open again.

'Mum?'

'Heather!' Fuck the pain. Relief swoops over me, taking my breath away as I throw myself at the door and bang my fists against it again. 'I'm in here!'

'The door's locked,' she calls back.

'See if you can find something to break it down. Are you alone? Where's Liam?'

'He's safe. He's . . . Ryan, over here!'

Wait . . . Ryan's here?

Why on earth would Ryan be here helping to rescue me? He doesn't have anything to do with this. He's a paid actor, which is still mind-boggling.

'Mrs Howden, stand back,' says Ryan.

I do as he says and back up as far as I can, which isn't very far because the room I'm in is tiny, but I hold my breath as a loud banging erupts in front of me. I cover my ears as the sound amplifies.

A few seconds later, the door bursts open. The first person I see is Ryan, holding a shovel in his hands. The lock has splintered, allowing the door to pop open. Heather pushes Ryan aside and throws herself into my arms.

'Mum!'

I squeeze my daughter tight, smelling her soft hair as I close my eyes and say a silent prayer of thanks to whoever is up there watching over us.

'Thank God you're all right,' I say.

'Me? What about you? Dad tried to kill you!'

'Not exactly, but he's . . . wait a minute . . . where is he? How did you find me? I thought he took you and Liam and made a break for it?'

Heather shakes her head. 'He didn't get the chance. Liam kept asking where you were, so did I. Then he got pissed off, said we were ungrateful, so he tried to drag Liam away and—'

'He did what?'

'He's fine though. Luckily, Ryan showed up and saved the day.'

Heather and I give each other space, even though all I want to do is hold her close for a little bit longer. I look past her at the teenage boy in front of me. A stranger. But it seems one of the few people who is on my side.

'Thank you, Ryan. I can't thank you enough.'

Ryan blushes pink. 'I should have said something earlier, but . . . well, Mr Hamilton was paying me well and . . .'

'It's okay. I understand.'

'No,' he says. 'I shouldn't have let it get so far. My job was to lure Heather away, keep her occupied, but then Mr Hamilton started saying he'd changed his mind. Your husband though . . . he got aggressive and that's when I realised this was all too fucked up to continue . . . Sorry,' he adds at the end, flinching as he swears. But I couldn't care less about his language.

'Wait . . . Heather, do you . . .' I can't blurt it out in case she still has no idea about who her father is. I never wanted her to find out, let alone like this. It's all blown up in my face and there's no way of keeping the secret any longer.

'Yes, Mum, I know Dad's not my real Dad.'

I hold my breath, waiting for the explosion I've been dreading, but it doesn't come. She clearly has a lot more she wants to say, but now isn't the right time. Even she must know that. I always forget how grown up she really is. I've wanted to keep her as a child for as long as possible, shielding her from a lot of things, but she's a young woman now, perfectly capable of functioning without me, her meddling mother.

'I'm so sorry I didn't tell you,' I say.

Heather purses her lips. 'Well, there's not much we can do about it now, but it does make a lot of sense.'

'In what way?'

'How I look nothing like him and have never felt a bond with him. Plus, Liam's whole blood type fiasco at the dinner table.'

I give her a small smile. 'I promise to tell you everything. Now, I think we need to call the police and get this straightened out, but first I need you to tell me where your father . . . where George is.'

At this point, Ryan steps forward. 'He's bolted. Gone. So has Glory.'

'What do you mean he's gone?'

'Mum, when Dad tried to drag Liam away, Ryan threatened him. Remember I told you that Ryan was good with technology and gadgets? Well, he has a drone he flies around and he caught Dad and Glory speaking in one of the rooms, talking about their plan, about how Dad planned to take over Victor's company and get revenge on you. He got everything.'

My mouth drops open. 'You're kidding!'

'Yep, but Dad's plan backfired massively when Victor changed his mind. George and Glory have disappeared. Turns out, after all this, they've got nothing.'

'Except me possibly going down for Victor's murder,' I say solemnly.

A grin spreads across Ryan's face.

'Mum, I just said that Ryan has a drone. He got everything on it.'

'Everything?'

'Everything. You're safe.'

Ryan reaches into his pocket and pulls out a USB stick. He hands it to me.

I take it, my hands shaking. This is it. After everything my husband put in place over the past year, the planning and dedication, it's all been foiled by a teenager with a drone. A teenager who was a part of the plan from the very start.

I watch Ryan and Heather talking and staring at each other, each with a faint blush on their cheeks. I realise my silly mistake. It's never been about me.

It's always been about Heather, and I couldn't be more proud of her.

CHAPTER 34

Turns out, George and Glory locked me up in the pantry of Victor's house. I only get as far as the kitchen by the time the police arrive, sirens blaring. Several armed response officers rush off towards the pool house, guns drawn, and I see PC Watkins stepping out of a marked car.

I can barely process what's happening. Heather holds my hand in a vice-like grip, clinging to me like she's afraid I'll blow away in the wind.

PC Watkins approaches me. 'Do you need a paramedic?'

It's then I remember my head injury. I reach up and touch it. 'Yeah, actually, that would be good this time.'

PC Watkins ushers me to the nearest chair in the kitchen and then uses her radio to call in an ambulance. Heather sits next to me, mute, trembling.

'Where's Liam?' I ask her, my voice a whisper.

'Oh shit, Liam!' says Heather. She lets go of my hand, pulls her phone out of her pocket and types a quick text. 'He's hiding. I told him not to come out until I texted him.'

Less than five minutes later, my son bursts into the room and flings himself at me, almost sending me crashing to the floor. PC Watkins makes a move to remove him from my arms, but I catch her eye and shake my head.

The whirlwind continues as the pool house is cordoned off and the investigation starts. Two paramedics turn up and check over my head wound, which requires stitches, and I need to go to hospital for observations overnight, but I refuse because there's no one around to look after Heather and Liam.

They eventually agree, but provide a list of symptoms to look out for in case my concussion gets any worse, and I'm to rest as much as possible. I'm a mother. Don't they know that mothers never rest? What even is the meaning of the word?

Heather pipes up that she'll look after me, and I almost fall off my seat again.

I provide a statement to PC Watkins, as do Heather, Ryan and Liam, who refuses to leave my side. He attaches himself to me like glue, grasping my hand tightly while I deal with the police and answer their questions. Heather finally lets me go when Ryan arrives, but she stays close, and even makes me a cup of tea.

I hand the USB over to PC Watkins. I haven't seen what's on it, but I trust Ryan. I'll have to go to the station to be questioned further soon, but I have no qualms with that. It's going to take time, but I'm determined to clear my name and get this straightened out.

There's enough evidence to pin everything on George and Glory, I'm sure of it. They may have disappeared when Ryan threatened them with exposing their plan, but they won't get far. It depends how quickly the police can go through the evidence and put a warrant out for their arrests.

George has been clever, thinking he could get away with it, but the minute things got too tense, too real, too risky, he's bailed and left his children behind without even a second thought. I always thought he was a good father. At times, he was. He took them on outings when they were young, played games with them and always said he'd do anything to protect them. Anything except face jail time, apparently.

Once I've provided my statement and the paramedics have finished stitching up my head wound, I'm allowed to go back to the cottage with the kids. It's been a long day and we're all in dire need of sleep, decent food besides biscuits and cups of tea, and a hot shower.

The main house is still off limits for a few more days due to the fire damage, but honestly I'm not sure I want to move back in. The house is tainted with George's deceit and, since he's still out there somewhere, I don't feel safe, which is why I triple-check the lock on the cottage door and reset the security system and change the code. Again.

Liam eventually detaches himself from me and drags his exhausted body up the stairs for a shower, but when I go to call him down for pizza half an hour later, I find him flat out on the spare bed, still dressed in his clothes. I tuck him up and kiss his forehead. When he wakes up, he's going to be as ravenous as a starving lion, but he clearly needs to catch up on sleep.

After Heather and I have showers and change into some clean clothes, we share a couple of pizzas, eating them on the sofa in the living room. The cottage is much smaller than the main house, but it's the perfect size for the three of us. I don't know what's going to happen with the house, considering it doesn't actually belong to me. It's still in Victor's name and he's dead. I'm assuming he's left a will, considering the assets and fortune he's left behind.

It's most likely going to end with us having to move out and find somewhere else to live. I don't relish moving back into a council house, but as long as I have my children with me, I don't care. Since I've left my job, I'll need to look for a new one, but I have no idea where we'll be living in the foreseeable future, so I can't make any rash decisions until I know more.

There's a movie on the television, but I'm only half paying attention. I can feel the elephant in the room, stirring between

Heather and me. She said she didn't want to talk about it earlier today, and that was fair enough, but now we're alone, now's as good a time as any.

'Heather,' I say quietly, 'there's nothing I can say that will make you forgive me for lying to you about who your dad really was, but . . . I hope you can, perhaps, understand the reason why I wanted to keep it a secret.'

Heather's eyes remain on the screen for a few seconds, but then she reaches for the remote and pauses the movie, stopping it just as Tom Cruise is about to leap from a skyscraper. It looks like he's hovering in mid-air.

'I do understand,' she says, and I can almost feel my heart sighing with relief. 'But . . . I still think it was wrong that you lied for so long, especially to Dad . . . George. I think he deserved to know from the start. He might not have stuck around, but . . . at least he wouldn't have found out the hard way, and Victor might still be alive.'

The depth of her wisdom astounds me. I know exactly what she means. She's right. If I'd told George the truth all those years ago, he could have walked out on me, knowing I was carrying another man's child, but I chose to hang on to him instead under false pretences.

Now, Heather's real father is dead and she never had a real chance to get to know him, nor did he get to know her.

And it's my fault.

Tears bubble up. I wipe them away with the cuff of my cardigan. 'I'm sorry,' I say. 'You're right. They both deserved to know the truth. I was so young and . . . it's no excuse. I made the wrong decision. I wish I could take it back, but—'

'Do you regret having me?'

Her question causes me to choke on air. 'What? No! God, no. Please don't ever think that. I don't regret having you, not even for a second. My only regret is that I didn't tell the truth from the start. I've hated lying to you, but George was a good dad, right?'

Heather nods. 'Yeah, up until about a year ago. Then he changed, but I guess now we know why. He wanted to take us away from you to punish you, but when the tables turned on him and he thought Ryan was going to dob him in, he took the chance and fled, left me and Liam behind like we mean nothing. That pretty much says it all really.' Heather stares at the screen again, at Tom Cruise in mid-air, and lets out a long sigh. 'We're better off without him anyway,' she adds. 'And . . . I'm sorry for my behaviour over the past . . . well, long time. I don't have an excuse.'

I let out a little chuckle. 'Yes, you do. You're a teenage girl. Trust me, I went through the same thing with my parents.'

'You never talk about them, you know.'

Her words stun me. My parents is a topic of conversation that has never been broached. Ever. 'No, you're right. I don't.'

'Why is that? I know they died before I was born, but you've never told me what they were like.'

More tears leak from my eyes and trickle down my cheeks. I can't keep the truth from her or from myself any longer. It's time I faced my past.

'They were . . . my adopted parents.'

Heather sits up straighter on the sofa. 'What? Why didn't you ever tell us that?'

I ignore her question. Now is the time to tell her the whole story, the real reason I didn't tell her who her real father was. It's time to tell her who I was, who I used to be.

'They were the best parents a girl could ask for, even throughout my worst times. I was a bit of a difficult teenager. I . . . I used to cut myself a lot, not to end my life, but it was the only way I could see to release the tension or bad energy inside me. My parents supported me through it. They understood and tried to help me, but I pushed them away, didn't want to know.'

I pause for a moment, my cheeks flaming. Admitting to my daughter about my scars feels both humiliating and freeing. To my shock, she doesn't say a word or even flinch.

I continue my story.

'I stopped cutting myself, but then . . . when I was eighteen, only a few weeks before I started university, they told me I was adopted. Literally, the day after my birthday. They said they wanted to wait until I was old enough to understand, but I didn't understand. I was so angry at them. Hated them. Told them I wished they were dead. I marched out of the house that night during a storm without a coat or any idea of where I was going. They went out in search of me in the car, driving around in the storm, but the whole time I was hiding in my old childhood treehouse.' I stop and wipe away tears. 'Dad skidded the car in the deep water on the road and hit a tree. Neither of them survived.'

Heather's mouth drops open, but she still doesn't say anything as I keep going, the words spilling from me for the first time in my life.

'As I was technically an adult, I didn't have to be put in foster care or anything like that. I had no aunts or uncles, not who I'd met anyway. I was due to start university, so I went and got on with my life, but inside I was a mess. I drank and did stupid things, but I didn't go back to cutting. I slept around a lot and then I found out I was pregnant. Everything was still so raw with my parents' death, and I couldn't make sense of anything. I blamed myself for their deaths, tortured myself every single day, but I never spoke about it to anyone. Since I was an adult, I wasn't offered any support or guidance to get through my grief, not like maybe a child would.' I stop, unsure if I really need to say much more. 'I never knew your father's name, so I was never able to find him, and then I met George and everything slipped into place. I saw a way out and took it.'

Heather seems to mull over my words for a few moments, biting her bottom lip the way she does when she's thinking about something complicated. Liam does something similar and sticks his tongue out. I call it his 'concentration tongue'.

'That's why you didn't tell me the truth from the start.'

'Yes, but it's not like I thought I was going to die in a fiery car crash. I just couldn't face you being as angry at me as I was at my parents. If I'd revealed the truth at the start, then George could have left. In hindsight, it would have been better if he did, but I was convinced I needed help to raise you. I had no clue what I was doing. I was weak and took the easy route out.'

Heather reaches over and squeezes my hand. That small gesture is enough for me to erupt into sobs, but this time it's more from relief and happiness that she hasn't turned her back on me.

'At least we have each other now,' she says.

'That we do,' I reply, squeezing her hand back.

'Thank you for telling me.'

'Thank you for listening,' I reply.

'What happens now though? Are we going to be allowed to stay and live here?'

'I doubt it, love. The house doesn't belong to me. I never won it. It was all a set-up. I'm going to start looking for a new home for us tomorrow, I promise.'

Heather nods, but I can tell she's a little apprehensive about our lives being disrupted again. I feel the same. All I've ever wanted is a stable upbringing for the kids, but George has ruined everything, all because he wanted petty revenge on me and he was greedy and wanted Victor's business for himself.

I lean towards Heather and we hug, with the pizza plate still balanced on the sofa beside us. Despite everything that's happened

— the late-night attack, the fire, the revelation that George has been behind everything and has been cheating on me, Victor's death — at least I still have my beautiful children with me. More than that, they're happy that I'm with them.

That's all that matters.

Now, I just need to get through the next few weeks, find somewhere to live and rebuild our lives. But George is still out there and I know I won't be able to relax and feel safe until he's behind bars.

CHAPTER 35

The next morning, Liam is ravenous as expected, so I make us all a full English breakfast. My head is pounding, but I've already popped some painkillers. Heather says I need to rest, that she's supposed to be looking after me, so we settle on her doing most of the heavy lifting while I supervise and explain what to do. She's never helped me in the kitchen before, so things don't go as smoothly as usual, but I'm grateful for her assistance.

The large wooden table is laden with plates piled high with far too much food for the three of us, but it enables me to keep busy and distracted because early this morning, I woke to my phone blaring to life. It was DC Watkins, who said she was dropping by later to talk to me and she was bringing Victor's lawyer with her, who also wanted to talk.

Since then, I've been a nervous wreck, and only manage a few nibbles of toast and a strip of crispy bacon before my stomach says no and starts clenching, so I drink copious amounts of coffee instead until I feel it slopping around inside.

'Mum, chill,' says Heather, helping herself to another sausage and a slice of toast.

I stop in my tracks, not realising I've been pacing up and down the kitchen while holding a pair of tongs. The extra bacon that Liam wanted is burning in the pan.

'Damn it,' I say, fishing it out with the tongs.

Liam stares at the blackened strip. 'It's fine. I like it crispy,' he says, reaching over to grab it.

'Yeah, but that's not crispy,' Heather replies. 'That's cremated.'

'Well, you burned the sausages,' comes the snippy retort.

There's a beat of silence and then we all burst into a fit of giggles. I drop the cremated bacon in the bin and fetch another from the packet on the side, dropping it into the hot oil, where it spits and starts curling up at the sides the instant it hits the pan.

'What time did you say Ryan was coming?' I ask.

'Like . . .' Heather looks at the clock on the wall. 'Any time now.'

'Okay . . .' I nod and turn back to the hob, determined not to burn the next round of bacon.

A few minutes later, Ryan knocks on the door. Heather greets him and he joins us at the breakfast table, where he helps himself to heaps of eggs, toast, hash browns and sausages, then tops it off with brown sauce.

'Thanks, Mrs Howden.'

'Fiona, please,' I say.

Ryan nods, gazing in astonishment at the array of food on the table.

Heather leans over. 'Mum's gone a bit overboard with the whole food prep. I cooked the sausages though,' she adds proudly.

Ryan takes a bite of a sausage and nods. 'It's very . . . well done.'

'It's burnt,' says Liam.

'It's fine,' says Ryan.

'Can I get you a coffee or tea or orange juice or . . .' I ask, then instantly grimace, hoping I'm not coming across as uncool, but Heather doesn't have the bitter tone of voice I'm used to, and whenever I ask her a question, she answers with proper words. The same goes for Liam. They're completely different kids.

'Orange juice would be great,' answers Ryan.

I pour him a big glass and hand it to him just as the crunch of gravel sounds from outside. Everyone stops with forks halfway to their mouths. I glance around the table.

'Okay, stay calm everyone,' I say, even though I'm by far the least calm out of the lot of us.

I open the door before PC Watkins has even shut her car door. She's with a tall man in a dark blue suit. The sight of her in uniform and him in the smart suit is enough to send my pulse sky-rocketing again.

'Good morning, Mrs Howden,' says PC Watkins.

'Hello, Officer,' I say with a slight head nod.

'This is Victor Hamilton's lawyer, Mr Boker.'

I nod my greeting. 'Come in,' I say.

We step straight through into the hallway. 'Something smells good,' says Mr Boker.

'My daughter and I have been cooking all morning. The kids were hungry. Would you like a coffee or something for breakfast or . . .'

'A cup of coffee would be lovely,' Mr Boker replies.

'Of course. Officer?'

PC Watkins shakes her head. 'Nothing for me, thanks.'

I gesture through into the living area, away from the kitchen/diner where the kids are still eating. 'If you'll head through there, I'll just grab the coffee.'

I leave them to make their own way and rush into the kitchen straight to the coffee machine. It's a lot smaller than the one in the main house, easier to use.

'Do you know what they want to speak to you about?' asks Ryan, his mouth half full of food.

'Not yet,' I say, a little tremor in my voice.

I press the button and the coffee trickles out below the nozzle, but I've forgotten to put a blasted cup underneath it, so it spills everywhere.

'Damn it,' I mutter.

Heather arrives next to me. She has a cup in her hand. 'Let me do it, Mum.' She starts prepping the coffee and puts a pot of sugar and a jug of milk on a tray.

I take a step back and lean against the counter, using the opportunity to inhale as deep as I can. She hands me the full tray when she's done.

'Thank you,' I say. 'I don't know how long this will take. They may want to speak to you again, I'm not sure, so please can you both stay close by until they leave?'

'Sure, Mum.'

Liam nods his answer, his mouth too stuffed with food to say any words.

I walk into the living area carrying the tray and set it down on the coffee table. Mr Boker has already made himself comfortable on the large, over-stuffed red chair and has several files and folders spread out on the coffee table as well.

'Thank you,' he says. 'You're probably wondering why I'm here to speak to you.'

'I'm assuming it's got something to do with the house.'

'Well, yes and no. First of all, I need to ask you . . . do you have DNA proof that Heather is indeed Victor's biological daughter?'

His question nearly floors me. He must realise I'm in shock by the way my mouth hangs open and I splutter. 'I . . . Well, no, but . . . I . . .'

He holds his hand up. 'My apologies. I'm not suggesting you're lying, but we will need to perform a DNA test before we can go ahead with the wishes noted down in Victor's last will and testament.'

'G-George said that he got a DNA test done. I think he gave it to Victor, but I can't be sure.' Then I pause a moment. 'What's this got to do with Victor's will?'

'Ah,' says Mr Boker. 'That's where things get rather interesting for you and Heather.'

'Okay . . .'

'Victor Hamilton, due to his vast wealth and assets, not to mention his business empire that's worth millions, had a very air-tight will drawn up right at the start of his career. He has kept it updated every few years, changing it if need be, but he hasn't done it since before he allegedly found out he fathered a daughter. He wanted to ensure that his legacy went to a suitable person who was related to him. He was always very specific about that.'

I shake my head. 'Oh my God . . . that means that Heather . . .'

'Allow me,' says Mr Boker, reaching forward and picking up a piece of paper from the coffee table. He begins to read and as the words float from his mouth, I have to slowly lower myself to sit on the nearest piece of furniture because my legs start trembling.

'I, Victor Hamilton, upon my death, do hereby bequeath the sum of one million pounds, my entire estate and business to my eldest child, whoever they may be. However, if they're not yet eighteen upon the date of my death, all assets will be transferred to the child's mother until the child turns eighteen. Upon turning eighteen, the child will have full control of the assets and can do with them as they wish. Upon writing this, I do not have a biological child that I am aware of, so a full DNA test will need to be carried out if a child or their mother ever comes forward claiming they're related to me.'

At this point, Mr Boker looks up from the page and at my face, which I can tell without looking in a mirror has gone white. My head spins. I'm glad I'm sitting down.

'There are several in-depth stipulations regarding his business empire that we'll need to go through in detail, but as soon as a DNA test is confirmed, I can draw up the paperwork and have you sign the deeds to your new home and business. You will also own the house you were living in previously as well, and you can choose to either sell or rent it out, however you see fit.'

More words come from his mouth, but I barely hear them. They're distorted because of the loud thumping in my head. I can't believe this . . .

Is this real?

How can this be possible?

I ask those exact questions to Mr Boker, who smiles. 'Yes, it's very real, Mrs Howden.'

'B-But . . . it doesn't mention us by name.'

'No, you're right. It doesn't, but Victor was . . . shall we say . . . popular with the ladies, especially in his younger days. He always wanted a child of his own as he got older, but never found the right woman to settle down with. As far as he was aware, he'd fathered no children during his years of enjoyment with the opposite sex, but he put this paragraph in his will, should anyone ever come forward that he did not know about before he died. May I ask, how old is your daughter?'

'She's uh . . . fifteen, nearly sixteen.'

'Then, in accordance with the will, you will be the main shareholder and controller of the business assets and money until she turns eighteen. At which point she can decide what she wants to do with it, but again, there are a few stipulations regarding the business as it is of such a large value and standing.'

I nod, but I feel stupid because I have no idea what any of that means. Hell, I don't know what Victor even *did*. As George rightly pointed out, I didn't notice when he changed jobs and joined Victor's company.

A thought occurs to me and I raise my hand like I'm a child at school asking the teacher a question. I quickly put it down when PC Watkins smirks at me, but not in a nasty way.

'Um, can I ask if my husband, George, knew about any of this? As I said in my statement, George told me he had plans to take over Victor's company and assets, but then Victor decided to change his mind about seeking revenge against me. I'm guessing he had no idea about what was in Victor's will.'

Mr Boker nods his head. 'Victor Hamilton was a very clever man. He did not allow anyone outside of his team of lawyers to view his will, so there's no chance your husband could have known about it. My guess is that he never planned on killing Victor, not at first. He expected to blackmail him into handing over part of the company or relied on Victor's revenge on you to outweigh his love and dedication towards his business empire and assets.'

This time, I'm the one who smirks. I wish George were sitting here listening to this, watching the past year of his life getting washed down the drain as he realises that, after all he's done to get revenge on me and destroy my life, he's actually the one who's handed me a vast business empire, two large mansions and a million pounds in cash.

It's enough to make me burst out laughing. I can't help it.

'May I speak to my daughter in private first?' I ask, rising to my feet, wobbling slightly as my head spins again.

'Yes, of course,' says Mr Boker.

I glance at PC Watkins, who gives me a nod of acknowledgement.

How am I even going to explain this to Heather? The fact that our family are now multimillionaires. I have no idea how to run an enormous technology company. I've worked part-time, menial jobs my whole adult life. I assume Victor has dozens, if not hundreds, of staff members who run most of it for him, but I'm going to have to make all the big decisions, sign all the cheques, dot all the i's and cross all the t's.

One thing is for certain — I'm going to have to learn fast.

But with Liam and Heather by my side, there's nothing I can't or won't do. I can't figure out if I'm the most unlucky person or the luckiest person in the world right now.

Whichever one I am, I sure have been dealt one hell of a lucky break.

EPILOGUE

'Thank you all for attending this meeting today. I realise that me taking over Victory Enterprises came as a shock to all of you five months ago, but I can guarantee it was a bigger shock to me.'

The entire table of boardroom members and staff chuckle and nod their heads, but every single one of them is hanging on my every word, sitting forward in their seats, eyes glued to me. I'm standing at the head of an enormous table with a large television behind me, on which is the presentation I've just finished delivering. I spoke clearly and confidently, only stumbling once or twice on the complicated numbers, which have never been my strong suit, but overall, I feel it went well and the room is full of smiling faces and nodding heads.

The meeting is being held in a glass-walled office on the top floor of a skyscraper in London. I'm dressed in a tailored navy-blue skirt suit with a killer set of bright-red heels, elongating my legs to the max. My hair is bouncing around my shoulders, not a strand out of place, while my make-up highlights my cheekbones and gives my eyes a dramatic yet professional look. I have barely pulled or tugged at my hair in months, something I never thought I'd be able to achieve, which means the straggly split ends have started to repair themselves and are looking much healthier.

I barely recognised myself when I looked in the mirror this morning before I got on the train to the capital, where I was due to meet the team of Victory Enterprises for the first time as their boss. Now I'm here, nervously shaking in my heels but feeling powerful.

I've come a long way in the past five months.

From domestic housewife to powerful businesswoman.

Heather was astounded to learn about Victor's will. She's already said she doesn't want the company or the assets when she turns eighteen. We'll have another discussion when the time comes as she may change her mind, and that's perfectly fine with me. But she's given me her blessing to take charge of the company and do whatever I want with it in the meantime, so here I am. I've never felt more out of my depth, but with the support of my children, I've never been more ready to face the big, scary world of running a multi-million-pound business empire.

Sometimes, when I think of Victor, I get a little sad that he never got to meet his daughter the way he would have liked to. I wish I could re-do a lot of things, but all I can do now is keep his legacy alive as best I can.

'Thank you all again, and I look forward to working with you more closely now I've got to grips with some of the paperwork and numbers.' Another murmur of chuckles echo around the table and then everyone erupts into applause. Some even stand.

My cheeks burn, but for once it's not from sheer embarrassment or humiliation. I'm proud of what I'm doing, what I'm achieving, about how far I've come. It's not like I didn't feel I wasn't worth anything when I had little money and lived in a council house, but standing here now with a captive audience, for once, I feel valued. Even at home, the children feel the same way.

George never valued me, but maybe that's because I didn't value myself. I'm not saying that money and power have made me worthy, but it has taught me that people look up to you, respect you more when you respect yourself. I value myself now for the first time in my life, and it has nothing to do with the expensive suit I'm wearing.

Everyone lines up to shake my hand and have a quick chat after the meeting has finished. My mouth is dry and I have to keep licking my lips to summon some much-needed moisture. There's a glass of water leaving a sweat ring on the table in front of me, which I'm dying to reach out and grab, but I don't want to come across as rude.

'I love your new ideas for the business,' says the woman in front of me. 'I always told Victor that this place needed a woman's touch.' She giggles nervously. 'Thank you so much for agreeing to listen to my proposal next week.'

'It's my pleasure. I can't wait to hear all about how to get more young girls into technology and business,' I say enthusiastically.

I manage to finally get through the throngs of people wanting to shake my hand and then, when the last one leaves the glass office, I grasp the glass of water and chug the lot. Thirst quenched, I reach for my handbag under the table and fish out my phone.

I have several new texts and a few missed calls, mostly from business associates and one from the head of marketing, who has been hounding me to set up a meeting while I'm in London. I'm staying at the Ritz for the next two nights while I get to grips with the business and attend meetings. They want me to make the trip into London every Monday and stay until Friday like Victor did, but I've told them that it's impossible.

I don't want to be away from my children for that long, which is why I'm handing over a lot of Victor's responsibilities to others in the business who have more knowledge than I do and who are more than willing to step up and take the reins.

I send a quick message to Heather, telling her the meeting went well and that I'm looking forward to celebrating with her this weekend. She passed all of her GCSEs except for Science, and has good enough grades to get her into a great sixth-form college, where she wants to study fashion design. I had no idea just how much she took after me and I can't wait to watch her grow into a talented young woman. She sends me a thumbs-up emoji and a heart. I assume that's it, but then they're followed by a message.

Proud of you! Xx

And it puts a beaming smile on my face for the rest of the day.

* * *

The two days finally pass and I'm one-hundred-percent ready to head home, kick off my heels and see my kids. My mind is exhausted from numerous meetings, where most of the conversations go straight over my head. My jaw aches from smiling so much. It's not been a forced smile either, completely genuine, but it's still exhausting to keep it going.

I'm settled in my first-class seat on the train back to the Cotswolds with my laptop open. Emails ping into my inbox every few minutes. Another pops up just as I finish replying to the last one. I sigh and close the laptop. Nope. It's after six in the evening on a Friday. I'm done.

I take a sip of white wine (some things never change) and lean back in my seat, closing my eyes. The rattling of the rails beneath are soothing as I'm gently shaken left to right.

'Excuse me, Ma'am, is this seat taken?'

My eyes flutter open and I stare at the most beautiful face I've ever seen. Unfortunately, it's one that also sends a tidal wave of horror through my body.

'Glory!' I grasp the armrests of the seat as if I've just had a collision. My body goes rigid.

'Hello, Fiona,' she says, sliding into the seat next to me. Her perfume is overpowering, stinging the edges of my nostrils. I'm in the window seat. There's no way for me to escape without climbing over her.

I glance around the train car, trying to catch the eye of any of my fellow passengers, but no one is looking around, too absorbed by their devices to notice how wide my eyes are.

'You look good,' she says, scanning the top half of my body. 'Love the suit. In fact, you look more than good. Money suits you.'

I bite back a snippy retort and instead say, 'I suggest you move along before the ticket warden comes around.'

'I have time.' Glory glances over her shoulder, then focuses back on me. 'So . . . I bet you think you're pretty clever, don't you?'

'I don't know what you're talking about, Glory. Let's be honest here. I had nothing to do with any of this. The fact Victor left everything to me and Heather in his will was something I never could have foreseen, and if it hadn't been for you and George killing him, it never would have happened, so I guess what I'm trying to say right now is . . . thank you.' I tilt my head and smile at her, feeling every inch a complete and utter bitch, but the look on her face is priceless. 'What are you doing here, Glory?' I ask while simultaneously edging my right hand towards the phone resting on the table.

Her eyes flick sideways. 'Don't even think about it,' she seethes.

'Then answer my question.'

'I came to deliver a warning.'

'Sounds serious.'

Glory stands up, towering over me. She shoves a stiff, pointed finger in my face. 'You're going to fucking regret ever—'

'I'm sorry, ma'am, but is this woman disturbing you?'

I look past Glory to see a very burly-looking ticket warden staring at us. We've also drawn the attention of all the other passengers on the carriage. Glory backs off, straightening her jacket.

'Yes, actually she is,' I say.

'Ma'am, I'm going to have to ask you to leave this lady alone. May I see your ticket, please?'

Glory's jaw is so tense that I'm surprised she hasn't broken a tooth. She backs away down the aisle, takes one final glare at me, then runs.

'Ma'am, would you like me to call the police?' asks the ticket warden.

'Yes, right away. That's the woman who killed Victor Hamilton.'

At the next stop, Glory is detained by the police.

I'm late getting home because I have to provide a statement and answer about a thousand questions, but I do get to see Glory being escorted into a police car in handcuffs, so that makes me feel better about missing Friday night pizza.

I have no idea why she thought it would be a good idea to hop aboard a train, follow me into the first-class carriage and verbally assault me, but then she always did seem like she had very little common sense.

By the time I'm dropped off by the taxi in the driveway and drag myself through the doors, I can barely keep my eyes open. I messaged the kids an hour or so ago to warn them I'd be late home, but then my phone died, so I couldn't confirm if they were okay with that.

I decided to keep Victor's house as our own and am in the process of selling the house I 'won' in the prize draw once the renovations to the fire-damaged parts have finished. I have no need for both. I've even tried to track down the previous owners of the dream house, the ones Victor paid off, but haven't had any luck yet.

As soon as I push open the front door, I know something is wrong. Call it a sixth sense. A mother's intuition. Whatever it is, the cold tingle up my spine makes me drop my bags on the floor and call out.

'Heather! Liam!'

There's no answer. The house is dark, but there is a faint glow coming from somewhere. The games room. They must be in there playing a loud game with their headsets on. Maybe Ryan's with them. He and Heather are dating now and he's here several times a week. It's a delight to have him.

'Kids?' I say, as I knock on the partly open door and push it open.

I expect to see them sitting next to each other on the giant beanbags, staring absentmindedly at the enormous screen, but that's not what I see at all.

What I see is a dead body on the ground, a giant pool of blood surrounding it.

My two children are huddled in the corner with their arms around each other, shaking and sobbing. I collapse to my knees at the sight.

'Mum,' sobs Heather. Liam's head is buried in her shoulder.

'W-What happened?' I ask, summoning the strength to get to my feet. I walk in a wide circle around the body and kneel next to my children, stroking Liam's head to let him know I'm here. He's in shock and . . . splattered with blood. So is Heather.

'Are either of you hurt?' I ask.

'No, we're not hurt,' answers Heather quickly.

'Tell me. Tell me what happened.'

Heather glances past me at the body on the floor. 'He attacked me, Mum. He tried to kill me. He tried to take Liam, wanted him to come with him. He was crazy, Mum.'

While Glory was threatening me on the train, my husband was here attempting to kill and kidnap our children. *My* children.

'Liam grabbed the hammer on the wall and hit him with it.'

My eyes swivel up to the empty space where Thor's hammer used to be mounted in pride of place above the pool table. Liam had loved it the moment he set his eyes on it in the previous house and had begged me to have it repositioned here. Now, it's lying on the ground, its heavy end covered in blood with bits of skull and hair stuck to it.

My son did that to his father. To save his sister.

There's a small pile of vomit nearby that's assaulting my nostrils, but I ignore it, turning back to Liam. 'Liam, can you look at me?' He slowly looks up. His eyes are puffy, his cheeks red and blotchy. 'I know you're scared, baby, but you don't have to worry, okay? I'm going to sort all of this out, make it all go away.'

Heather gasps. 'Mum . . . you can't.'

'Yes, Heather. We can. I am not going to let your father and his piece on the side ruin what we have now. Do you hear me? Now, have either of you left this room since it happened?'

'No. We tried to call you, but . . .'

'I'm sorry. My phone died. I was delayed because Glory confronted me on my way back from London, but she's been detained by the police now. It's over. But first, I need to get this cleaned up.'

My children stare at me intently, waiting for my next set of instructions. It's the strangest feeling in the world. To have their undivided attention. There's nothing I wouldn't do for my children.

A low groan comes from behind us.

I look over my shoulder to see George's left hand twitching.

'Oh my God, he's alive!' cries Heather, who rushes to her feet.

'No!' I shout as I grab Heather and pull her back down to the floor.

Liam's face is awash with relief. He must have been so scared, thinking he'd killed his father. I must admit, I'm relieved too. It makes the next part much easier.

'Mum, we should call an ambulance,' says Heather.

'Love, I think it's too late for that. Please take your brother upstairs, straight into my bathroom, and take it in turns to have a shower and wash up. You can change into the bathrobes hanging on the back of the door. Do not go anywhere else in the house, do you understand? Not until I tell you.'

'Mum . . . what are you going to do?' asks Heather, her voice trembling.

Another groan.

I stand up and face George, who is attempting to lift his head. Blood is oozing out of his mouth and a gaping head wound, rather like the wound he gave me five months ago, but much, much worse. There's no chance of saving him. Even if I called an ambulance now, there's no way he'd survive. My son would go down for murder, and even though it was through self-defence, this would destroy his future.

'Mum?' asks Heather again.

'I'm going to do what I have to do,' I say. 'Now, go.'

Heather and Liam stand up. Liam moves in next to me.

'Did I kill him, Mum?'

'No, love. You didn't kill him.'

Liam looks up at me, his eyes brimming with tears. 'Love you, Mum.'

'Love you more, baby.' I kiss the top of his head while Heather takes his hand and pulls him out of the room. I wait until their footsteps sound on the stairs, then bend down next to George. He's stopped trying to get up, but he's trying to say something.

I don't care what he has to say.

Gently, I cover his nose and mouth with my hand and squeeze until he stops squirming.

The room descends into silence.

I take a deep breath, knowing that this night is far from over.

My right hand rises to the side of my face, but instead of grabbing a strand of hair and tugging it, I scoop it up into a messy ponytail and, using a tie from my bag, I tie it up at the back of my head.

Time to get to work.

THE END

ACKNOWLEDGEMENTS

A huge thank you goes to the whole team at Joffe Books who works on my books, especially Kate Lyall Grant, who has helped and guided me from the start. It's a true honour to write for Joffe Books and for the team to bring each book to life with their social media presence, editing and proofreading skills and more.

Thank you to all my readers who continue to read my twisted thrillers, support my author career and post about my books. None of it goes unnoticed because without you, I wouldn't be where I am today. Here's to many more books to come!

THE JOFFE BOOKS STORY

We began in 2014 when Jasper agreed to publish his mum's much-rejected romance novel and it became a bestseller.

Since then we've grown into the largest independent publisher in the UK. We're extremely proud to publish some of the very best writers in the world, including Joy Ellis, Faith Martin, Caro Ramsay, Helen Forrester, Simon Brett and Robert Goddard. Everyone at Joffe Books loves reading and we never forget that it all begins with the magic of an author telling a story.

We are proud to publish talented first-time authors, as well as established writers whose books we love introducing to a new generation of readers.

We won Trade Publisher of the Year at the Independent Publishing Awards in 2023 and Best Publisher Award in 2024 at the People's Book Prize. We have been shortlisted for Independent Publisher of the Year at the British Book Awards for the last five years, and were shortlisted for the Diversity and Inclusivity Award at the 2022 Independent Publishing Awards. In 2023 we were shortlisted for Publisher of the Year at the RNA Industry Awards, and in 2024 we were shortlisted at the CWA Daggers for the Best Crime and Mystery Publisher.

We built this company with your help, and we love to hear from you, so please email us about absolutely anything bookish at feedback@joffebooks.com.

If you want to receive free books every Friday and hear about all our new releases, join our mailing list here: www.joffebooks.com/freebooks.

And when you tell your friends about us, just remember: it's pronounced Joffe as in coffee or toffee!

Printed in Dunstable, United Kingdom

79711030R00150